FADEAWAY
JOE

FADEAWAY JOE

A NOVEL

HUGH LESSIG

CROOKED LANE

NEW YORK

Published in the United States by Crooked Lane Books, an imprint of The Quick Brown Fox & Company LLC.

Crooked Lane Books and its logo are trademarks of The Quick Brown Fox & Company LLC.

Library of Congress Catalog-in-Publication data available upon request.

ISBN (hardcover): 978-1-63910-436-9
ISBN (ebook): 978-1-63910-437-6

Cover design by Sarah Brody

Printed in the United States.

www.crookedlanebooks.com

Crooked Lane Books
34 West 27th St., 10th Floor
New York, NY 10001

First Edition: August 2023

10 9 8 7 6 5 4 3 2 1

For my dad, Davey, who told stories of the road

JOE

1

J OE PENDERGAST SPENT last night with a case of the walk-abouts. He prefers that term over wandering, which is a doctor word. Wandering implies aimlessness, and Joe is anything but that. He knows today is March 21, and he knows what year it is. He knows the sun has just risen, and he's sitting in the dewy grass of his backyard with muddy shoes, his ass getting wetter by the second. He knows the walkabout included moments of lost time, but at some point he spoke to someone while standing in his front yard. He knows that it was a short conversation and the person walked away. Alive.

He pushes away the jumbled images with a vigorous shake of his head. Whatever happened, it can't stand in the way of tonight.

Standing up, Joe adjusts his Tidewater Shuckers ball cap and brushes off his work pants. Maybe his neighbor Donna saw him walking around and can fill in the blanks. He moved here only last month, but she's already volunteered to invade his bathroom and label everything so he doesn't shave with toothpaste or gargle with sandalwood cologne. But Joe doesn't need that yet. He can keep the contents of the bathroom straight in his head, and the same goes for his living room and kitchen. The doctor said he was high functioning, a medical term he can accept.

That said, he must have fallen asleep here in the backyard. The doctor doesn't need to know that.

Smart as a whip, that doctor, and pretty as a high school prom queen. Fired questions like a game show host. Name the season. Name the current president. Name your hometown. When she asked about family members, Joe said, "My parents are long gone, and I'm an only child. I've known a man named Maxie for forty years. He's the closest thing I have to a brother."

When she smiled, Joe shot back: "He fired me because my brain is turning to oatmeal and I can't manage his restaurant. His words. So there's that too."

Joe walks along the side of his house, toward the front yard. Donna's place is all buttoned up, and her little sports car is gone. The birds are quiet, the air stilled. It reminds Joe of those shocked moments after the commission of violence, when a man's teeth are on the ground and people wait to see if he'll pick them up.

It makes Joe think of tonight, and he smiles for the first time today. Maybe the last.

In his tiny front yard, a food truck sits in the driveway, freshly painted and emblazoned with the banner saying "Joe's Takeaway." It takes him a moment to remember why it's there. The food truck belongs to him. It is his new job, the not-so-dreamy one.

His rented beach house faces Seneca Lane, a short, dead-end road that stops at Donna's property. Tall seagrass grows on the opposite side of the road, shielding a small inlet with a boat slip. When Joe moved in, he inherited a twelve-foot johnboat from a sailor shipping out of Naval Station Norfolk. Joe remembers that the sailor transferred to Puget Sound with his nice wife and daughter. The guy couldn't take the boat and asked Joe if he wanted it. The movers were in the midst of hauling in Joe's furniture, and Donna was already peeking out from behind her curtains, curious about the new neighbor, and Joe was a little foggy from all the activity, so he said sure, why not? The sailor did woodworking on the side and made Joe a little ownership plaque, affixing it near the bow: "Joe Pendergast, Skipper."

Joe figures a nice boat ride might clear his head and help him remember last night. He cuts through seagrass along a narrow path. He takes one look at the boat and freezes.

It is pooled with blood. A hank of gray hair floats in the pinkish water.

He couldn't have killed Maxie last night, even if he was wandering.

Right?

2

THE GRAY HAIR might have come from Maxie's head, but it's hard to say. Maxie disguised his male pattern baldness with an elaborate combover plastered in place by various gels and sprays. It curved around like the seams of a baseball. He is sixty-four years old (or maybe he *was*, looking at this mess), and Joe is two years younger, with a silver and black mane that Maxie grabbed by the fistful whenever he wanted a highball or needed Joe to knock on someone's door.

Joe closes his eyes and exhales through his nose. He tells himself to think it through. The scalp and the blood do not necessarily translate into a murder. Two men could have fought here last night. Joe knows nothing of this neighborhood, and no one except for Donna, even though he grew up a few miles down the road in Buckroe Beach. Virginia was a lot different in the sixties.

He decides to clean the boat. That plaque bearing his name is screwed in tight, and a boat filled with blood and hair and labeled with your name is not something that should stand, even if it won't matter after tomorrow. He gets a bucket from the garage and sloshes water into the boat. He bails it out and tips it sideways. He puts the hair aside.

Fifteen minutes stretches into half an hour of routine work. He's cleaned up enough blood in his day that this doesn't bother him. Even though it's only March, the sun is warm on his neck, and the air smells of water and seagrass. He's just finishing as Donna's sports car putters down Seneca Lane. The car lurches to a stop twenty feet away. The top is down, and Donna's little dog is harnessed in the passenger seat.

"Hey, Joe. Heading out for a boat ride? You should put a coat on. It gets chilly on the water."

Donna P. L. Fallon is the forty-five-year-old love child of trailer park hippies who walked around naked half the time. She had matriculated from high school cheerleader to performing at gentleman's clubs near Hampton Roads military bases, and from there to getting her real estate license. Her middle initials stand for *Peace* and *Love*. Again, hippies. Her bright smile sometimes gets lost in a jangling wreckage of floppy hats, oversized bracelets, and hoop earrings. Donna's superpower is oversharing, according to Donna.

"Mr. Pendergast, you could at least say good morning."

"Ah, good morning, Donna. Dressed to the nines, I see."

"I came down from Richmond. You know, another real estate conference." She rolls her eyes, as if Joe understands. "Butterbean and I could have driven back last night, but we got a room. Didn't we?"

The dog is a teacup something or other. It stares daggers at Joe, as if he knows all about the bloody violence in the boat. Joe holds the dog's gaze until Donna breaks the spell. "What's that you got there?"

She's spotted the hair in the grass.

"Probably came from an animal," he says, tossing it into the bucket. "Hard to tell what it was."

"Good God in heaven, go wash your hands! No, wait." She reaches back into a saddlebag-sized purse and tosses him a small bottle of hand sanitizer. "Use that. It kills germs, and you'll smell like chocolate cherry marshmallow for the rest of the day. Keep the bottle." She sighs contentedly as he rubs the smelly stuff up to his wrists. Then comes The Question. "So how are you doing with the . . . you know."

When Joe moved in, Donna had introduced herself and handed him a pineapple upside-down cake. Joe joked that it represented his brain. He told her straight off about his dementia diagnosis, half hoping to scare her away. But her hippie dad had died of Parkinson's, so she jabbered on about pill trays and the importance of keeping a routine.

"I'm doing good," he says now. "My pill tray is made up three weeks out, and I've labeled my bathroom stuff with sticky notes. The doctor says I can still be high functioning for quite some time. I've spent most of my life on the medium- to low-functioning end, so that's an improvement, right? I've had a few foggy spells, nothing serious. I know who I am and who you are, plus Butterbean here. I know it's the first day of spring, and I'm in Buckroe Beach."

"Buckroe Beach is down the road, Joe."

"Right. I'm closer to Phoebus. Still the city of Hampton. In Virginia. In the United States. Satisfied for now?"

"It can be tough. That's all I'm saying. You're in a new home, a new environment. That's a challenge for anyone."

"Nights are more dicey," he says. "I may have been walking around last night. If anyone says anything, let me know."

She unclips the dog's harness. It saunters over to the cleaning bucket and lets loose a yellow stream near Joe's leg. "Butterbean likes you," Donna says. "If I had a girl dog, I was going to name her S-I-N-D-E-E. That was my dancer name. I may have told you that."

"You have not, but that's a new detail I'll add to the list. I've known you briefly, Donna, and yet it seems like forever." He glances at the boat, now reasonably clean. "I should get ready for tonight."

She snaps her fingers. "That's right. The debut of Joe's Takeaway, soon to be the best food truck in Hampton Roads. The Moonbeam Brewery is a nice venue for a Thursday. I'd like to show up tonight, but I signed up for a webinar. I want to hear all about it tomorrow morning."

"That will be fine."

She doesn't realize there won't be a tomorrow morning for Joe. He may not remember how last night ended, but he knows how it began. He called Maxie and left a message: *Come to the Moonbeam Brewery Thursday night to help christen the new food truck.* Maxie responded with a message of his own, saying he'd be pleased to come, and he was happy Joe was no longer upset about how things had ended. It's the sort of bullshitting that goes on between violent men who don't want to tip their hands.

"It's just hotdogs and such," Joe says. "It should be fairly uneventful."

3

After Donna goes inside, Joe swishes through the seagrass to look for a body that's missing some of its hair. He finds a business card that looks brand new, for the George Pickett Grill. The Pickett is out near the Air Force base. He pockets the card and finds little else: a few discarded fast-food wrappers and beer cans. The Pickett sticks in his head for some reason, unrelated to blood or boats or the onset of dementia.

"Joe, do you have a minute?" Donna again. She's coming across the road, staring at her phone.

"Yes, Donna. What's up?"

"Was there an incident last night of any sort?"

Joe squints hard, pretending to dredge up memories lost in the brain sludge. "Like I said, I may have been walking around, but I don't know for sure. Why do you ask?"

"My security camera focuses on the front door, but it gives me a partial view of the road. I replayed the tape from last night—it's a habit after I've been away—and came across this little scene."

She tilts the phone so Joe can see the black-and-white video. Donna's front porch takes up three-quarters of the screen, and a short stretch of Seneca Lane fills the background. Joe fears he'll see himself strutting naked down the middle of the street with a lawn mower blade, having just cut a guy to pieces. But like a bad accident, he can't look away. In the background, a hooded figure stumbles into the frame from the direction of his house. He can't tell if this slender person is a man or woman. The figure walks to the center of the screen and stops dead. Both arms come up in a gesture of mock surrender. The head bobs up and down.

"It looks like a conversation is going on," Donna said. "Whoever it is, they seem agitated. Are you sure no one came by your house last night? This is time-stamped at 10:32 PM." She looks over his shoulder to the tall seagrass. "Did you notice anything when you cleaned up over there?"

The hooded figure takes several steps toward Joe's house and stands on the edge of the frame, hands on hips, as if surveying the property.

"They're looking at your yard, Joe, not the road. You should check to see if someone was skulking around last night. This is supposed to be a safe neighborhood." Donna looks behind her, as if expecting a hooded thug to drag her away. "Maybe you should get a dog. Butterbean isn't much, but he makes noise."

"I'll consider that," Joe says. "Say, have you ever gone to the George Pickett Grill?"

She makes a sour face. "Ugh, no. That whole corridor on King William Street is seedy. Mom and Dad used to protest there. Back in the sixties, they had a sit-in at the lunch counter. At least, I think it was George Pickett. I can't remember."

"I believe you're right," Joe says. "I was ten years old in 1965, Donna. Different times back then. The sit-in at the Woolworth's lunch counter downtown was a big deal. The

Hampton University students pushed that, I believe. But there was also some excitement at the Pickett."

"Why are you asking?"

He holds up the business card. "Found this in the grass. Just made me think of it."

After she leaves, Joe takes the bucket into the garage and pulls a black garbage bag from a big roll. He puts the chunk of scalp in the bag and tucks it at the bottom of the chest freezer that stores his hotdogs, brats, and Italian sausages for Joe's Takeaway. He tries to remember the encounter from last night, but it's a jumble of images, like pieces of a jigsaw puzzle scattered across a card table. That hooded figure in the video moved like a young person, not someone with gray hair.

Christ, losing your mind shouldn't be so stressful.

He goes inside and climbs the stairs to his living room. Donna has described Joe's new place as a classic beach house. The living room, kitchen, and master bedroom are on the second floor, with French doors that lead to a deck. The ground floor accommodates another bedroom, a second bathroom, and Joe's office. Joe walks to the fridge and touches the photo of Kathy that sticks on the door. It shows her working behind the bar, leaning forward with a tired smile. Then he flops on the couch and jiggles his laptop to check email. He's got something from Jennifer, his new online counselor.

Dear Mr. Pendergast:

Did you get the whiteboard and easel I sent? It's handy for writing down major items or a to-do list. With that new food truck, you'll be making lots of lists. LOL.

As I've written before, I am not a professional counselor, simply a volunteer who wants to do good. I've had some experience with dementia survivors close to me. I guess that's how we got paired up.

According to the Facebook page for Joe's Takeaway, it looks like you'll be at the Moonbeam Brewery tonight. Please let me know how it goes.

Your friend,

Jennifer

The whiteboard and easel came yesterday. It stands in the corner of the main room, where you might put an extra chair if you weren't totally alone in the world. On the left of the whiteboard, Joe has listed all the food he'll need for tonight. On the right is another list of important reminders.

Maxie is visiting the Moonbeam.
Take care of him before he takes care of you.
Lead police on a chase with the food truck.
Go out in a blaze.

THE MOONBEAM BREWERY is two miles from Joe's house, and he spends part of the afternoon looking at its website. The bar is the dreamchild of a retired NASA-Langley engineer, who erected a warehouse-type building near the water and installed a rocket-shaped bar. He hung old photos of the seven Mercury astronauts who trained at NASA-Langley in the late fifties and early sixties, before everything moved to Houston and Florida.

Joe magnifies one photo that shows astronauts Alan Shepard and John Glenn participating in Hampton's "Mercury Day" in 1962. Back then, Joe was a gawky little kid with bristle-brush hair, who wore plaid shirts, white socks, and black shoes. He stocked shelves and sliced lunch meat at his parents' corner grocery store and dreamed of sneaking onto a moon rocket to escape the seventh level of hell that was Pendergast Cut-Rate. He wasn't freed from bondage until 1976, when his parents died within months of each other. By then, Joe's childhood had burned up in the atmosphere. He looks at that photo and thinks of the old days. He remembers being behind the counter the first time Maxie came in. Joe was sixteen and Maxie was only two years older, but he engaged Joe's dad in a man-to-man conversation about a loan. Joe is still thinking of those days when his phone alarm goes off.

It's five o'clock. Time to crank up the food truck and face his old boss.

He drives to the Moonbeam and parks the truck away from the other cars. The bar opens up like a garage, with tables outside and people milling about. The lone bartender is a black woman who wears a track shirt and runner's tights. Flowered tattoos form a sleeve up her left arm, and her cornflower hair is coiled into braids that look strong enough to tie down cargo in a hurricane. Her smile is all business.

"I'm here with Joe's Takeaway," he says.

She gives him a blank stare.

"The food truck that was affiliated with Captain Maxie's in Norfolk? I took it over and renamed it. The truck had a standing gig here Thursday, and the contract should have transferred over."

His chest tightens in momentary panic until her eyes light up in recognition. "Right, right, I got an email from a Kathy someone. Let's go outside and I'll show you where to set up." She talks as she walks, showing Joe her back and raising her voice so he can hear. "It must be awesome to get a working food truck with current licenses and gigs transferred over. I guess Captain Maxie's is getting out of the food truck business."

Joe lengthens his stride, to keep up, and scans the outdoor tables. The place looks about half full. He wonders if they'll go for a simple menu of hotdogs and such—not that it will matter after tonight. "They're definitely getting out of the food truck business," he says. "The owner of Captain Maxie's has bigger things on his mind. See, he has this project you might have read about . . ."

The bartender points to an open corner of the lot. "That's your spot. What else do you need from me?"

"Nothing," he whispers. "I'll either be dead or in jail by this time tomorrow."

The bartender smiles and cocks her head. "Sorry, what was that? Something about a project?"

"Oh, never mind. I'm just talking to myself."

In his head, he goes over the sequence for setting up the food truck. Two Crock-Pots with mac and cheese should run on the highest setting for the first thirty minutes. Then he should turn on the propane and light the grill. Italian sausages and brats go on first because they take longer than hotdogs. Right before opening, he'll set out the condiment table and the ice chest with sodas and water to let everyone know he's ready for business. But even as this sequence replays in his head, another set of events runs in the background, like a scene that keeps repeating.

A little over a month ago on Valentine's Day, he and Kathy were eating dinner at their favorite place in Norfolk when Kathy began describing Maxie's hotel-casino project south of Virginia Beach. It was news to Joe, and the next day he confronted Maxie about it. They were at the restaurant, standing between the bar and the kitchen. Joe asked why he'd been kept in the dark about this big project. The staff and customers could see them.

Maxie saw everyone watching and lowered his voice. "I was going to tell you, brother. But you got enough to do here. Speaking of which, we need talk about how you run things at night."

"Night manager is my dream job," Joe says. "You know that. Whatever you want me to do, I'll do it."

Maxie smiled and took Joe aside, never a good sign. "This job has gotten the best of you, brother. The books aren't balancing. Supplies are off. You were better working the door, am I right? I think you should go back there. Captain Maxie's needs someone new at the helm. I'm sorry, Joe. I'm making Kathy the night manager. If you don't want to work the door, we can find something else for you to do. Sweeping up or something."

Joe saw his life crumbling before his eyes. "No, no, Maxie. I can get back on the beam. I've just been a bit confused lately. That's all. I can't be sweeping up. Not after all this time."

"I'm sorry, Joe. Decision's been made."

Joe knew that look. He struggled for something to say. "Look, maybe I could get in on this casino project. You won't need a bouncer, but you'll need a greeter. Someone to say hello and direct people to the right place. I could do that. Wear a fancy suit and whatnot. Play off my reputation as the best bouncer in Hampton Roads."

"That was just a magazine story, Joe. It was three years ago, and it didn't mean anything. I'm sorry, you can't be part of the casino project. There's money missing from Captain Maxie's. This is my flagship bar. I've known you for forty years, and that's why I'm not calling the police. Working the door will keep you away from the cash drawer."

At that moment, Joe's right fist took on a life of its own and slugged Maxie in the temple. The next few seconds happened in slow motion as Maxie toppled over a deuce table, and his heavy framed eyeglasses skittered across the floor. Joe was still processing the scene when Maxie scrambled to his feet and threw a left. Joe ducked, but Maxie caught him with a right to the head. He followed with a left to the jaw and another right between the eyes. Joe fell back and hit the floor hard. He got to his knees and instinctively counted to eight, as if they were kids back at the gym.

"Get out of here, you bum," Maxie said. "You and I are done."

Joe stumbled out and walked around Norfolk for hours, reliving all the things he had done for Maxie over the years, breaking laws and breaking bones, making men cry in front of their children. All in the name of collecting debts for illegal poker games that Maxie ran in the back room of Captain Maxie's. Later that night, Kathy found him and went with him to the ER. He had a nasty gash on his head, either from Maxie decking him or from falling on the sidewalk at some point. At the hospital, they took X-rays and called the prom queen doctor, who fired off her questions and told him the ugly truth.

The bartender at the Moonbeam snaps him back to the present. "You should get ready to open. Time's a-wasting."

"Sorry. I was lost in thought."

"You must have worked at Captain Maxie's a long time to get their food truck. Allowing you to rebrand it, that's awesome."

"I worked there almost forty years," Joe says. "I got the food truck instead of a gold watch."

It was Kathy's idea to let Joe have Captain Maxie's truck as a form of dementia-related severance payment. Food trucks are manageable. Everything is always in the same place and within arm's reach. She thought Joe could handle it. It was Kathy's idea to let him keep two weekly gigs, the Moonbeam tonight and tomorrow during lunch in downtown Newport News. It was Kathy who gave the food truck a new name, transferred all the licenses to Joe's Takeaway, and found the beach house next to Donna's for him. It was Kathy who sent an email to the Moonbeam so tonight would go smoothly. But it wasn't Kathy's idea to break up with Joe after two years of living together. Maxie insisted on that. And Kathy, for all her ability to slap down unruly men at the bar, is both scared to death of Maxie and loves his pursuit of money. She arranged the details of

Joe's new life and promptly dumped him. Apparently greed trumps romance in Kathy's world, even when you throw in a healthy dose of guilt.

"I should get back to the bar, Mr. Joe. Looks like people need refills."

"Pendergast. Joe Pendergast."

"But you're Joe's Takeaway. That's how I'll remember you."

"We'll see how you remember me. You know, back in my day, you wouldn't see an African American working behind the bar. It was so different around here. Did you notice the theater a few blocks up the road? It has main seating and a balcony. In my day, the whites would sit downstairs and you would have had to sit upstairs. But you could see better in the balcony. Also, you could drop pieces of popcorn onto the people below."

Her face freezes for a moment, then she breaks into a grin. "You sat upstairs with the black folk, Mr. Joe?"

"I did. I had a crush on someone."

"It ever come to anything?"

"No, ma'am. And I regret it to this day."

She sticks out her hand. "My name is Christina but I go by Charlie. You need anything, you holler. I run this place."

"I thought an engineer from NASA-Langley owned it?"

"He owns it, but I run it. This is my baby. My dream. This is what I'm all about."

When she leaves, Joe goes through his routine of preparation and stands at the open window. He's as ready as he'll ever be. Crock-Pot, propane, sausages, brats, condiment table, and cooler. Kathy said running a food truck would be good for his condition—her words—because everything is always in the same place. But when the first customer arrives five minutes early, Joe begins to tremble. It's as if a countdown has begun.

"I'll take two dogs, and please don't beat me up." The man wears khaki shorts and a shirt with a popped collar, and somehow has a suntan in March. "This story is quite the thing."

Posted on the truck next to the menu is a laminated cover of *Tidewater Coast* magazine from three years ago. They did one of those goofy reader polls on the best place to hook up, best place to watch a sunset—that sort of thing— and that's when Joe was named Best Bouncer in Hampton Roads. His picture made the cover.

"The owner of Captain Maxie's is quoted in that story," Joe says. "According to him, I was the younger brother he never had. He might show up tonight. And when he does, there might be fireworks."

"Big reunion planned?"

"Something like that. You never know what will happen when old friends meet."

CHAPTER

5

J OE HANDLES THE initial rush of customers with no problem. He gets into a comfortable routine and is restocking the grill when a knock comes on the window. He turns
and expects to see Maxie, but it's Charlie the bartender
again.

"Didn't mean to startle you," she says.

"I'm good."

"A customer mentioned he got an odd vibe from you.
Like you were nervous."

"I'm not nervous at all."

"This guy is a boater. Has a suntan. He's forty and tries
to look twenty, so maybe it's just him. He's also a bit catty.
But you're new and I wanted to make sure everything was
copacetic."

"I know who you're talking about. He was my first customer. Maybe I came off as nervous. First customer. First
gig. That sort of thing."

"Perfectly understandable. I like to check out the smoke
before it becomes a fire." She notices the magazine story.
"The boater mentioned this article. It looks like you were a
badass back in the day, Mr. Joe."

"That was from three years ago, so perhaps I still retain some of my badassery. If you ever need a bouncer, let me know."

"Maybe I'll take you up on that," Charlie says. "Then again, you might hit on me, and I'd have to kick your ass."

"I bet you could. I've broken up fights between men and women. Let me tell you, women know how to fight, and it didn't start with mixed martial arts and fighting in the octagon nonsense. I'd rather break up a fight between two guys." He gives her a wink. "Then again, some girls like bouncers."

Charlie throws back her head and laughs. "Is that a fact? You must have honed your moves in that theater, up in the balcony. I can see this crew-cut white boy hanging out in the cheap seats. You yawn. You stretch. Pretty soon you got an arm around a black girl, and she's like 'what just happened?' Yep, I can see it now."

Now Joe is laughing. "You're a piece of work, Charlie. You know something? My dad ran a cut-rate grocery store in Buckroe Beach back in the sixties. Basically, he was Klan. I'm not sure he was a flag waver, but that's a distinction without a difference. He went to the meetings and talked the talk. He said it was good for business."

Charlie keeps her smile. "And you with a crush on a black girl. That must have been tough."

"You'd be surprised how kids adjust," Joe says, letting his mind wander. "As you get older, you get more set in your ways. Less willing to change."

"More likely to push back," Charlie says.

"Exactly."

After Charlie walks away, another rush hits. The flow of business allows him to stay calm and plan his next move. He imagines Maxie showing up and making a smart-aleck comment about what a comedown it must be, slinging hotdogs

instead of managing a restaurant. He'll ask if the ladies in
the new neighborhood are fuckable, or if date nights consist
of his right hand in the shower. That smirk. The casual put-
downs. Joe will shuffle his feet and flash his "aw shucks"
grin. He'll open the back door and invite Maxie into the
truck. Then he'll press that smirky face against the hot grill,
maybe stab him with a long fork or just beat him to a pulp.
He'll have time. Most folks would rather watch a fight than
break it up.

After it's over, Joe figured he would dump Maxie's body
in the parking lot and speed away. Someone would take a
picture of the mangled corpse and post it, and that's how
the old boss will be remembered. Meanwhile, Joe could lead
police on a slow-speed chase. Get up on I-64 and go through
the bridge-tunnel. The papers will play it big the next day,
and when the police find out what's going on inside Joe's
head, they'll put him in a hospital instead of jail.

But now he's thinking about Charlie.

This might kill her business: a psycho food truck guy,
a body in the parking lot. She'll feel lousy that she checked
on Joe because she smelled smoke, then walked away. She'll
replay it in her head. The Moonbeam is her baby, and Joe
would be shitting all over it. Maybe the NASA engineer
who owns this place will fire her. She won't have the satisfaction of screaming at Joe—telling him she'll pay extra to
carve *asshole* on his tombstone—because by then Joe will
be drooling into a cup and won't give a shit one way or the
other.

Goddamn it. Now what?

He's still thinking about it thirty minutes later when
Maxie shows up. Joe spots him from a distance, talking at
an outside table. Maxie looks at the truck, locks eyes with
Joe, and returns to his conversation. *So that's how it will
be.* He will make Joe wait. Everything happens on Maxie's

schedule or not at all. If only dementia could erase all the times Joe said, 'Is there anything else I can get you, boss?' or 'Where should I put your dry cleaning, boss?' If only he could forget groveling for a casino job, offering to wear a monkey suit and be a glorified Walmart greeter, knowing he was already out the door.

Motherfucker. Get over here and get your beating.

"Excuse me, I ordered a dog." A young woman with a mohawk strip on her shaved head hunkers forward, almost sticking her head through the window. "Sometime today maybe."

"I'm sorry, honey. I'll get that right now."

"I'm not your honey. And maybe a little coleslaw on the side."

"You either pay for coleslaw or you get bubkes. You've got a loud voice, honey. I hope you turn it down when you're in church."

She rolls her eyes. "Funny man. Yes, I'd like a side of coleslaw for the going rate." She leans away from the window and looks to the side. "Best bouncer in Hampton Roads? I never heard of *Tidewater Coast* magazine. Must have been back in the day."

"You're the second person who has said 'back in the day.' That was three years ago. If you want back in the day, go inside the bar, and look at those old photos. You probably don't know about John Glenn or Scott Carpenter or the others." He fixes a hotdog and a spoons coleslaw next to it. "Here you go. Enjoy it in good health."

The young woman gives him a smile, and it brings back memories of working the door at Captain Maxie's, joking and jousting with people in line. Over the years, he honed his patter to a carnival barker's edge, keeping people engaged while they waited. As she walks to the side, Maxie approaches the window. He wears a tan sport coat and a polo shirt. His pants are white, his shoes brown. He appears to be alone, but someone might have driven him.

"You look ready for summer, boss," Joe says. "Your bruise healed nicely."

Maxie smiles with capped teeth. "It wasn't your punch; it was falling over that damn table. I lost my balance." He steps back and assesses the truck. "I like the paint job and the name, and I see you scaled back the menu. That's a good call, Joe. Too many of these trucks have complicated menus. You order food and get a fucking pager, then you wait around for forty-five minutes. You're keeping it simple. Kathy was right to let you have the truck."

"How is Kathy?"

Maxie ignores the question. "I hope this works out. It may be a right-sizing thing—enough to keep you busy, but not too big so you get confused, good for someone in your condition."

Always with the putdown. "You want a hotdog, boss?"

"Bad for the cholesterol. Smells good, though. I bet your homemade mac and cheese will be a hit with the crowd."

Silence settles between them. The drinkers at the outdoor tables seem a world away, their raucous laughter a distant serenade. Maxie steps closer and opens his sport coat. He often carries a .25 caliber shooter clipped to his belt, a left-hand pull. Maxie follows Joe's eyes. "I'm not packing, Joe. You invited me here, and I came to issue some friendly advice. You know everything about my business, from way back. Not just poker, but the other stuff."

"You mean loan sharking, where I beat up people who owed you money? Yeah, I seem to remember that was before your poker games started to pay off. You were still working for your crooked father back then."

"Keep your voice down, idiot."

Joe clenches his fists, his knuckles cracking. "When I was a kid, you'd come into Pendergast Cut-Rate, dressed to the nines, smelling of cologne. You'd ask if I could come to the gym after work and spar a few rounds. My dad thought it was good exercise, but you were training me to throw punches, knowing you'd need a goon down the road. You were only two years older than me, but you were always scheming. Like a snake."

Maxie's eyes flash in anger. "You should have seen yourself stocking shelves as a fourteen-year-old. Knowing you'd never play football or fuck a cheerleader after the game. Knowing that piece-of-shit store with the stale bread and dusty soup cans would be your life. I got you out of that hellhole."

"The bread was always fresh."

Maxie steps closer, his nose nearly touching the window. "I'm not here to argue, Joe. We start talking about my dad or your parents, that gets us nowhere. I'm asking you politely, man to man, to keep your mouth shut about what you know. I'm going legit in a big way. I have to testify before city council, present blueprints before planning commissions, make small talk with politicians—all that shit. I got reporters calling me. I can't have you shooting off your mouth."

"Or what?"

He leans inside the customer window and sticks out his right hand. "Let's keep this civil and shake on it. That will be our bond. You and I go back forty years. It didn't end so good between us, but that's how it is with family sometimes, am I right? I want you to be well, Joe, even though you hit me."

Maxie tries to smile, but his mouth curls in derision. He's clearly thinking what a loser Joe Pendergast turned out to be, slapping hotdogs on buns and pretending to be happy. He's thinking of a good insult, and he'll mumble it while walking away.

"Joe, you still with me?"

"Sure. Let's shake on it." Joe tightens his grip. Maxie tries to pull away and nothing happens.

"Joe, let go of my fucking hand."

6

J OE ADMIRES MAXIE's pinkie ring with the sparkling red stone. He twists the little finger at the base of the joint a quarter turn. Maxie closes his eyes and refuses to acknowledge the pain. His voice is a fierce whisper: "You want to muscle me in public? You think that's good for your long-term health? You baboon!"

"I can't seem to let go," Joe says.

Maxie tugs at his arm and gives up. His shoulders sag, and he goes back to being Maxie the businessman. "Joseph, I come here in good faith. You're creating more trouble by pulling a stunt like this. I got a right to my dreams. My dad ended up in prison on a chump charge, disgraced for life. For so long, people looked at me and saw him. I can step out of that shadow. A man is remembered for the last thing he does, brother."

"You kicked me to the curb, *brother*. You separated me from the only woman I ever cared about. Don't give me your sob story."

"You socked me, Joe. And you did it in front of people. I had already decided to let you go—that's true—but I could have taken care of you. Better than this. Better than serving hotdogs to the rabble."

"Kathy."

"Kathy is twenty years younger than you. She needed to move on because she's no caregiver. When you get worse, she won't be able to deal with it. It would have been an ugly breakup. A good, clean break now is better."

"Thanks for making that decision for me. I got a halfway decent savings account that can disappear in the blink of an eye, but sure, her being a caregiver is a problem."

"Money was missing from my bar."

"I didn't take it."

Maxie closes his eyes. It is a deliberate gesture. "I've lost my fucking patience with this hand-holding. I could beat your ass any day of the week, and we both know it. Just because you cold-cocked me on your way out the door doesn't make you invincible."

Joe torques the pinky finger and nearly snaps it at the base.

Maxie hisses but does not cry out. "*You crazy shit bird.* You no-good, lousy thug. You just killed yourself. It won't be quick and it won't be painless. That much I promise. God damn your soul, Joe Pendergast."

"Come inside and do it," Joe says. "We can't fight through a window. Come around to the side and be quiet about it, and we'll settle this."

Joe closes the customer window so people won't stand in line. He opens the rear double doors and steps away. He plants his feet. Maxie won't let an injured pinky stop him from fighting, not when his blood is up. He can throw elbows and slam foreheads like a young man. A small voice inside Joe's head tells him to move the fight away from the Moonbeam for Charlie's sake. Maybe they could go for a ride. But it's too late now, and, well, Charlie is someone he just met. A nice woman who could be a friend if things were different, but her dreams are not Joe's problem.

Maxie steps into the truck and closes the door behind him. The bitterness between them is like a freight train that can't be stopped. Joe bends his knees and scooches his right leg a few inches, getting comfortable with his balance. He looks at the hot grill. Maxie looks in that direction too.

"You were always the boss," Joe says. "Now it's just us."

But Maxie bends down and comes. up with the .25 pea-shooter. It was in an ankle holster all this time. He holds it steady, his finger away from the trigger guard.

"I needed you to make the first move, Joe. And that's what you did. Maybe I'll shoot you dead and burn myself on the grill, say you tried to disfigure me, that you went a little nuts. It's the old story of a disgruntled employee. Your brain is turning sour, to boot. I'm sorry, Joe. We had a good run."

Joe stares at the gun and sees where he screwed up. He had wasted time thinking about Charlie. He should have shaken hands with Maxie like a gentleman and invited him inside. Made him feel comfortable so he wouldn't pull the gun. But Joe could never act differently from how he felt. He could never put on airs. He would have been a lousy greeter at the casino.

"Better make the first shot count, boss. That's not a very big gun."

"Oh, I will." His face is all business.

Someone taps at the customer window. The tap turns into a hard knock and a voice calls out. "Hey, I hope you two are done making out in there, because gay geezer sex is not my kink. Get a room or something, yeah? And if see any yeti hairs, I'll puke up my hotdog."

The girl with the mohawk is back.

CHAPTER

7

THE GIRL'S VOICE pierces the bubble. For those few seconds, Joe heard nothing but Maxie's voice, saw nothing but those glittering eyes and the gun. Now he hears the laughter of the beer drinkers, the slamming of car doors, the sizzle from the grill. He smells the meat and the tang of booze.

Maxie lowers the gun and steps back, his pinkish white lips stretched into a grimace. Joe resists the urge to punch him in the liver on general principle. The two are separated by three feet, but it might as well be a football field.

"You should go to a doctor for that finger," Joe says. "It'll swell up. I think a ligament or two might have popped."

Maxie puts the .25 in his pocket and cradles his hand. "It's too bad, Joe. You can't be put out to pasture now. You got to be put down. I need to work out how it will happen, and I will enjoy it." Maxie turns and leaves. He doesn't seem angry or sad—just lost in thought, as if he's been presented with a complex math equation and needs a blackboard.

Joe watches him go, knowing he has become just another problem in Maxie's grand scheme, like a building that must be demolished or a piece of land to be plowed under. As he opens the customer window, the girl with the mohawk props her elbows on the sill and stares straight ahead, not meeting Joe's gaze. "That man had a gun," she whispers. "Shouldn't you be calling someone?"

"No, and you shouldn't either."

"Because you two were friends? You called him 'brother.'"

He slaps both hands on the table. "If you want food, I can get you food."

"I'm good," she says. "I was walking past and saw you two facing off, and I made the joke, but then I saw the gun."

"If you don't want food, I got customers behind you."

She steps aside as Joe fills orders for the next few minutes. When the rush passes, she sidles up to the window and leans in like they are old friends. She passes a few crumpled bills toward him. "Now that I'm thinking about it, give me a side of mac and cheese. Is that guy with the gun coming back?"

"Probably not tonight."

He scoops mac and cheese onto a plate. She grabs a plastic fork and walks off to the left, then changes her mind and goes right. She flips up her hoodie. When she moves across Joe's field of vision, hunching forward from left to right, the image connects with a bang. The slender figure, the strange walk.

She's the person in Donna's video.

8

J OE CLOSES UP around ten o'clock. He's out of mac and
cheese and Italian sausage, running low on hotdogs and
coleslaw, but his head is full of ideas. Before leaving, he
walks inside to say goodbye to Charlie. The Moonbeam is
going great guns, and she's in her element, navigating the
landscape, managing her dream. Joe catches her attention
and waves.

"Hope everything went okay," she says, raising her voice
above the noise.

"A few surprises. Nothing I couldn't handle."

"Then I'll see you next week."

"Yeah."

He drives twenty minutes to Newport News to scout
out tomorrow's lunchtime gig. According to an email, they
want him to set up on the sidewalk outside the courthouse
near City Hall. It sounds safe, but he wants to see it at night,
without people. He wants to see angles and corners in case
Maxie sends someone with a gun, although a drive-by killing in public isn't his style. The city of Newport News is
shaped like a pencil, three miles wide and twenty-eight miles
long. At the southern end, government buildings cluster in

the shadow of the Newport News shipyard, where the towers of aircraft carriers rise in glorious Navy gray against the backdrop of the James River.

Joe finds the spot and parks the food truck. He cuts the engine and opens the customer window to let in the cool breeze. If he goes home now, someone could be waiting in the bushes or in the house. The scenarios flip past like his old baseball cards. Maxie keeps several men around him these days, drivers and gofers, men with no brains and gym muscles, who might carry guns or saps. In the early years, Joe was the only guard Maxie needed, the only messenger, the only driver, the only problem solver. And Joe was dumb enough to be proud of it.

He spends a few minutes gazing into the empty valleys of downtown Newport News before driving back to Hampton. He wrestles the food truck into his little driveway and notices a shadow moving in Donna's front window.

He climbs out of the truck and stretches. If someone is inside with a gun, they'll have a good target. A bullet could drop him in the driveway in these next ten seconds. But the moment passes and Donna opens her front door. She's wearing a Virginia Tech shirt, track pants, and thick, heavy socks. She scurries across the lawn, wide-eyed and nervous.

"Butterbean was in the backyard, barking his fool head off. I went out to get him and saw—I don't know— movement, a shadow in the backyard. Maybe a large dog but maybe something else. Maybe I'm seeing things."

"Now look, Donna. I'm the one on this street who's supposed to have hallucinations. Don't go invading my territory."

"Joe, this isn't funny."

"Was this movement toward the back end of the yard or closer to the house?"

"Toward the back end."

"Did it move quickly? Did it flinch or anything?"

"No. It . . . it slid. Like a person sneaking around."

"Did you hear anything?"

"Just Butterbean."

Joe wants to ask if she has more security footage of the strange person on Seneca Lane. If nothing else, he might solve the mystery of Mohawk Girl and the blood in the boat before this person in the yard decides to shoot him.

"I'll go inside," he says. "I'm sure it's nothing."

"No, sir. I'm going with you and taking my pepper spray and stun gun. I danced at a club, Joe. I know something about defending myself in the dark hours after last call. And don't tell me I'm a hippie's daughter so I have to be a peace lover. That's a nasty stereotype."

The house is as empty as Joe's future. Downstairs, the sliding glass door is closed but unlocked. Joe can't remember if he left it that way. Donna goes upstairs, turning on lights and stomping from room to room before coming downstairs. "All clear," she says. "That's the proper term, right?"

"That's what the detectives say on TV. We make quite the team, the old codger and the hippie's daughter. We could get a show on Netflix."

"We should market it."

They share a nervous laugh. Donna hasn't calmed down, and now Joe is feeling the rush of adrenaline that sometimes came after he collected one of Maxie's debts, after the poor loser pleaded and got beat for his trouble, the sound of broken bones like ice cubes cracking in a tray. How many times did he go to the wall for that man, walking into danger because someone owed Maxie money? Now he's risking Donna's neck for no good reason.

She lingers at the door.

"Something else, Donna?"

"That whiteboard upstairs. What you wrote. I couldn't help but see it. Maxie visiting, take care of him before he takes care of you, lead police on a chase. It's an odd list."

"Pay that no mind," Joe says. "I was rambling."

"Maxie is your old boss, right? The guy who runs Captain Maxie's and wants to build the casino."

"He is. Did I tell you that?"

"I googled you and found a story from a few years ago about you being the best bouncer around. It says you worked for Maxie, and he's in the news these days. Are there problems, Joe? The way things are going around here—people in the road, people in the bushes—I'm going to worry."

"Don't be nervous."

"Stop with the tone. I'm not a nervous Nellie. If something is going on with you, I want to know about it."

"Nothing is going on with me. Promise."

"How did it go tonight at the Moonbeam?"

"Smooth as silk. Now get a good night's sleep and go sell houses tomorrow."

As she turns to leave, her hand rests on the doorknob. "Joe, can I make a confession?"

"If it's about dancing at clubs, I'd rather not hear it."

"I didn't see a shadow in the yard. I just wanted to come in here and make sure everything was in its proper place given your condition. Does that mean I'm terrible?"

He pats her arm. "It means you're a good neighbor, but I really am feeling fine."

He goes upstairs and takes his pills. From under his pillow, he checks the .44 snub nose revolver he's carried with him on occasion, a gun he has only fired once. Later that night, he falls asleep on the couch. The gun stays under the pillow.

CHAPTER

9

JOE GETS TO Newport News a full two hours before the gig is supposed to begin. Someone from the city staked out his spot with orange traffic cones, and he edges the food truck into place after a couple of tries. The customer window provides a view of the sidewalk and a small park with benches and trees. Last night, his eyes were drawn to the lights of the shipyard, and he looked right past this little park. In the bright light of day, the area looks harmless. Maxie won't try anything here.

Downtown lunch customers turn out to be a different breed from drinkers at the Moonbeam. They want their food and they want to leave. Back to their meetings. Back to their desk with pictures of kids and golden retrievers. Back to networking, or whatever they call goofing off these days. The steady march of customers continues for the first hour. Joe manages to restock the grill and put on another Crock-Pot of mac and cheese without closing the window, but when he turns around, five people stand in line.

The woman in front wears a scarlet blouse and white skirt. Her giant hoop earrings dangle on either side of her heart-shaped face, and she bobs her head with a nervous energy. "You got quite the cash cow here, Mr. Joe Takeaway. There you go. That wasn't so hard."

"Ma'am?"

"You just smiled. Don't look so grim. Life is good."

"If you say so."

Mohawk Girl shows up around one o'clock. She stands in the park and pretends to read a history plaque. She's facing away, but there is no mistaking that racing stripe of black hair. Joe wonders if she wants to be seen, or if she figures he is too busy to notice her. As he works through another rush of customers, she sits cross-legged on the ground, still facing away, her backpack on the ground. The food supplies start to dwindle. The hotdogs go first, then the Italian sausage. With ten minutes left in the gig, Joe is down to brats and coleslaw, with no customers. He closes the window and trots into the park. The girl is listening to music through earbuds. Up close, she looks maybe part Latina or black—those white earbuds stand out against the light brown skin. He hooks his finger in the backpack, lifts it off the ground, and walks back to the truck.

It takes her a minute to realize her backpack is gone. She looks right and left, then walks in circles. Joe locks the double doors to the food truck, shuts the customer window, and opens the backpack. Inside the flap is a card you fill out in case someone finds it. It has the name of Paula Jessup and a phone number, but no address. The backpack contains two cans of pepper spray, several energy bars, a decent first aid kit, feminine products, a pocket knife, a larger jackknife, a flashlight, and a whistle. There is no wallet, no money, no other identification.

He's still rifling through her stuff when she knocks on the window.

"Gimme my stuff, pervert."

Joe opens the window. "Hello, Paula. We're out of hotdogs, but the brats are good if you'd like one. On the house.

Stalking someone must take a lot of energy. You need to keep up your strength."

Her clothes are identical from the night before: blue jeans with frayed knees and a T-shirt with a sequined pattern that's impossible to decipher without staring too hard at her chest. A stiff breeze comes in off the James River and sails through the little valley of office buildings. She hugs herself against the March wind.

"You need a jacket?" Joe points to the corner. "I got one hanging over there. It's the first day of spring, but still."

"I'm fine. I need my backpack."

"You got quite the arsenal in here."

Her face twists into a grimace. "Come on, man. I want my backpack."

"How about you tell me where you live and I'll bring it to your door? I don't see an address in here. Fact is, you have me at a disadvantage. My schedule is on Facebook. You can show up whenever and ambush me. But I can't show up where you are. Can I at least keep that big knife?"

"I need everything in there," she says, almost whining now. "I'm on my own."

Before he can finish, she reaches in and tries to grab the pack. Joe has a good hold, and they play tug-of-war for a few seconds until she lets go and starts to cry. Backpedaling into the park, she looks right and left, her face twisted in grief.

"Hey, I'm sorry," Joe calls out—maybe he took this too far. "Sometimes I don't know when to stop kidding around. Here, take your stuff."

Instead, she runs into the park and cuts around a corner as if someone is chasing her.

THAT NIGHT, JOE double-checks the lock on the sliding glass door in his office. That's where Maxie's men would enter. The front door only works for cops and thugs collecting debts, but that big glass door is a beacon for someone wanting to break in. He examines it for scratches or marks and finds none. He steps outside onto the redwood deck, which is just big enough for his grill and two camp chairs in the unlikely event he would have a guest. He should install a motion light out here. Then again, a light would not scare the type of man Maxie would send.

Joe figures he'll have a week, maybe less, and stalking Maxie won't be easy. He has a couple of offices in Norfolk and keeps a rotating schedule. He lives in a gated community with a guardhouse. He can't walk into Captain Maxie's waving a gun because other people might get hurt. Hell, he felt bad about Charlie the bartender, and he barely knows her. He may have to wait for someone to show up and decide matters.

Sighing in resignation, he trudges upstairs and sits on the couch next to Paula Jessup's backpack. In the time he has left, maybe he can figure out this girl's story. She's on the run from something or someone. That much was clear from this morning.

"I should have given you back to her," he says to the pack. "I joked around too much. I did that working the door sometimes. People got pissed about not getting inside, and I could make them smile, even when they were waiting. And you know what? Sometimes I'd give them a break. That's why they named me best bouncer, not because of my fists." He closes the pack. This girl's got someone chasing her. He thinks of his boat, the blood, the hank of hair.

He puts the backpack aside. In two years as Captain Maxie's night manager, he hired kitchen help and waitstaff. In the process, he taught himself how to do background searches on job candidates. He ran names through prison databases. He subscribed to a website that told him if someone had declared bankruptcy or got sued in federal court. Another tool allowed him to see old versions of websites. For a moment, Joe pretends he's sitting in his little office at Captain Maxie's, surrounded by CO_2 cylinders and boxes of napkins, and Paula Jessup has just applied for a job as a waitress or a cook. Last call has come and gone. Chairs are up on tables, pointing their legs to the sky like passed-out drunks, and he has the building all to himself.

Time for a deep dive on Paula Jessup.

She has a Facebook page that hasn't been updated in more than a year. She graduated from Phoebus High School four years ago, so that puts her around twenty-two years old. The most recent post is from eighteen months ago, a group photo taken at the York River Comedy Club. It was the final show of the season, and eight people are crowded shoulder to shoulder. Paula appears to be laughing at something off camera. Her comment reads: "What a great group. If only we could laugh like this all the time."

She lists no family, relationships, or jobs.

Paula Jessup does not show up in the state prison system or federal court. A simple search of news stories turns up her high school graduation list, nothing more.

He searches general news for the last name of Jessup and skims though dozens of entries. Jessup is a community a few miles south of Baltimore, Maryland. Several campuses in California make up William Jessup University. Stanley Jessup is running for sheriff somewhere in Oklahoma, and Maya Jessup is an art student at the University of Minnesota, with her own blog. Joe searches for "Paula Jessup" and "Virginia" and finally hits on a news story from a dozen years ago.

Late on a February night, Michelle Jessup, a resident of Berkeley County in central Virginia, died when her car crashed into a bridge abutment on a rural road a few miles from the Daisy Court Trailer Park, where she lived. Michelle had been drinking at a bar around midnight, and police believe the crash happened around one in the morning as she drove home. Several empty beer cans were found in the wreckage.

Michelle was a single mom. Friends said she was a self-taught mechanic who enjoyed working on cars. One neighbor said Michelle could "replace your brakes, swap out your plugs and was a serial oil changer, and she hated cars with computers. She wanted to fix things herself." Her restored 1975 Chevy Nova was demolished in the wreck. Besides her father, Michelle was survived by her ten-year-old daughter, Paula Jessup.

There is no mention of Paula's father.

Joe searches for Paula Jessup in Berkeley County and finds nothing. At some point, she moved to Hampton and graduated from Phoebus, but how did she get here without a mother? Where does she live now? Questions run together as he tries to assemble a time line. A wave of vertigo washes over him. He holds his head to stop the spinning and closes his eyes. He leans back on the couch, hands at his side, legs out straight.

He wakes up.

It seems that some time has passed.

The house is dark.

There is no power outage. The refrigerator is humming, and the blue digital numbers on the microwave stand out in the dark. He doesn't remember turning off the lights. Without moving his head, he scans the living room. Stairs lead up from the ground floor, and he can see the top steps. His eyes shift to the whiteboard, then back to the stairs and—*there.*

A movement in the shadows. Someone standing at the top of the stairs just now, then moving down to avoid being seen.

Pushing up from the couch with a loud groan, he shuffles toward the kitchen, then into his bedroom. He pulls the .44 snub nose from under the pillow and counts to three. He listens for movement and hears none. He strides deliberately from the bedroom toward the top of the stairs and sees the shadow moving farther down, into the darkness.

Joe pulls the trigger. The gun kicks in his hand.

He runs downstairs and sees a bullet hole in the wall above the door. A breeze hits his back, coming from the office. The sliding glass door is wide open, and the glass is broken near the handle, which is sticky and wet.

A woman comes into the backyard and calls his name. She wears a Virginia Tech shirt and sweatpants, and wants to know if he's hurt. This woman doesn't work at Captain Maxie's. He's sure of it. And he was just in his office, doing a background check on a new hire, the kind of thing Maxie never thought a two-fisted thug like Joe Pendergast could do, but by God he did it. Kathy had showed him a few websites, but Joe figured out the rest himself.

This woman reminds him of Kathy in some ways. Maybe she's a cousin.

But she shouldn't be here.

Just to be safe, he points the gun at her head.

11

"You don't work here," Joe says. "Get back in your car and go home."

The woman puts her hands in the air and stares at the gun. Joe doesn't recognize this corner of Maxie's parking lot. Someone must have planted pine trees along the back border and not told him, but he doesn't patrol the grounds. He's not a fucking groundskeeper. He's the night manager, for Christ's sake. He hires and fires people. Twenty years of working the door until he got his dream job, and no one can take it away.

"You're not supposed to be back here," he says to the woman. "I could shoot you for trespassing. If you're too drunk to call a cab, I can call one for you, but just this once. I'm not a dispatcher, and I don't the work door anymore. I run a tight ship. I've tossed out girls as well as guys. Sometimes the girls fight harder. You got blood on your hands? Because there's blood right here on this handle. I'll stop talking now. You got me rambling."

The woman shows him both palms. "There is no blood on my hands."

"That's good for now."

The woman smiles. "I want to put my hands down, and I want you to lower the gun. Can we do that?"

Joe doesn't know why he's holding the gun. Nothing good happens when someone brings a gun to a bar. But this whole thing is confusing. There shouldn't be grass in the parking lot, and the pine trees don't make sense.

"I want you to think," the woman says. "You know me."

"You look like one of Kathy's cousins. She doesn't have a sister. I've often told her, 'God forbid there'd be another like you in the family.'"

"It sounds like Kathy is very special." This woman acts like she has all day. Her expression is so sincere, as if Joe Pendergast is the most interesting man alive, and she can't wait to hear more about his life.

"Kathy is my girlfriend." Joe's voice always catches on the last word because he can't possibly believe it. "She's a good twenty years younger than me, but I think she has daddy issues. She came here to Captain Maxie's a few years ago and runs the kitchen on day shift."

"Came here to Captain Maxie's," the woman repeats, looking around the yard. So she's confused by the trees and the grass too. "I get it. Are you just dating, or are you living together?"

"Living in sin," Joe says. "That's what Kathy calls it. She was raised as a churchgoer, but she don't bother with it now, and I never did. My parents worked every Sunday at Pendergast Cut-Rate. No one remembers it now. It was up in Hampton. I worked there seven days a week." He eyes the woman again. "Kathy's got red hair like you. I thought there was a resemblance. But she's back home now, sleeping. She manages the kitchen. She's smart as a whip too. I let her handle my email and my banking. She does banking over the computer, lickety-split. And I don't care about my email. Half of it's junk anyway."

"You must trust her a great deal. How long have you been living together?"

Joe searches his memory. "It seems like a long time, but it probably isn't. She knows all my secrets."

"She must be a special person, because we all have secrets."

"I've got secrets up the yin yang," Joe says. "I killed a guy and left him in a burning car. A cop can't walk today because of me. And I never went to see him, never apologized for one damn thing. He was a good cop. Maxie says people who apologize are weak, and he wouldn't let me talk about it with anyone, not even Kathy."

The woman who could be Kathy's cousin doesn't move. "That sounds awful. Why did you kill someone and leave them in a burning car? Was this a bad man?"

Joe chuckles. "He was a deadbeat. And he was obnoxious. That's what got him killed, not the deadbeat part."

"And the police officer—what happened to put him in a wheelchair?"

He's about to tell her when a small dog comes yapping along. It's a tiny thing, like that dog in *The Wizard of Oz*. The woman seems relieved and calls the dog "Butterbean." Joe connects it to the little dog in the sports car and connects that to his neighbor Donna and connects that to the face of the woman standing before him. Donna has stopped by for a visit. That's all this is. Relief washes over him.

"How are you doing, Donna?"

"I'm good, Joe," she says. "I forget what we were talking about. Do you remember?"

Joe looks down at the blood on his hand, then sees it on the door. "This isn't my blood. I guess I had a break-in. I don't know. I'm confused. I got a gun, though. No one's gonna sneak up on me."

"Why don't we walk upstairs and get you settled?" Donna cradles her dog in one hand and steps inside. She carefully closes the sliding door and picks up shards of glass from the carpet and drops them in a wastebasket. She asks Joe if he has a vacuum cleaner. Joe tells her not to worry about it. Donna leads him upstairs and tells him to sit on the couch. She goes into the kitchen and comes back with his pill tray.

"It looks like you didn't take your pills tonight," she says. "See here? Friday evening is still full."

Joe stares at the plastic container with its tiny compartments. "Yeah. Looks good."

"But you should take these pills. Do you want some water?"

"That'd be good, Donna. Thanks."

Donna goes into the kitchen and opens the fridge. She seems to take a long time getting a bottle of water and comes back shaking her head. "That fridge is a mess, Joe. All those boxes of hotdogs and sausages opened up. The top is off the coleslaw. Which hand should I slap?" She laughs and waves him away. "I'm kidding. It's your fridge, and you can keep it however you like."

Donna must be mistaken. He'd left the inside of his fridge buttoned up with everything in its proper place and labeled, like always. The dog curls up next to him. Before nodding off to sleep, he sees Donna staring at that whiteboard as if she's trying to solve a complicated math problem. Joe looks at it too. It's not his list from before. The writing is in a red marker.

He doesn't use red.

CHAPTER

12

JOE WAKES TO sunshine streaming through the shutters. He shields his eyes and feels around for the dog, but Butterbean is gone and so is Donna. It's just after eight in the morning. He goes into the bathroom and makes correct use of his toothpaste and shaving cream. He checks his laptop and finds an email from Jennifer, his friendly counselor.

Mr. Pendergast:

I wanted to follow up on Thursday's email. How was your first "gig" at the Moonbeam Brewery? I can't wait to hear about it. Did you have to throttle any drunks? Given that you worked as a bouncer, I bet everyone behaved. LOL!!! Anyway, send me a message when you have time.

Your friend,

Jennifer

He walks toward the deck, figuring the morning sun might do him some good. Passing the whiteboard, he sees the writing in red.

Got my backpack. Took some food on the house.

Maxie didn't send someone to break in last night. It was that Paula Jessup.

He searches the rest of the room. The backpack is gone from the couch and Donna was right: the fridge is a mess. Someone took a twelve-pack of hotdogs and a scoop or two of the coleslaw. His gun is on the kitchen counter, and he's not sure how it got there. Maybe Donna put it there for safe keeping after they talked in the backyard. She sure is nosy. He makes himself a fried egg sandwich and eats it on the upper deck.

As he's finishing, Donna comes outside and looks up at him, shielding her eyes from the sun. "Just checking to see how we're doing after last night's excitement," she says. "I think I got all the glass from the broken door."

"Thanks for doing that," he says. "We were jabbering away, weren't we?"

"We sure were." She pretends to zipper her mouth shut, as if protecting some great secret. "Any idea who broke in? Whoever it was left a note—something about taking food and a backpack."

"It was a mix-up with a customer yesterday. It's nothing."

Donna switches on her real estate–agent smile. "It sounds like more than a mix-up, Joe. I know a guy who sells security systems and he could get you a good deal. We've got a hooded figure walking along the street, and now you've got a break-in. Did you see the news this morning?"

"I don't watch much news."

"They found a body floating near the bridge–tunnel. A something-something Jessup, which isn't a name I know around here." She shrugs, as if this news is neither here nor there. "Well, Butterbean and I have errands. You have a good day, and let me know if you need anything. Did you take your pills this morning? I put your pill tray on the counter near the gun. Put that gun someplace safe, okay?"

But Joe is already walking inside, trying to swim through the brain sludge and remember exactly what happened last night. *Any idea who broke in?* He paces the room, looking for his laptop, and spots it on the coffee table. Of course it's on the coffee table. Where else would it be? His hands tremble. Paula Jessup was here. She took the backpack and opened the fridge. Her backpack had been on the couch. He could have reached out and strangled her and dumped her body in the water, and the police could have fished her out this morning.

What else happened last night? Why did Donna zip her lips like she was keeping a secret?

He can't look at the news story. He can't see her face staring back at him.

Then he thinks.

A body in the water near the Hampton Roads Bridge–Tunnel.

How would Paula get all the way out there?

He checks the gun and sees that one round has been fired. He remembers being at the top of the stairs and finds the bullet hole above the door. He runs down to the garage and searches his Hyundai Accent. A layer of dust has settled on the hood. It hasn't been driven recently. The food truck is locked and doesn't appear to have been driven last night.

But maybe Paula Jessup has a car. He could have stolen it and driven her body somewhere.

Just be a man and look at the damn story.

He goes to his laptop, calls up a website for a local news stations, and looks under breaking news. He's hyperventilating. *Just look at it,* he tells himself.

A body was found floating in the water near the HRBT. The victim was wearing a life jacket, and police are not commenting on the cause of death. They found a wallet with the body, and it had a Virginia driver's license.

The dead man is Anthony Jessup.

Joe breathes.

You're such a pussy. It's all a big coincidence.

Or maybe not. Joe googles the name and finds the obit of Michelle Jessup he read last night. He reads how she wrapped her 1975 Chevy Nova around a tree and how she liked to work around cars. Farther down, Anthony Jessup is named as Michelle's father. He is the grandfather of ten-year-old Paula, who lost her mother in that accident and whose father was already long gone. Chances are, Paula was raised by her grandfather into adulthood.

So now Anthony Jessup is dead, and the granddaughter is galivanting around the neighborhood.

It's a nice mystery. Fascinating to figure out if he had the time.

Joe slams down the laptop lid.

Except he doesn't have time. His brain can only handle one rabbit hole at a time, and even that will be dicey. Paula Jessup wants to play a game with Joe, but she needs to find another partner or learn solitaire. He looks at the whiteboard and chuckles. "I'm sorry, Paula Jessup. Good luck with your dead grandpa. You're on your own. I got my own killing to plan."

He spends the rest of Saturday cleaning the house.

PAULA

13

PAULA JESSUP WAKES up in the front seat of her 1976 Chevy Nova SS. The air is stale and close. Her bloody hand sticks to the vinyl, and she peels it away by fractions of an inch. A sudden movement outside the window forces her upright. The skin rips and she screams as blood drips across the seat. Two men on sleek bicycles glide past the car in gales of laughter.

She presses the open wound against her jeans. It's a clean slit, nothing more. With her free hand, she reaches for the combat knife that fits into the scabbard strapped to her ankle. It's still there. An elderly couple walk past the window and look down their noses at her bedraggled clothes. Or maybe it's the mohawk. Old people hate the mohawk.

So much for spending the night at her happy place.

She's at Fort Monroe, the former Army bastion with historic homes and brick apartment buildings, which opened to the public a few years ago. The seawall and beach attract cyclists, dog walkers, and joggers. Old concrete bunkers that once housed artillery to guard the Chesapeake Bay now stand as silent sentries. Paula parked here last night after fleeing Joe Pendergast, who shot at her with a hand cannon and missed by a mile. She'd broken in through a sliding glass door and carelessly grabbed a sharp edge while running out. But she managed to snag her backpack and some food from his fridge.

She rolls down two back windows, and the stiff breeze sweeps away the stench of blood and sweat. It's just after eight o'clock on Saturday morning, and Mia would be serving breakfast. Paula calls her and gets the answering machine.

"Hello. You've reached the Benedict House, a shelter for homeless women and their children. If this is an emergency, call 911. Otherwise, leave contact information and a brief description of your situation."

Mia Newsome.

* * *

Paula had seen her on the news, being interviewed about human trafficking. She'd googled her, learned that Mia Newsome had been the most feared campaign manager in Virginia, responsible for a string of Democratic successes at the state and congressional level. One day she'd up and quit, declaring that winning elections wasn't enough, and set out to help people in need. She'd testified before the General Assembly in Richmond about trafficking, and ran the Benedict House, named for the patron saint of the homeless.

She was the woman to hear the story Paula needed to tell.

They'd met seven months ago on a warm September morning. On the day Paula knocked on the door, Mia ushered her into a nearby park, where they could talk in private.

The woman was in her early fifties but looked ten years younger, with short silver hair. She wore thick black glasses with horn-rimmed frames and blue jeans.

"I can see you need to talk," Mia had said.

And Paula had, about how she'd grown up in central Virginia with her mother, who'd died in a car crash when Paula was ten; how she'd moved in with Grandpa Tony in the same trailer park; how she'd learned that he ran with a crew who stole TVs and appliances. About how she had to wash her own clothes and couldn't always get it done, so she would wear dirty clothes to school, easing past the school bus driver, who wrinkled her nose. She learned to make her own meals and ate a lot of bananas and ramen noodles; learned to avoid Grandpa Tony when he was planning a job or when he was drunk, which accounted for most of his waking hours.

Then Paula told what she had never told anyone: what had brought them here. How, on a night when she was fourteen, she woke to find the guy who ran the crew, Chauncey, straddling her. Her grandfather heard her screams and interrupted before anything happened, but a few months later moved them here to Hampton. He had a friend who worked at the George Pickett Grill, and he got a job there. He rented a house, and Paula moved into an apartment above his garage.

"It was rent-free and had a washer/dryer combo," she said. "He gave me his password to Netflix and HBO, and I could come and go as I pleased. But we never talked."

"Not about Chauncey the rapist?"

Paula shook her head. She thought about that night, how her grandfather, instead of being furious when he came upon Chauncey trying to hump his granddaughter, got a look like, *"Hmm, how do I handle this?"*

Then Paula got to the point, the story she needed to tell. A few months ago, she'd come home from the comedy club, early in the morning, after partying with her friends, and she'd seen a group of young girls trooping out of her grandfather's house and piling into a van. Young girls, like middle school age—all Hispanic. At four in the morning.

Grandpa drove them away. After they left, she went upstairs in the main house, which she'd been told was off limits, where she'd never been and which she'd never asked about. She found two rooms, military-style cots, rumpled clothes, stuffed animals, cigarettes, and condoms.

She started watching the house before sunrise. The girls left at the same time. They looked exhausted, strung out. She followed the van, saw where the girls were dropped off. She visited the Pickett for lunch, casually wandered back past the restrooms, saw some of the girls working in the kitchen.

Paula sweated as if the sick truth was oozing from her pores.

Mia had waited before speaking, and seemed to choose her words carefully. "It sounds like the Pickett is engaging in labor trafficking at the very least, maybe sex trafficking," she said. "These girls are recruited out of poor conditions in their home countries, with the lure of work in the states. Once they arrive, someone takes their important papers— allegedly for safe keeping. They don't know the language or the area. They have no money or friends. It's forced slavery."

Mia's mouth twisted into a frown. "You could call the police, but the owners of the Pickett could plead ignorance. Maybe they'll say the girls provided false documents. They'll get off with minor offenses, and the girls—the children— will be the one who suffer."

Paula shifted on the bench. "Tell me what to do," she said. And Mia did.

"Watch the restaurant. Hang out in a far corner of the parking lot. Try to talk with the girls if they leave the building. Try to figure out where they come from."

Over the next several weeks, Paula watched the Pickett and noted when the girls took smoke breaks behind the restaurant. At first, Paula walked by and nodded. Then she started talking to them. Three months ago, she'd convinced one girl to leave and seek refuge at the Benedict House.

Mia had sent her news stories, studies, and brochures about the different forms of human trafficking. Paula had the papers on the front seat of the Nova and read them during her stakeouts. That's what had gotten her in trouble with her grandfather. That's what led to Wednesday night.

* * *

Wednesday was three days ago, but it seems like a lifetime. That night, her grandfather walked up to her apartment and opened the door without knocking. He held a fistful of human trafficking literature in his massive hand.

"These were on your car seat," he said.

"I hope you didn't break a window getting in."

"Let's go for a ride and talk about this, hon."

He never called her hon. It scared the hell out of her, and she pointed to her gym shorts. "Let me change first. That night air is cold." She put on a hoodie and jeans, strapping the combat knife to her ankle.

She drove the Nova, and he directed her toward water. He said very little. When they hit a random dead-end street with a boat slip, he told her to stop and get out. She stepped onto the street, bent down, and pulled out the knife. Her heart hammered. She fought to control her breathing in the still air. Silent grandfather was bad grandfather. He pushed her into the boat and stepped in after her. He donned the only life jacket, smiling as he put it on. Then he had her row the boat into the inlet that led toward the Chesapeake Bay. A hundred yards from shore, he told her to stop.

"You got into my business, Paula," he said. "You never should have done that, and this ends now."

She stared at him. Was this the warning, out here in open water? Was this how he wanted her to back off, him with a life jacket and her with a hoodie? Was he going to dump her overboard, make her swim for shore to teach her a lesson?

Then he spoke again. "I'm very sorry about this," he said. "But your momma should have never checked out early. Truth be told, she didn't want a child, so maybe this is just as well." He reached back into his waistband, where he always carried his favorite piece, a .38 caliber revolver. Somehow, she wasn't really shocked when he pulled it out.

He was going to shoot her and dump her body in the water, as if she was nobody, nothing, not his flesh-and-blood kin he helped raise? Or maybe he was bluffing. This didn't seem real. But she saw the look on his face, she saw him move to raise the gun, and she lunged, surprising him, knocking the gun away. But then he locked his hand around her neck, those strong hands, hands that never offered her any comfort or affection. As his grip tightened, scenes rushed past her: Chauncey the pervert, doing her own laundry, momma's death as an inconvenience, those poor girls who slept in his house, never caring, never helping. She had the knife in her hand, holding tight, and she reached up and jammed it in as hard as she could. For a moment nothing happened, and then his grip loosened. She pushed his hands off her and pulled away, sucking in air, staring at him. The blade had gone in beneath his Adam's apple. He reached up touched the hilt and she saw the fury in his eyes, saw him pull it out, saw him lunge for her, and somehow he was over the side, in the water. She grabbed for him, a granddaughter's instinct buried somewhere in her DNA. Her fingers dug into loose skin, and she came away with a clump of hair as he went over.

She screamed into the air, a wordless, wrenching shriek, and fell back into the boat.

The air had turned suddenly cold. She shivered. The boat was drifting toward open water and the bridge–tunnel.

She grabbed the oars and rowed toward her grandfather, but the current swept him farther out, and she watched him go. She picked up his gun and flung it far away into the dark. She wailed into the night while rowing back to shore, the bottom of the boat sticky with blood. Her shoulders and neck ached by the time she made it back to shore, and she was shaking with cold. The bottom of the boat was filled with gunk as she climbed out and stumbled onto the dead-end road. At first, she walked the wrong way, then turned and found her car.

An old man stood in his front yard, staring into space.

"What the hell are you looking at?" Paula asked, her voice trembling. "You want to kill me too?"

He worked his mouth, but no words came out. Whatever he saw wasn't the car, she realized. Whatever he thought didn't concern her. A food truck was parked in his driveway. She noted the name, "Joe's Takeaway."

"You must be Joe," she said. "Nice to meet you, Joe. If you don't mind, I need to get back and clean out my apartment. This car is so great that I'll be living in it for a while. How do you like them apples?"

As she drove away, the old man followed the car with his eyes.

Paula hasn't talked to Mia in two weeks. It's time to tell her about the boat and the strange man in the yard.

14

Paula calls the Benedict House again and gets the answering machine. This time, she leaves a message: *I've had a week. It started Tuesday night and there's stuff you need to know. Since you don't like surprise visits, this is fair warning. I might need another walk in the park. Maybe the jets will be flying out of Langley today. I could use some inspiration.*

She leaves Fort Monroe and detours past Grandpa's house for a slow drive-by of her now-abandoned garage apartment. After watching her grandfather float away and then leaving the boat, she fled back to the apartment and packed up the Nova, concentrating on anything that would betray her identity. The apartment isn't in her name. There is no lease, no documentation. If the police searched it, she wants them to think a nameless hobo squatted there. It took about an hour to clean out the place, a shockingly efficient operation, considering what had happened. Maybe she'd wanted to leave for so long that it just came naturally.

Now, two police cruisers are parked outside the house. She drives past with both hands on the wheel, eyes straight ahead. A block later, she checks her mirrors. A white Mercedes-Benz van has come up behind her. It's just like the one her grandfather drove to work. The George Pickett Grill had three or four identical models, always parked in the far corner of the shopping center. They let Grandpa take one home at night for the girls.

She turns at random—from Hope Street to Sagar, then to Willard, then back to Hope. The van stays with her. The Pickett logo is emblazoned on the side.

Shit.

Shit. Shit. Shit.

Visiting the Benedict House is impossible now.

At a stop sign, the van pulls to within inches of the Nova's bumper. A man with a buzz cut leans forward on the wheel. A heavy-set white guy sits in the passenger seat. They stare straight ahead, saying nothing. She pulls onto Mercury Boulevard and heads toward Newport News. Mercury Boulevard is a major four-lane highway with a lot of stop-and-go traffic, and it will be hard to lose them. At the first opportunity, she turns toward I-64. On the interstate, the Nova will leave that van in its dust. She takes it east toward Norfolk and Virginia Beach. Three-quarters of a tank of gas will get her to North Carolina if that's what it takes to lose these assholes.

She could stop at Brady's Auto Parts, even though she's not due at work until tomorrow, her ten-hour shifts running Sunday through Wednesday. She could hang out in the break room and make sure the Mercedes doesn't double back.

Wait, are you kidding? They can't know where you work.

They must have been waiting for her at the garage apartment. They haven't heard from Tony and figure something went wrong.

She takes the ramp onto the interstate, and the Mercedes settles in behind her. She eases the Nova to sixty-five and pulls into the passing lane, its V-8 purring. Momma would be proud of this car. Back in the day Momma worked for hours on her own Nova, a 1975 hatchback with a black vinyl roof and mag wheels. Paula sat cross-legged on the ground and passed tools—three-eighths-inch ratchet, Philips head screwdriver—and imagined owning a muscle car when she grew up. She bought the SS three years ago from Jack Brady, who was so impressed with her knowledge of older engines that he hired her to work at his store.

The Mercedes pulls closer. Paula eases the Nova to seventy, then seventy-five. She weaves into the slow lane to get around a truck, then shifts into the passing lane. The Mercedes stays with her. Approaching the bridge–tunnel, she sees a string of brake lights. It might be nothing, she tells herself. Then she comes to the flashing overhead sign.

"TRAFFIC STOPPED. HRBT BLOCKED."

15

PAULA CAN SEE the problem from where she sits: A too-tall truck has tried to enter the tunnel. This happens when the driver ignores height restrictions and gets dinged by a sensor. VDOT folks flag down the truck before it descends into the tunnel portion of the HRBT, which goes under the Chesapeake Bay and comes up onto a bridge. The driver is now trying to maneuver his rig into a pull-off area. This takes about fifteen minutes—not the worst thing that can happen on this stretch—but people have no patience in stopped traffic. Everyone envisions a six-car pileup and thinks they'll be here all day.

Case in fucking point.

A Cooper Mini has somehow wedged itself between herself and the Mercedes van. The driver gets out and stretches. It's been thirty seconds, but he can't keep his ass in the seat. To Paula's right, a man wearing a Navy ball cap steps from a black GMC Yukon, hands on hips, shaking his head. Paula shrugs at him, and he smiles back. Sailors are okay. They come into Brady's Auto Parts looking for chrome gas caps, sporty mufflers, or hood pins to trick out their Hummers or sports cars. Men purchase these items when they don't actually know how to work on cars, but to be fair, sailors have other priorities.

The doors to the Mercedes open. Paula now recognizes the driver, Buzz Cut, as an employee of the Pickett. He was always there during her lunchtime scouting missions, always giving orders to Grandpa, running a hand over his sandpaper scalp. The heavy-set white guy is a stranger, his bullet head catching the sun. They walk over to Cooper Mini guy and pretend to admire his ride. Cooper Mini guy points to the tunnel and shakes his head. They continue talking while the truck maneuvers into the pull-off. The Cooper Mini guy seems to be jabbering a blue streak: "So you're into labor trafficking? I hear that's a growth industry. Those girls make good sandwiches, I hope. You fuck any of them?"

The two men continue toward Paula.

She takes the pepper spray from her backpack, flips up the red button, and shifts it to her left hand, under the closed window. Buzz Cut stops just outside the door. Bullet Head is on the other side. Paula stares straight ahead.

"Bad traffic," Buzz Cut says over the roof of the Nova.

His heavy-set buddy grunts in agreement.

"It sucks when you're trapped and can't move." He rests his arm on the roof and drums his fingers on the metal. His buddy does the same. It sounds like rain falling on the double-wide trailer back in Berkeley County. She grips the steering wheel in both hands and revs the engine.

"Anything could happen in a situation like this." Buzz Cut takes out a set of keys. "Someone could scratch the paint on a nice car and you'd have to sit there and take it." He touches the tip of a key to the Nova's hood, which is painted a sparkling sky blue. Jack Brady gave her a good deal on a paint job, and Paula waxes the Nova every three months. The hood is the most important feature. That's what people see first.

He drags the key across the metal ever so lightly.

Paula rolls down her window and shows him the pepper spray. "Get away from my car."

He pockets the key and turns to her. "Morning, Miss Jessup. They found Tony in the water not too far from where we're standing. Stabbed and bled out. The police called the restaurant because he listed me as an emergency contact. Imagine that. There should be a news story this afternoon. You can read about it." He looks toward the water and shakes his head. "You screwed the pooch on this one, sis. We were willing to shoo you away as a nuisance. You're not a nuisance anymore."

"Steer clear of me," she says.

He looks at the back seat. "You sleeping in this car? Sure looks like it."

Traffic starts to move. The driver of the Cooper Mini rushes to get behind the wheel. Buzz Cut lingers for a moment, then taps the roof of the Nova and walks away.

Everyone keeps to thirty miles an hour through the tunnel, but a NASCAR race breaks out on the other side. The Cooper Mini darts into the slow lane, comes up on a truck, and tries to pull in front the Nova, but Paula is still in third gear. She slams it into fourth, and its two hundred and ninety-five horses pull away from the pack. For the next mile, the Cooper does a decent job of staying with her, but the driver's heart isn't it. He falls back, and the Mercedes isn't even a white speck.

Buzz Cut will bide his time. He'll keep looking.

Paula needs a plan. She drives for another hour, taking Route 17 toward the Great Dismal Swamp before turning around and heading back toward the Benedict House. It's safe to go there now. Maybe Mia will have some ideas.

16

M IA IS IN a mood. She hunkers forward on her desk, having listened to how Paula killed Grandpa, followed by the adventure in stopped traffic with the Mercedes twins. Her office is nothing more than a large closet, and Paula stands with her back against the closed door. There isn't room for another chair, and Paula gets the impression that Mia seldom brings people into this little room, and when she does, the door is always closed.

"Back to gramps," Mia says. "You're in the boat and he pulls out a gun. All because you stacked those brochures in the front seat. I hope you realize how careless that was."

"I had my knife," Paula says.

"A knife almost wasn't enough." Mia shakes her head. "Men and their guns. Where would we be without men and their guns? Back up a second. There is no particular reason you both ended up on Seneca Lane, correct? There is no connection to the strange food truck guy?"

"No reason, but I got the feeling Grandpa wanted to find water. When he saw the boat slip, he looked pleasantly surprised. I don't think he knew the area."

"He probably planned to drown you in the shallows, not actually shoot you. Your death would be a mystery. He'd come and claim the body and shed a few tears. There might be a story in the paper. Maybe the York Comedy Club would dedicate a show to you. And then you'd be forgotten."

"That's really dark."

"It's the truth." She eyes Paula up and down. "You look recovered."

"It's great that you're being supportive through this trying time. You'd think that leaving politics and running a shelter for homeless women would have turned you into a caring nurturer. God forgive me for thinking the obvious."

"It doesn't pay to be a slum angel. Homeless people work their own angles sometimes. Do you still have the knife?"

Paula pulls up her pant leg to show Mia the knife in its scabbard.

Mia can't hold back a tight smile. "Point taken. How far did the boat go out?"

"We were maybe a hundred yards from the shore, heading toward the bridge–tunnel. That's when it happened. There was no one, and I mean no one, on the water. No small boats, no cargo ships coming in or out of the port, no Navy ships."

"Good. So you saw the gun, there was a struggle, you stabbed him, then game over."

"I'm not finished. Jesus, do you ever shut up? I'm not pissed that I killed him in self-defense. I'm pissed that it took me until I was in my early twenties to do it. I should have run him over with a car when we lived in Berkeley County. I'm not in shock and I don't have PTSD. I don't need a counselor. I need to know why I waited so damn long." And she wondered—but didn't say—why she'd made that last futile attempt to reach out to try to save him.

"Because he's your grandfather," Mia says. "He was your last tie to your mother. You held out hope. You're thinking maybe the boat trip is a scare tactic and that he'll tell you to lay off. I blame myself for this, Paula. I told you to watch the Pickett and gather information. I should have done it myself or hired an investigator."

"He bled like you wouldn't believe. I tried to keep him from falling into the water and came away with a handful of hair."

Mia frowns at her phone. "And you felt nothing?"

"Cold. Outside and inside. But I'm fine now. I think."

"Uh-huh." Mia pinches the screen, enlarging whatever she's looking at.

"What's so interesting on the damn phone?"

"I'm reading the news. The top story is about a Hampton man found dead in the water near the bridge–tunnel. Police are investigating the death."

"Are they saying it's homicide?"

"Look at you with the legal phrasing," Mia says. "They haven't said one way or the other. But considering the police are investigating, as well as your encounter with the Mercedes, I wouldn't walk around in the open. You can crash upstairs in the third-floor room. But first pull that hot car of yours around back. It attracts attention. And go say hello to Rosa. See if you can get any more details about what happened to her at the Pickett. We might as well keep looking into that."

Paula smiles at the mention of the girl's name, then turns serious. "I also need to tell you about the weird food truck guy who has problems of his own." Paula describes how the man stood in his yard that night, followed by the encounter at Moonbeam Brewery, then downtown Newport News the next day. For now, she doesn't mention breaking into Joe Pendergast's house to retrieve her backpack, stealing his food, writing on his easel, and getting shot at.

"The night at the Moonbeam was intense," Paula says. "Some guy got in his face. Joe bent his finger, and the guy threatened to kill him."

Mia listens with closed eyes. "I'll do a background report on this Joe Pendergast, since he knows your name. I'll treat him like he's a candidate running for office. If he has any skeletons, I'll let you know."

CHAPTER

17

PAULA TAKES THE stairs to the second floor of the Benedict House. She stops near the end of the hallway and knocks on a door with a crayon drawing of a unicorn leaping over a rainbow. She whispers, "Rosa, it's me." Shuffling noises come from inside. The door opens a few inches, and a girl's face appears, eyes down.

"Can I come in? Unless you're having a private party in there, in which case I'll take the guys for myself. Stupid drawing, by the way. You're not fooling anyone with unicorns and rainbows."

Rosa opens the door, flops on the single bed, and hugs her knees. She is fifteen years old with the eyes of a beaten-down adult who has seen too much of life. Track pants cover her bony legs. A flimsy tank top with food stains down the front hangs from her narrow shoulders. Tousled hair and chipped toenail polish complete the look. It's been two months since Paula lured her away from the George Pickett Grill. That day, her dark eyes sparked with hope and promise. Now she looks at the sheets, at the floor. Everywhere but up.

"Mia treating you well?" Paula asks.

"It's all good."

"You don't look like it's all good."

Rosa rolls away from Paula and stares at the wall. "It's nothing. This place is fine. I feel protected here. But I've got nowhere to go. I can't work anywhere. I've got no ID, no money. No one will hire me."

"I think it goes deeper than that. On the night you got into my Nova, you told me about a man who assaulted you. Groped you. How happy you were to get away from him. Since then, it's been nothing."

"Mia sent you up here to pry more details out of me. She's been asking about it."

"She's concerned, Rosa. We both are. I wish you could get a job at Brady's Auto Parts. I could work the counter, you could make the deliveries. You'd have to get a driver's license, but that would be sweet. We could drive into work together and hang out afterward."

"That's a nice fantasy," Rosa says.

"Don't underestimate Mia when it comes to finding jobs for the girls here. She got that local cosmetology school to accept a few. Two other girls ended up at a landscaping firm. She even placed someone as a welding trainee at one of the smaller shipyards. She won't give up on you, Rosa, so don't give up on yourself. You've already come a long way."

Rosa came from Guatemala. Paula didn't know her whole backstory, only that she'd landed in Florida, worked her way to Hampton Roads, and ended up on the street before working at the Pickett, allegedly for room and board. She wasn't among the girls who had stayed at Grandpa's house. She slept in the backroom of the restaurant and never left the building except for smoke breaks. Rosa doesn't smoke, but she pretended to love cigarettes just to get outside and breathe fresh air.

"Maybe I'll find a boyfriend," she says.

"Don't depend on a man to rescue you. Draw strength from your passion. You could help other people in your situation. Given time, you could run a shelter like the Benedict House, a place where women could be protected. We could do that together."

"Not likely."

"The night you escaped from the Pickett was the best night of my life," Paula says. "I was able to do something that mattered because you had five times the courage of an ordinary person. What you've been through would have broken most people. But you're not broken. Trust me."

Rosa hugs her knees and turns on her TV to the Hallmark Channel. They pass a few minutes watching a Christmas movie, and Rosa starts talking about hot guys and cute kids.

"I need one of those Hallmark boyfriends," Rosa says now. "Some white dude with a crewneck sweater whose wife died a few years ago, and he's raising a kid on his own."

"Boy or girl?" Paula asks, humoring her.

"Definitely a boy. He would need a mother's touch. He'd be afraid of me at first. He might even hate me. I'd accidentally spill something on his favorite shirt or break his computer. But then he'd come around. That would be a nice story."

"Yeah," Paula says. "It sure would."

This goes on for a good thirty minutes. Rosa has an entire make-believe world mapped out, complete with conflicts and happy endings. She would end up running a flower shop. She would do ice sculptures. She would enter her cooking in a local contest and beat out the snobby soccer moms from the PTA. Her stepson would love her for it.

"Come to Brady's Auto Parts with me one day," Paula says. "Hot guys come in all the time."

"But do they have crewneck sweaters and golden retrievers and call themselves Chad? I want a Chad."

Paula grabs the control and turns off the TV. "Rosa, there are no Chads. Get your head out of your ass and stop watching TV. Move on with your life. It won't get any better until you do, and you can't stay here forever. Get up and get out in the world."

Rosa glares at her. She appears on the verge of saying something, then takes a breath and seems to think better of it.

"Spit it out," Paula says. "If want to hate me, that's fine. Whatever gets you up and moving. I get that it's tough. I really do. But sitting on your bed won't make things any better."

Rosa's eyes smolder with anger. "Maybe I could live above your grandfather's garage."

"I'm not there anymore."

"Too bad. Because I'm sure your grandfather would want to come visit me. He could never take his eyes off me when I worked in the kitchen. You should ask him. Ask him about Rosa just for the pleasure, just to see the look on his face."

Paula's mind starts to spin. Grandpa didn't have a woman in his life. His own wife—Paula's grandmother—had left him soon after Paula's mother was born. He never talked about her. In fact, he never talked about women at all. Money, yes. Booze, definitely. But never women. And yet he kept middle school–aged girls in his house. Girls who kept condoms by their bedside.

"Rosa, I . . ."

From the hallway, Mia's voice cuts through the tension. "Paula, come downstairs. I want to show you what I've found. Your Mr. Pendergast turns out to be an interesting fellow."

18

As an opposition researcher in politics, Mia knew how to find legitimate dirt, the kind that can't be refuted. Unpaid taxes and past due child support. Zoning and code violations on rentals (because politicians can be shitty landlords). A master's thesis from thirty years ago that said the Civil War was about state's rights, not slavery. She found old versions of websites, did reverse image searches. She combed through divorce decrees, wills, and property transfers. She made friends at courthouses and police stations. She researched parents and grandparents, children, and grandchildren. Coworkers and bosses. High school classmates and football coaches. Their fraternity and sorority. When Mia said someone's background was "interesting," it meant skeletons were falling from their closet like clowns from a microbus.

The Benedict House has a screened-in back porch where the girls like to hang out. Mia leads Paula to one corner, where computer printouts cover a card table. "Before I get into what I found, what else can you tell me about Joe Pendergast? Go over your encounters again."

"He never talked to me after I got off the boat. He stared straight ahead. I had my grandfather's blood on me. I'd just stabbed him. I'm not even sure what I said. The next night at the Moonbeam, I wanted to see if he remembered me. I made a pest of myself, but I don't think it clicked because he got into that argument with an old guy."

"Interesting," Mia says.

"The next day, he was doing lunch in Newport News. I got careless. I wanted to wait him out, talk to him. But the bastard stole my backpack and got my name. I got pissed and broke into his house later that night to get my stuff. He'd fallen asleep on the couch. I might have written some snarky stuff on an easel he keeps in his living room."

"It bothers me that he knows your name," Mia says, "but there's nothing we can do about that. Joe Pendergast is a dangerous man. He spent decades working at Captain Maxie's bar in Norfolk. Back when he started, it was a rough place. It only went upscale in the past few years. The owner is Max Smith. He's alleged to have run illegal poker games out of the bar, possibly a sports gambling ring, possibly loan sharking. Joe Pendergast served as his gofer, delivery boy, and leg breaker. He might have done worse. He collected on Maxie's bad debts for years."

"There's a magazine story about him being named best bouncer in Hampton Roads three years ago."

"It's bullshit public relations material, designed to put a friendly face on the folksy old man who works the door and talks to people. Joe Pendergast and Max Smith go back a long way."

"How did they connect?"

"That magazine story says Pendergast's parents ran a corner grocery store in Buckroe Beach, and Maxie would come in to chat. There's probably more to that story, but steer clear of Pendergast. He's professional muscle, and he's been cut loose by his boss for reasons unknown. On Captain Maxie's website, he's still listed as the night manager.

I called down there and got the 'he's no longer with the company' line. That means he was fired or there was some kind of breakup."

"I noticed a pill tray on Pendergast's kitchen counter. He kept a list of medications stuck to the door of the fridge. Ari something."

"Aricept?"

"That might be it."

"Ah. He's got dementia. That would explain why he was staring into space when you were in the road. He might have been wandering."

As Paula shuffles through the printouts on the card table, a photo of an older man catches her eye. He's wearing a gray suit and a white shirt open at the collar, and he's smiling at the camera. "This was the guy who got in Pendergast's face at the Moonbeam. The guy who threatened to kill him."

"That's Maxie."

"There wasn't a whole lot of brotherly love between them."

"Keep thinking about what you saw," Mia says. "Even if it you remember it days later, let me know. It's impossible to tell exactly what's going on without more digging. Meanwhile, let me repeat my previous advice. Steer clear of Pendergast. I've known a retiree from the Norfolk Police Department for years. He's a good man. When I dropped Joe Pendergast's name over the phone, it got an immediate 'uh-huh,' as if he couldn't tell me everything he knew. But he provided the background on Pendergast as a debt collector. It saved me some time."

Paula lets that sink in and tries to remember what she saw on the whiteboard before writing her own message in red. Something about taking care of someone. As she thinks back, a girl stumbles onto the porch, cigarette in hand, then stops at the sight of Mia and Paula.

"Sorry," she says.

"No problem," Mia says. "We're almost done here."

When the girl leaves, Mia begins gathering up her printouts. She takes a long look at a Google map that shows a rural area south of Virginia Beach. At the bottom is a parcel outlined in red, labeled with a name.

Ledyard Aloysius O'Brien.

"I went down a brief rabbit hole of Maxie's business dealings," Mia says, noticing Paula's interest. "He's got some casino-hotel complex planned, assuming state lawmakers approve casinos in the near future. He's bought up tracts of land south of Virginia Beach, but this dude holds the key." She points to the strange name. "He owns fifty acres, much of it road frontage. It's impossible for the project to succeed without Maxie buying that land."

"Has Maxie bought it?"

"Not that I can see. This O'Brien might be holding out. But like I said, I've only been at this for an hour. Meanwhile, you need to lay low. The name of Tony Jessup is in the news. Stay here for the time being. I'm assuming nothing in your apartment will identify you, and you've taken down your social media accounts?"

"Yes and yes. My driver's licenses still has my old Berkeley County address. Same for vehicle registration."

"Good. You're off the grid, sort of. Feel free to claim the bedroom on the third floor. The girls hate it because it's small, but it'll do in a pinch. Anything else on your mind?"

"Rosa said something about my grandfather. I think he's the one who groped her."

Mia looks to the backyard, where a small plot of grass that borders an apartment complex. "If that's true, then Rosa isn't the only one. Try and get some sleep."

19

You could drive past the Benedict House and have no idea what goes on there. It looks like any other sprawling family residence in a nice neighborhood, and Mia takes pains to keep it that way. Neatly trimmed shrubs border the house, resting in fresh piles of mulch. The sidewalk in front of the house is always swept clean, as is the flagstone walkway leading to the front door. Stray pieces of paper or fast-food wrappers that blow in off the street don't linger. As Mia gathers her printouts, Paula offers to take over the yardwork to show her gratitude.

"Don't worry about that. Just hide that muscle car for now," Mia says. "Bring it around back. Remember, your room is on the third floor. I put blankets and a pillow on the cot, but make your bed. I want to see the corners tucked in."

"Yes, Sergeant."

"Don't be a smart-ass. You play by the rules like everyone else, which means in bed by ten. If you interact with the neighbors, it's 'yes sir' and 'yes ma'am.' I jumped through hoops for a zoning variance from city council to run a homeless shelter in a residential neighborhood. The folks on the street have been politely supportive, but they'll turn on me if the cops start showing up or we start howling at the moon. And I wouldn't blame them." Mia half smiles. "Now chop chop."

Paula drives the Nova around back and begins unloading her belongings salvaged from the apartment. The third floor is a wide-open space, so Mia fashioned a room with partitions in one corner. It's enough for a cot, a nightstand, and a functional chest of drawers. A small flat-screen TV hangs in one corner near the ceiling. She stuffs her clothes in the chest of drawers and unfolds the sheet and thick blanket. After carefully making the bed, she finds the remote. It's too early for local news, so she finds a news story on her phone about her grandfather.

Body Found Floating Near HRBT

The body of a Hampton man was found early Saturday in the water near the Hampton Roads Bridge–Tunnel, state police reported.

The dead man was identified as Anthony Jessup of Long Street, in the Phoebus neighborhood. Police would not comment on the cause of death, pending further investigation. Jessup, 64, was wearing a life jacket, according to onlookers who spotted the body just before sunrise.

Josie Miller, 32, a pharmacist, was on her way to work at the Hampton VA Medical Center when an accident in the tunnel stopped westbound traffic coming Norfolk. "I got out to stretch because I knew it would be a while—it always is," Miller said. "When I looked over the railing, I saw him."

Jessup worked as a short-order cook and assistant manager at the George Pickett Grill in Hampton. He moved from rural Berkeley County a few years ago

*and quickly became a valued employee, according to
owner Sean McTavish.*

*"This is a sad day for everyone here at the Pickett,"
he said. "Everyone loved Tony."*

Other TV stations offer versions of the same story. One
has a photo of McTavish. He's definitely the buzz-cut driver
of the Mercedes who chased her onto I-64.

"I see you got the penthouse suite."

Rosa stands in the doorway. Paula darkens her phone
and pats the bed. Rosa sits next to her, smelling of talcum
powder and soap, and her short black hair falls in wet curls
around her face. Then she pops up and opens a drawer in
the dresser. Her hands sift through Paula's things.

"Are you perving on me?" Paula asks.

"Just checking. If you've put clothes in the drawer,
you're staying here. I guess this means you're homeless too.
Mia reserves this room for girls who break the rules, get in
a fight, or otherwise need a time-out."

"Great. I'm in solitary confinement at a homeless
shelter."

Rosa matches Paula's socks and folds them into little
balls. "I'm glad you finally killed him."

"Excuse me?"

"You killed him," Rosa repeats. "You stabbed him in a
boat. Then you got off the boat and ran into some guy staring into space. The guy runs a food truck. You stalked the
food truck guy at the Moonbeam Brewery, and there was
some weird encounter with a Maxie person. Then the next
day," Rosa says, picking up two more socks, "you found the
food truck somewhere else, and he stole your backpack. He
has an odd name and he's dangerous, and Mia wants you to
steer clear of him. Also, food truck guy has dementia."

"You were listening to our conversation on the porch."

"And you broke into his house to get your backpack."

"Jesus, was there a microphone out there? Is it on You-Tube yet?"

"Tammy, the girl with the cigarette who stumbled onto the porch, was sent down there on a spy mission." Rosa smiles. "She was standing just beyond the door the whole time. I could see you had something on your mind. With the number of eyes and ears around here, the place might as well be bugged. So why'd you kill Tony? It wasn't because of me."

"Self-defense. He pulled out a gun and was going to kill me."

"Because you got me out of there, I bet."

"I didn't get you out, Rosa. You left on your own. I supplied the car—which turned out to be the problem. Mia gave me all this stuff on human trafficking, and I left it piled up on my seat. My grandfather saw it. And they knew someone was talking to the girls on their smoke break, trying to get them to leave. He connected the dots. Or someone did for him. I tried to hide my face when I was there, but maybe I didn't do a good job."

Rosa shakes her head and flops back on the cot. "So you're hiding from the police now?"

"More like hiding from Sean McTavish." Paula describes the car chase on I-64 and the confrontation in stalled traffic. "I eventually lost them—nothing keeps up with the Nova—and they don't know this place. But I can't sit here and wait for things to happen."

Rosa nods in an agreement. "Your grandfather was a pervert, always slapping my butt and pinching me. But McTavish is dangerous. Any girl who stood up to him was gone the next day. Did he have another guy with him, some stupid-looking muscle dude?"

"The guy riding shotgun had a shaved head and lots of muscles."

"Yeah, that guy is serious trouble. When he shows up with McTavish, someone gets gone. Who's this Aloysius fellow? Tammy couldn't figure out how he fit into the mix."

"Tammy the spy didn't prepare a transcript of our conversation for your review?"

"Just tell me."

Paula explains Maxie's proposed hotel-casino complex and how Ledyard Aloysius O'Brien owns land blocking the project. "This Maxie is the former boss of food truck guy. And Maxie has bad intentions toward food truck guy . . ." Paula waves her hand. "What am I saying? You know everything I know. Tell me what to do next."

Rosa stares at the ceiling, her eyes wide and full of secrets. "Go to the morgue and find your grandfather's body. Cut off his balls and stuff them in his mouth. Then cut him up some more. That way, he'll go into the afterlife hobbled and ugly and useless."

Paula leans back on the cot. She touches shoulders with Rosa and lets the words sink in. "I may have stabbed him, but I still tried to keep him from falling into the water. Who does that?" She puts a hand on Rosa's arm. "You said he groped you. If he did more than that, you can tell me."

Rosa's eyes go dark again. "You're a good protector. But who will protect you?"

"I've never needed a protector."

"You do now."

20

MINUTES LATER, MIA clomps up the stairs. Even though she's a slip of a thing, she sounds like a weight lifter when she walks. Peeking around the partition at the two women, she points at Rosa and says, "Paula and I need to have a word. Go downstairs for a minute, please."

Paula waves it off. "Rosa knows everything. There was an eavesdropper on the porch."

Mia fixes her with a stare. "Yeah, I figured you dispatched Tammy as your eyes and ears. She is a blabbermouth of the first order. Fine, we're all up to speed." Mia shakes her head, sputters a breath. "So this is what I've come to say: You have to leave, Paula. I was out pruning shrubs, and a white Mercedes van drive drove past. It had the George Pickett Grill logo. Then it turned and made a second pass. Some guy with a shaved head was at the wheel. He looked right at me. They must have followed you here."

"No way," Paula says. "I lost them on the interstate going toward Virginia Beach."

"Maybe they waited near the bridge-tunnel and picked you up coming back. It doesn't matter. They've figured it out. I can't risk a confrontation. It would affect all the girls, especially you, Rosa. You escaped from the Pickett, and they can't know you're here."

"I hate it when you're right," Paula says. "But yeah, I've got to go."

Thirty minutes later, Paula is back on the road and looking in her side mirror for a white Mercedes van. She drives around Hampton aimlessly for the next hour, turning over different scenarios in her head. Moving back to Berkeley County is a dead end, and going on the road is a nonstarter. Sooner or later, police will discover that she is Tony Jessup's granddaughter and start looking for her. Sean McTavish could leak her name to the police, but he probably won't. He doesn't want Paula telling stories about what goes on at the George Pickett Grill. No, McTavish's only strategy is to get rid of her. Meanwhile, the police will keep looking for clues. No other boats were in the water that night, but someone could have watched from shore. A boat that left the dock with two people and returned with one would have raised alarms.

Oh, shit. The boat.

The boat was filled with blood and gore, and she had just walked away from it. The owner must have called the police by now.

Paula drives into Phoebus, avoiding her old garage apartment, and parks around the corner from Joe Pendergast's house. She cuts through an alley and sees a wide, grassy strip that runs between homes. It looks like an old right-of-way, and she comes upon Seneca Lane from the dead-end side. Ignoring her hammering heart, she crosses the road, swishes through the sea grass, and sees the little dock where the boat is tied up.

It is clean.

Almost pristine.

Paula squats down and runs a hand along the stern. It smells of bleach, and the two oars are packed neatly away.

Near the bow, a small metal plaque is fixed to the side. Paula takes one look and almost falls into the water.

"Joe Pendergast, Skipper."

Food truck guy owns the boat.

Food truck guy cleaned up her mess.

Maybe he saw the blood and feared he killed someone in a dementia-induced rage. But is that how Alzheimer's works? Maybe he can't talk to the police on general principle. That retired Norfolk cop said Joe Pendergast was a badass back in the day. A gofer, leg breaker, and maybe worse, Mia said. Maybe he didn't want to report that his boat was full of blood?

But he'll have pieced it together by now. Tony Jessup's name is in the news. He knows a young woman named Paula Jessup was stalking his food truck. He could go to the police with that information. But Joe Pendergast has problems of his own, namely, his old boss threatening to kill him. Maxie can stake out Joe's food truck just as Paula did, and he probably knows about Joe's house here on Seneca Lane.

So Joe Pendergast needs a protector too.

Maybe they could help each other. Pendergast wouldn't put up with Sean McTavish and Bullet Head playing their little car games. But how could Paula return the favor and protect Joe from this Maxie? She thinks back, trying to remember bits of overhead conversation from that night at the Moonbeam. Maxie told Joe to keep his mouth shut because he was "going legit in a big way." And Maxie said something about "knowing my business from way back."

That's it.

Joe Pendergast knows all the dirt on Max "Maxie" Smith, a man who is stepping out of the shadows into high-profile business circles. Maybe Pendergast can write down all the dirty secrets of Maxie's operation and lock it away somewhere, put documents in the cloud or in a safe deposit box at a bank, then tell Maxie to leave him alone. But she can't just knock on Pendergast's door with a sales pitch.

Mia would tell her to do some homework first.

She leaves the boat and gets back in the Nova. Thirty minutes later, Paula Jessup walks into Captain Maxie's bar and grill on a mission to gather intelligence.

21

As Paula's eyes adjust to the darkened interior of Captain Maxie's, shadows morph into hard lines. Booths are along the right wall, tables run down the middle, and a J-shaped bar is on the left. A small stage holds an acoustic guitar on a stand. The woman behind the bar is a forty-something redhead. Paula pulls up a stool and hunkers forward, eyeing the beer taps.

The redhead makes a beeline for her, asks, "Got some ID?"

Paula takes out her driver's license, hoping the bar TVs aren't turned to local news. It's six o'clock, and she doesn't want to look up and see a photo of dead Tony Jessup. The redhead holds the license to the light. "You don't look this old, but that's a real license, all right." She hands it back with a smile. "Welcome to Captain Maxie's. Saturday night awaits and we're just getting started."

"That makes two of us," Paula says.

She nurses a light beer, orders nachos, and keeps her head on a swivel. The place is about half full. Farther to the left, beyond the bar, a pair of pool tables sit empty. Paula considers shooting a game by herself so someone will challenge and she can ease into conversation with a random stranger. *My first time here. Doesn't this place have that famous bouncer?* She's about to slide off the stool, when a door opens near the pool tables. Its outline is barely visible in the wall. Out steps Maxie, his silver hair carefully arranged. A red polo shirt tucked into expensive jeans shows off his hard belly. As he passes the pool tables, Paula notices the bandage on his pinky finger.

"Hey," he says to the redhead. "We need some more drinks in back."

The redhead flips a bar towel over her shoulder. "I'll get one of the girls to handle the beers."

Maxie frowns and walks into the dining area. He goes from table to table and asks if everything is to their liking, acting like he's the owner of a four-star restaurant, when he's only serving burgers and wings. The redhead dispatches a waitress through the half-hidden door. Then she checks on Paula.

"Get you another?"

"I'm fine for now. "Quite the boss you have there."

She rolls her eyes. "He's just breaking balls."

"Men always think they're so witty," Paula says. "If they only knew."

"True that." She pours a beer and puts it in front of Paula. "On the house, as payment for your fine observation."

The waitress who was sent into the secret room has returned and is asking for towels. "We've some spillage," she says. "They're getting a bit restless in there."

The door hangs open. Paula slides off the stool and walks that way, heading to the restrooms. Passing the open door, she sees groups of men at tables, staring at playing cards. She keeps going and stops near the ladies' room, where a framed newspaper article hangs on the wall, from August 4, 1956.

Cotton "Candy" Smith keeps them smiling in Phoebus

Never let it be said that smiles do not rule the sidewalks here in Phoebus, for that would be to deny the existence of one Cotton Smith, better known as Candy.

The 35-year-old Army veteran and entrepreneur rules this neighborhood with a tip of his derby and a friendly nod. With his tall frame and shock of white hair, he cuts an imposing figure on his daily strolls.

For the record, he is the owner and operator of Smith's Candy Kitchen on Hope Street. One would not have imagined a strapping Army veteran who fixed Jeeps and trucks during his time in the service would turn to chocolates and hazelnuts.

"I always had a sweet tooth," Smith explains. "I figured to make the most of it."

Today is the 10-year anniversary of its opening. Its bustling business alone would earn Smith recognition. But his work doesn't stop here.

He's donated to various charitable causes in and around the neighborhood. He launched an overcoat drive last winter and will do so again. He helped spearhead the campaign three years ago that resulted in Phoebus and Elizabeth City County consolidating with the city of Hampton.

"I know what the community needs because I have my ear to the ground," Smith says. "I have a little secret—"

Paula stops reading and takes a photo of the newspaper story to read later. On the wall next to it is a faded rectangle, as if another frame had recently hung there. As Paula returns to the bar, Maxie is watching her.

He acts like he's seen her before.

22

P AULA AVOIDS EYE contact with the old man. She slides back onto her stool as the redhead brings nachos and walks off. A woman takes the stage and strums a few practice chords on the guitar. Paula pulls her plate closer and shields it with her forearm.

Maxie comes up behind her. "You been in prison?"

"Excuse me?"

"It's a simple question. I asked if you'd been in prison. That's how you eat when you're inside, always protecting the plate. You don't look old enough to be in prison, but you never know these days." He steps around her and sits on the adjacent barstool. Up close, Paula can see that his nose has been broken, maybe more than once. He tries to hide his bandaged hand.

"Let me guess," Paula says, eyeing the finger. "Kinky sex games got too rough, and she bent it the wrong way."

His smile shows a healthy row of teeth. "You're vulgar. That's not attractive in a woman, but then you've got that hair. You'd probably have nice hair if you'd let it grow. Put on some makeup. Wear a skirt or something nice. Grow a ponytail."

"I didn't realize fashion advice came with the service at Captain Maxie's. I'll have to tip higher than my usual two percent."

Maxie invades her personal space. His gray eyes do a little dance and he smells of cigarettes and musty air. "I'm wondering why you took a photo of that newspaper story."

"It seemed interesting. I like local history."

"You from up that way, in Phoebus?"

"York County. But I know Phoebus."

Maxie nods. "Phoebus used to be called Little Chicago because of all the bars and brothels. Now it's got nice restaurants and antique shops. Go figure. When my dad walked those streets, he was a respected individual. He tipped his hat and the women nodded. The men shook his hand. He was a lot more than a candy store owner. He contributed to causes. He helped the downtrodden. People forget that." Maxie taps his temple with a forefinger. "People have selective memories."

"I believe the article touches on that. I took a photo so I could read it later."

"You won't use it on social media to make fun of him, I hope."

"I see no reason to do that. I just thought the story was interesting, that's all."

"A girl as young as you with that haircut, I can't imagine you're into history. Also, that beer's gonna sprout legs and walk away if you don't pay attention to it."

Paula downs half the beer in a couple of gulps. Maxie continues to study her. "I can't place you, but I seen you before. It wasn't in this bar, and it wasn't in this neighborhood. A girl like you walking around Ocean View, I'd remember. Ocean View once had this big amusement park facing the water. A wooden roller coaster was the big attraction. When they wanted to close the park, some director had the bright idea to make a movie called *The Death of Ocean View Park*. They tried three times to dynamite the wooden roller coaster. The damn thing refused to budge until a bulldozer yanked it down. That's Ocean View. It's old-fashioned, but it's hanging on. And it has better things in store."

"Like you," Paula says.

"Yeah, like me," Maxie says. "What brings you down here, missy?"

"Just drinking beer."

His smile shows he doesn't buy the explanation. "You don't have to tell me why you're here. It's a free country. But I'll be watching to see if that story pops up anywhere. I don't like people making fun of my pop."

"I won't do that. Promise."

He pats her on the shoulder with a heavy hand. "That actually sounds believable. Maybe I misjudged you. It wouldn't be the first time I made that mistake. I'll stop harassing you now. Enjoy the food and drink."

He types a text into his phone, walks to the door of the poker room and disappears inside. Paula surfs the web for other references to Cotton "Candy" Smith. She uses keywords like *shame* and *downfall*, because people must have made fun of him. A few minutes later, she finds a different story than the one on the wall. This is from 1997.

Former gambling kingpin Cotton "Candy" Smith dies in prison

Cotton "Candy" Smith, 77, was found dead Tuesday morning in his cell at Red Onion State Prison, where he was sent after a money-laundering conviction brought disgrace to the once popular gambling king of Hampton.

Smith came of age during the Great Depression and enlisted in the Army after the Japanese attack on Pearl Harbor. He worked in a logistics unit and met his wife in England during preparations for D-Day. It was here, by Smith's own admission, that he became adept at playing poker, hosting games that lasted into the night. When the war ended, he returned to Phoebus with his British wife and opened Cotton's Candies, a confectionary shop.

"Back then, the men were breadwinners, and I needed something to entice them to enter a candy store," he told a Reuters reporter in a jailhouse interview. "So I began hosting informal poker games on Friday nights. The players would buy my candy because they felt guilty about leaving their wives and kids at home."

Soon he was staging high-stakes poker games, and that led to the establishment of an illegal sports betting ring in the late 1940s, which covered entire sections of Hampton Roads. By the mid-1950s, Smith was a well-known figure in Phoebus, praised for his many charitable donations. Behind the scenes, he was a political kingmaker, backing candidates for local and state offices.

He started a side business, selling political buttons, stickers, banners, and other items to candidates for their campaigns. That proved to be his downfall.

Authorities in 1996 charged Smith with using the political trinket business to launder money from his vast gambling and loan-sharking network.

The buttons, stickers, and other items were made in United Arab Emirates by an American ex-pat, Roderic Campbell. According to authorities, Smith bought the items at inflated prices and paid with gambling *proceeds. Campbell then transferred the excess money to UAE accounts, where Smith accessed it.*

The scheme fell apart when Campbell was arrested on unrelated child pornography charges in the UAE. Facing a long prison sentence, Campbell confessed to his relationship with Smith.

Smith was preceded in death by his wife, Clementine, and is survived by one son, Max "Maxie" Smith, who owns Captain Maxie's, a popular bar in the Ocean View section of Norfolk.

"I knew Pop wouldn't last long behind bars," the younger Smith said. "Seventy-six years old when they put him away. Ridiculous. Everyone looked up to Pop. When he walked down the street, he stopped traffic."

23

PAULA CONNECTS THE dots. Maxie's father ran high-stakes poker games in Phoebus decades ago. Captain Maxie's has a room where men play cards with cash on the table. She wants to walk around the building and see what else she can find, but the bartender is watching her like a hawk. Every time Paula reaches for her beer, the woman glances over.

Paula calls up the website for Captain Maxie's. It opened in 1980, a full seventeen years before Maxie's father went to jail. The site says it began as "a neighborhood tavern that served as a focal point in the Ocean View neighborhood." There is no mention of Max Smith being the owner. Paula finishes her nachos and pushes the plate forward. The red-head takes the bait and walks over.

"Nachos okay?" she asks.

"Very yummy, thank you."

"You merited a visit from the boss," she says. "Are you two acquainted?"

"Not at all. I like local history and took an interest in that story about his father. Your boss seemed concerned. I got the impression that his father faced some criticism back in the day."

"You might say that. Maxie's dad went to prison for money laundering." The bartender scans the bar, as if her boss is within earshot. "But it was how he went to prison—frog-marched from his candy store and tossed into a police car on a Friday night in full view of everyone. Police tipped off the media, and the images were everywhere—ol' Cotton with his head down, hands cuffed, sobbing like a baby."

"That's awful."

"It hurt Maxie to see that." She takes the plate. "Are you sure he doesn't know you? I've seen that look on his face. He thinks he's seen you somewhere."

Paula rubs her head. "It must be the haircut. Makes me stick out. Have you worked here very long?"

"Four years. It's been quite a ride."

"I bet you make a lot of friends in a place like this."

"You also meet people you'd like to forget." Her phone buzzes. She looks at a text and quickly swipes it away. "On balance, it's been a good place to grow." She eyes the door, where a group of customers just entered. "We'll start to fill up pretty soon. If you're meeting someone, I'd suggest saving a stool. It will soon be occupied by hipsters asking for sour beer. That's what this world has come to."

"I couldn't help but notice the card games behind that door. It looked like a big deal."

She shrugs. "Just a bunch of friends playing cards. That's all." The answer is quick and rehearsed, as if people ask this all the time. "Are you a journalist or member of law enforcement?"

The question sends a chill down Paula's spine. "Me? No. I'm just drinking beer."

"I always ask that when people wonder about the card games. Everyone has conspiracy theories. So you're just drinking beer in a strange bar, is that right?"

"I guess so."

"You're from up in York County?"

Paula hadn't told the redhead she came from York County. She'd told Maxie, and no one was within earshot at the time. Maxie sent a text to someone before he walked away, and the bartender has been watching her since then. Maybe Maxie told her to chat up this strange customer he's seen somewhere before.

"Get you another beer, young lady?" she asks.

"I'm good."

"If you fancy yourself a poker player, those games are strictly by invitation only. That's the other thing I'm supposed to say."

"I don't play cards. I'd be awful at it."

"You noticed the activity. That's all I'm saying." She grins and takes the glass. "It's all good. Let me top this off for free."

The bar starts to fill up, and Paula stares into her glass, waiting for people to crowd around her. But it seems like she's sitting in a dead zone. No one takes the stools to either side. No one reaches over her to get a drink. She's relieved when her phone buzzes and she recognizes the number of the Benedict House.

"Mia?"

"No, it's Rosa. You need to get the hell back here."

"Calm down. What's wrong?"

"That guy in the Mercedes van drove by again. Then he stopped and knocked on the door. Mia met him with her stun gun. You can imagine what happened next. She's okay. Everyone is okay. But the police are here. It's a bit of a mess. I'm only slightly freaking out. I'm on the back porch, trying to hear parts of the conversation. The police are searching the yard. I'm also digging into Mia's printouts. What kind of name is Ledyard Aloysius O'Brien?"

"Don't worry about Ledyard Aloysius O'Brien," Paula says. "I'll be right there."

Paula cuts the connection and looks up as the redhead makes a beeline for her with a look that is all business. Paula smiles and says something about settling up.

"Please don't say Ledge sent you," the redhead says. "I didn't think he knew anyone so young."

"Huh?"

"You just said his name."

Ledge.

Ledyard Aloysius O'Brien.

"I said I wanted to settle up," Paula says.

The bartender swipes the glass from the bar. "That's probably a good idea. You need to be careful, hon. Take that advice from me. It might be best if you don't come back here."

24

T HE PARKING LOT was half empty when Paula arrived, but now it's full. Back in the Nova, the steering wheel helps steady her trembling hands. Her garage apartment has been searched by police. The Benedict House is marked. The Nova has a target on its back. She needs a fourth corner, a place in the shadows. She starts the Nova and mashes the accelerator. The engine revs and the car doesn't move.

Right.

Transmission in park.

Shifting into gear, she pulls onto Chesapeake Boulevard and heads toward the interstate. Saturday night traffic is fast and hostile, everyone looking for booze or a hookup and just wanting to cut off the nearest driver. Paula sets her teeth and stays under the speed limit. She might as well start practicing good driving habits. A cop who pulls her over will notice her last name. Her phone buzzes as she hits the interstate. It's a text from Rosa.

What is happening? Are you on the way? Call me.

Paula makes the connection, and Rosa picks up immediately. Sirens and rushing wind obscure the connection.

"I'm walking in the backyard to keep moving. Shit. The police are coming through the house and talking to everyone. I can't talk to the police, Paula. I have no ID, nothing."

"Go out beyond the backyard. There's an apartment complex. You can hang out near the dumpster. Was anyone hurt when those guys knocked on the door?"

"Mia ducked a punch to the face. She's fine. The other guy got a stun gun in the neck, I think." Rosa take a few breaths. "I'm working my way toward the apartment complex now. I want to read more of Mia's printouts. Where were you?"

Paula explains her trip to Captain Maxie's and how she ran into trouble after saying Ledyard's name aloud. Traffic on I-64 slows near the bridge-tunnel. She looks to her right and left. No cop cars or Mercedes vans are following. Rosa clears her throat, says, "That's very interesting."

"What is?"

"The reaction to that man's name. Mia made a printout of the Google map that shows Ledyard's property. You probably saw it. On top she wrote, 'Maxie's weak spot.' I guess that's because this Ledyard dude is blocking the casino project, and this Maxie can't do anything about it."

"I should tell Joe Pendergast. He's got Maxie breathing down his neck. I was thinking how I might help the old guy, then get him to help me. I don't have anything to offer, except now I know Maxie's weak spot."

Rosa almost chuckles. "You should talk it through. That's what you always told me. I'd be standing out by the dumpsters, and you'd be trying to convince me to leave. You must have said, 'Talk it through, Rosa' a hundred times."

Traffic slows to a crawl near the bridge-tunnel. Paula lets the Nova coast. "All right, I'll play along. Dot number one: we know Maxie's weak point is needing Ledyard's property. Dot number two: if myself or Joe Pendergast were to somehow control that property, Maxie would have to respect that. Dot number three: the two men in the white Mercedes will slowly kill me."

"Be serious," Rosa says. "Forget the white Mercedes for a second."

"I am being serious. I make next to minimum wage at an auto parts store. How do I, first, find money to buy the land, and second, convince Joe Pendergast to trust me? Last time I checked, he stole my backpack and tried to shoot me when I came after it."

"So you need to get more money. That's all."

"I had no idea it was that simple. Just steer me toward the money, and we can finish this conversation."

Rosa says nothing for a moment. The silence stretches to thirty seconds. "This Pendergast runs a food truck, right?"

"He calls it 'Joe's Takeaway.'"

"And he takes credit cards, right?"

"He's got one of those sliding squares on his smartphone. So what?"

"There's a way to start acquiring money," Rosa said. "It will take a while, but it might convince this Pendergast that you're serious.

JOE

CHAPTER

25

J OE WAKES UP Sunday morning feeling refreshed. Cleaning his house yesterday was like a tonic. He stayed away
from TV news, erased Paula Jessup's name on the whiteboard, and damn near forgot about her. Hell, forgetting is
his new superpower, so there's that. Now it's time to find a
new line of attack on Maxie. He can't wait for his old boss
to make the first move. Joe needs to find a way to get him
alone. Limit collateral damage. Maybe do another round
of food truck gigs just for fun while he figures out another
plan.

He turns on the TV, and Anthony Jessup is all over the
news.

He worked at the George Pickett Grill, which explains
the business card that Joe found near the boat. He and
Joe share the same birth year, 1955. Someone named Sean
McTavish owns the Pickett, and he's all broken up about
Jessup's untimely death. He cries for the TV cameras. The
door of his restaurant is draped in black bunting. Joe spends
all morning on the couch, replaying news clips over and
over.

He can't stop laughing.

Sean is putting on an act, and it's not that convincing. Joe has a finely tuned bullshit detector when it comes to sob stories, thanks to Maxie's poker games. In the heat of a gaming night, Maxie would sometimes loan money to men who foolishly thought their luck was about to turn. When they lost a few more times and exhausted the loan, they tried to slink away—ghosted Maxie, as the young people say—thinking they could repay at their leisure or maybe Maxie would forget it. The next day, Joe received a list of names and addresses of the deadbeats along with the amount of the loan. Then he went knocking on doors. If the guy wasn't an asshole, Joe played nice in front of the family. He'd say Captain Maxie's mistakenly undercharged for drinks and dinner, and maybe they could talk outside about how to settle up. But most guys said they didn't have the money and pleaded hardship. The hot water heater busted. The transmission on the family minivan went out. One guy insisted he spent five grand because his dog had leukemia just before a healthy Pekinese bounded into the room.

Sean McTavish is cut from the same phony cloth. He's trying too hard to be sad.

"Let me tell you about Tony," he says. *(Look down at your shoes. Gather strength to go on.)* "Tony lived a hard life. Worked hard. And yeah, he played hard. His daughter died in a tragic car accident when she was in her twenties, and Tony raised his granddaughter out of the goodness of his heart."

Off camera, someone asks how he came to Hampton Roads.

"I knew him through a friend," McTavish says. "Tony was getting up in age and lived over in Berkeley County. He wanted a different line of work. I asked him to help out in the kitchen. He learned the business by working nights and weekends. The guy had no ego. He was salt of the earth."

Any problems at work? Any enemies?

"I'll let the police comment on the accident, the incident, whatever they're calling it. I know that he was well loved here at the Pickett. Customers thought the world of him."

The police don't say much. All angles are being investigated, and they're not commenting on the cause of death. Joe scours newspaper websites and finds nothing new. Around two in the afternoon, he falls asleep watching TV and wakes up to a knock on the door. The sun is setting. He checks his watch and sees he's been napping for about five hours.

A cop is standing in the driveway. She's got a big smile.

"Good afternoon, sir. Well, good evening, I guess. How are you doing today?"

Joe has talked to countless police officers in his time, usually after settling a dispute at Captain Maxie's by knocking someone into next week. Those conversations are easy. Trouble has occurred and you talk about it. Trouble sets boundaries and provides a focus for the conversation. But a cop who smiles and says good afternoon like nothing is wrong, that's bad from the get-go.

"Good evening to you, ma'am," Joe says, matching her smile. "How can I help you?"

She hands him a business card with the police department logo. Her name is Suzi Robinson. "We're looking at boats in this area for a possible connection to a case," she says. "Does that johnboat down there belong to you? The one at the end of the road?"

"It was actually gifted to me by a sailor who shipped out of here a few weeks ago. I just started renting this house."

"Mind if I take a look at the boat?"

"Go right ahead."

She'll either find something or she won't, but Joe is fairly certain he's cleaned it thoroughly. The boat has no distinctive markings other than the plaque the sailor made for him. Officer Robinson spends a few minutes at the boat slip, then swishes around the seagrass before coming back.

"When did you take it out last?" she asks.

"I haven't been out yet. I'm not really a boat person, but like I said, the sailor couldn't take it with him." Joe can tell she knows something.

"What was the name of this sailor?"

"Luke something."

"Any way you can get a full name?"

Joe squints hard, pretending to think. "I can't. To be honest, I've got early-stage dementia, Officer. I had to quit my job a while back at Captain Maxie's down in Norfolk. Now I've got this food truck here. If you want, I could show you my pills and medical records." It occurs to Joe that she hasn't asked for identification, so he pulls out his wallet and hands her his driver's license. "That's me. Is there a problem with the boat?"

"We're going to have to impound it, Mr. Pendergast. It's possible it was used in an incident we're investigating."

"Oh, good grief. What happened?"

"We pulled a body from the water out by the HRBT this morning. You may have seen it on the news. Some commercial fishermen said they noticed a white johnboat in the water the night before. Two people seemed to be arguing, even fighting."

"There are a lot of johnboats around here."

"True. But the body was wearing a life jacket. It had a name tag for Lucas W. Williamson. He's a sailor on the USS *Theodore Roosevelt*. The aircraft carrier recently switched homeports from Norfolk to the West Coast. The address on the tag was the house across the street. We talked to Mr. Williamson by phone, and he said exactly what you just said. He gave the boat to a neighbor when he left. So that's good on you, Mr. Pendergast. I appreciate your honesty. Funny thing, but he couldn't remember your last name either. He said the guy's name was Joe, that he just moved to the neighborhood, and he had a food truck."

"That would be me."

"From the descriptions we received, two people were in the boat that night. One was the victim, but the other person couldn't have been you. It seems like someone took your boat, returned it, and cleaned it out."

Joe waves his hand as if dismissing the boat from his life. "Take the thing, Officer. Do all that NCIS stuff and let me know what you find." Joe shakes his head and plays the helpless fool who doesn't know a damn thing. Even if the police find a strand of hair or piece of skin that belonged to Tony Jessup, who's to say it didn't happen just like Officer Robinson described? Joe doesn't know Tony Jessup and has never been to the George Pickett Grill.

Put him on a lie detector, for Christ's sake.

Well, maybe not.

26

THE POLICE COME for the boat the next morning.

Joe busies himself in the kitchen as they go to work. He's half expecting Donna to knock on the door, but she's not home. Monday must be a good day to sell houses and impound boats. He boils elbow macaroni and sets up evaporated milk, eggs, whole milk, and shredded cheddar cheese on the kitchen counter. His mac and cheese went over well during his first two gigs. He rechecks the recipe, but he tells himself that's not because of the dementia. He's done that all his life.

The prom queen doctor said he should keep busy, establish a routine. When Joe said he enjoyed cooking, she practically applauded. He can't wait for the follow-up visit. *"Besides the food truck, my boss wants to murder me, but I may want to get him first. Meanwhile, the police questioned me about a second murder that involved my boat. I know the girl who did it, but I think she's okay. So yeah, I'm keeping busy."*

He mixes the ingredients in the Crock-Pot and turns it on low. He sets the alarm on his phone for six o'clock that evening, eight hours from now. Checking his email, he finds yet another message from Jennifer. She just emailed him yesterday, asking about the Moonbeam gig.

Good morning, Joe:

Sorry to blitz your inbox again. I forgot to mention something yesterday. When you see the doctor again, it's best not to mention our exchange of messages. Sometimes the doctors get a little funny about so-called "amateur" counselors. They think it's like a Facebook scam. But we know better, yes? We're just talking, you and I.

Have a great day,

Jenn

So it's Jenn now. Her mention of Facebook gives him an idea. Joe's Takeaway has its own Facebook page with a photo of the truck, his menu, and a calendar that lists gigs. Kathy worked it up before he left, part of his severance package. So far, Joe has a couple of good reviews from Moonbeam customers and one from the lunch gig in downtown Newport News.

The police will no doubt monitor this page. They'll want to make sure Joe Pendergast is pursuing legitimate business, doing all the right things. Typing with two fingers, he pecks out a message and posts it. *"So glad to get my first two gigs under my belt. Thank you for the support. Now I need to stock up on food. Heading to Bulk Warehouse this morning for some supplies! See everyone at the 'Beam next Thursday!"*

He keeps the Hyundai in the garage and takes the food truck. The Hyundai is a decade old, with a puke-green paint scheme and needs to be nursed along. And the food truck will be easier to follow if the cops are watching. His

phone beeps several times during the drive. People are liking his Facebook message. One person posted a comment:
"Can't go wrong with hotdogs and brats!"

At the Bulk Warehouse, he parks in the far corner of the
lot, away from other vehicles. The police will see that he has
no problem being out in the open. Inside, he fills a shopping
cart with meat and buns, plus the ingredients for his mac
and cheese and a few tubs of coleslaw. He makes small talk
with the cashier while checking out and finds the food truck
with no problem. As he throws open the rear double doors,
a shadow appears behind him. Someone is standing there.
People stare at their phones all the time and don't know
what they're doing, so this could be nothing. Or it could
be someone who recognizes the food truck. It could also
be a cop, but that's fine and dandy. Joe Pendergast wants to
cooperate with the police. He's already told the truth to that
nice officer, and he's not hiding his presence here.

Best to ignore it.

The shadow does not move as he unloads the buggy.

"That's a lot of food."

He turns and sees Paula Jessup. She looks like she slept
in her clothes.

"You again," he says. "Did you have fun scoping out
my house the other night? I know it was you. He points
to the gauze that covers her hand. It's a bad wrap job,
already coming loose. "That's what you get for breaking
the sliding glass door. I didn't mean to shoot at you. It
just happened."

"Listen to what I'm about to tell you," she says. "You
don't know me. I just walked up and started a conversation."

"But I do know you. Don't try to confuse me."

"Two guys are approaching us right now. I want them
to think this is a completely random conversation. I should
have seen them earlier. I should have been more careful. But

they're coming now, and you need to act natural, like we just met. So to repeat: you do not know me."

Her eyes jump with fear. Joe remembers the last time he saw her in Newport News, turning a corner like someone was chasing her.

"I got it," Joe says. "Just act natural. I got a question, though. What race are you? Because the way the sun hits right now, you look different."

27

Two men approach them. Joe recognizes one as the Irish fellow from the George Pickett Grill who was crying fake tears on TV. He looks shorter in real life, and wears a polo shirt with the Pickett Grill logo and a pair of skinny jeans that make him walk like he's got a board up his ass. His companion trails by a few steps, as if Paula might run. His bald head is shaved to a bright shine, and he looks like every losing fighter Joe has ever seen.

"Good morning, gentleman," Joe says. "Great day to be outside."

"It sure is." The Irish fellow points to Paula. "Do you know our little friend here?"

Joe shrugs. "She's curious about the food truck. I'm looking to hire a helper, and she might be it." Joe remembers the man's name now: McTavish. First name Sam or Sean.

McTavish whistles in surprise. "That's very odd since she's already got a job. In fact, she should be at work right now. Brady's Auto Parts in Norfolk, right, Paula? We went down there. They said you normally work Sunday through Wednesday, but you asked for today off. Nice people to give you that. They had no idea where you might have gone."

"And yet you found me," Paula says.

McTavish shrugs. "That car of yours is hard to miss."

The silence drags out a bit. Shoppers push their buggies past the little group, unaware of what could happen at any second. The shiny-headed man repositions himself and sets his feet.

"I was just about to show this young lady the inside of my truck," Joe says. "Young lady? Step this way." He ushers Paula through the double doors. The shiny-headed man puts one foot on the bumper.

"You don't need to come in," Joe says.

"Oh, I think I do."

"Have it your way. I'm old, but agreeable."

Joe walks toward the front of the truck and gently pushes Paula ahead of him. McTavish stays in the parking lot as Shiny Head steps inside. Joe turns and acts like he's ready to shake hands. "Welcome to Joe's Takeaway," he says, taking the man's thumb and bending it backward. The man falls to his knees, eyes clenched in pain. His free hand goes for a back pocket.

"Don't reach for anything," Joe says quietly. "If you do, I'll break your thumb. Right now, I'm ready to dislocate it, and that can be worse when it comes to healing. A broken bone, they get you surgery and screws and such, but a dislocation has to heal on its own. It gets all swollen. God won't tell you when everything is okay. God acts like that sometimes. What's your name?"

"Fuck you."

Joe adjusts his grip by a fraction of an inch. The man yelps in pain.

"Wendell," he says.

"Your lips are turning white, Wendell. They are stretched thin across that ugly face of yours. Not a good look. Now I'm thinking you need to leave my truck. I don't like you, Wendell. But I don't like a lot of people, and I don't cause them trouble. If the police were called, your boss is wearing a shirt with the name of your business. Not a good look for customers. What do you think, Wendell? Are you worried about public relations and all that?"

McTavish steps to the double doors but doesn't come inside. "We're fine, Mr. Joe's Takeaway. I can see you're a tough guy. We have no quarrel with you."

Joe releases his grip and steps back. "That means we can go about our respective days with no worries. Am I right?"

McTavish stares at Joe a long time, his face impossible to read. Then he smiles broadly. "You are exactly right. We'll go about our day with no worries. See you around, Paula."

They walk to the end of the row and climb into a white Mercedes van with the Pickett logo emblazoned on the side. Joe stands at the back bumper and watches them leave. Paula stays near the driver's seat, hugging herself. She was a rebellious little pistol at the Moonbeam. The next day he stole her backpack and that knocked her down a peg or two. Now she's three or four pegs below that, shoulders slumped, looking like she might cry.

"That guy might have torn ligaments to deal with," Joe says. "I thought I felt something pop." He tries to smile. "You want to tell me what's going on with you?"

She takes a breath and gathers herself.

"I should ask what's going on with you," she says. "Your old boss is after you. He runs poker games from the back room of Captain Maxie's. The door is almost hidden. I was there last night and saw a bunch of guys, a lot of money on the table. You used to work for him, bouncer of the year and all that. Now you're running a food truck. What's with you two?"

"Tell me why you killed Tony Jessup. He was your grandfather."

"Jesus. Quiet voice, please."

Joe looks over the parking lot. "No one's here. The police have impounded my boat. It sounds like they have a description of the two people in it. I thought they might suspect me, but they don't. I'm just an old man who's going around the bend. I'm harmless, relatively speaking. But you're a killer and I'd like to know why. I don't believe Tony Jessup was a good person. A man cried fake tears for him on TV. That can't be good."

"You saw me at your house that night. You could have asked me then."

"I neither saw nor heard a damn thing."

"I got out of the boat and came up the road. We were less than twenty feet apart."

Joe points to his temple. "I got early-stage dementia. I woke up in my backyard that next morning. I didn't realize you were standing in the road until I saw you at the Moonbeam that night. It doesn't matter. My neighbor, Donna P. L. Fallon—the initials stand for Peace and Love—has security footage of you walking up the road. And yeah, it looks like you're talking to someone off camera, so you probably talked to me, I'm thinking. I don't know if the police have that footage, but they might."

"Can you tell it's me from the footage?"

"It's a young person in a hoodie. When I saw you at the Moonbeam, I could tell it was you by how you walk. Whether that's good enough for the police, I doubt it. They'd probably need prints or a good face shot. I cleaned out that boat, including a piece of your grandpa's scalp."

Paula smiles.

"You think that's funny? What kind of person are you?"

"You had a falling out with Maxie," she says. "What was it?"

"Don't change the subject. You're in my food truck and I shooed those guys away. The least you can do is answer my questions. But let's go back to my place first. I bought frozen food, and it'll melt by the time you get to the damn point."

"My Nova won't like following a food truck. It's got a three-fifty under the hood. How do you start this jalopy anyway—with a hand crank?"

"Funny."

"I'm mixed race. My father was black, my mom white. You asked about my race. Do you remember?"

"I do. It was just a few minutes ago. I'm not completely lost yet. How the sun is hitting you, that's what caused the question. You look different when the sun is hitting you."

"I'm sure it's about more than that, old man."

Joe thinks back to his boyhood crush. Her name was Cheyenne. "I got stories to tell about how it's more than that. But I don't know you well enough to do that."

28

Paula's car is a classic, painted a sparkling green, with shiny wheels. A thick blanket covers the back seat, and Joe wonders if she's sleeping there. It doesn't look like she's changed clothes in a while. But she jabbers on about the car like it's her firstborn. In a way, maybe it is.

"No wonder those guys from the Pickett followed you here," he says. "You can't miss this thing. I wouldn't know a three-fifty cubic-inch engine from a pull-start lawnmower, but this car looks fast just sitting here. A Chevy Nova, you say. I'll take your word for it."

"Yeah, the car sticks out, sure, but so do white Mercedes vans. If they followed me here, I didn't see them, and I was looking in my mirrors the whole time. And yesterday afternoon? This car was parked behind a house—totally hidden from street view—yet they drove past the house like they knew it was there. It's uncanny."

"Those two hyenas didn't seem very canny," Joe says. "Let me ask you something, speed racer. Did they ever come in physical contact with this car? Maybe you had it parked somewhere and they found it."

"They followed me on I-64 and traffic stalled. Everyone got out for a few minutes. They stood on either side of the car, trying to scare me. I just looked straight ahead. But yeah, they were close enough to touch it."

With an exaggerated groan, Joe bends down to survey the undercarriage. The bottom of this car is cleaner than most kitchen counters, which makes the GPS tracker easy to spot. It's in the wheel well on the passenger side, a black disc with a strong magnet. He tugs at it for a few seconds before it breaks free. The Nova lurches.

Paula stoops to look over his shoulder. "Did you just break my car? Because you're dead if that happens, Alzheimer's or not."

He straightens up and hands her the tracking device. He's used these a couple of times to find guys who wouldn't come to the door and pay their debt. You just wait until they get gas or stop at the grocery store. "They knew the location of this car the entire time. Now answer a question for me."

She stares at the tracker.

"I said, answer a question for me."

"Um, yeah. Sure."

"We know how they found you. How did you find me?"

"You posted on Facebook that you'd be here this morning, buying supplies. A food truck is pretty easy to spot in a parking lot."

"Shit. The Facebook page. Now answer another. Why did you follow me?"

She settles her shoulders as if preparing to reveal a great truth. "Ledyard Aloysius O'Brien," she says.

"That name sounds familiar."

"Before we're through, he'll be your best friend." She smiles as if she knows a secret.

"We're already through, you and me," Joe says. "No offense, but I want nothing to do with you. Chances are you'll be arrested for murdering your grandpa before the month is out, and maybe you want to murder me too. Taking advantage of a doddering old man." He points to her bandaged hand. "You've already broken into my house."

"To retrieve my stolen backpack," she says. "Let me ask you something. Those two guys from the Pickett, do they look like people who run a restaurant? You've been in that environment all your life. Can you imagine them greeting customers and asking about their meal?"

"They look like thugs."

"They are thugs. And when you hear my story, you'll know why I did what I did."

Joe surveys the parking lot. He doesn't want this young lady hanging around his house, but she's already broken in once. Maybe he should keep her close, figure out her deal. Also, she's come down a few rungs since Wednesday night. She did her homework on Maxie, and there must be a reason for that. This Ledyard O'Brien name dances on the edge of his memory. It has something to do with Maxie's casino-hotel project.

"Follow me back to the house," he says. "You can help me unload the truck. But first, let's make sure that Mercedes is nowhere to be found. Drive your Nova over to the food truck."

"You can get in."

"I'll walk."

The Nova growls to life, and its smooth, throaty rumble breathes new life into Paula. She straightens and her eyes focus forward. By the time Joe walks to his truck, she's found a space nearby. Joe doesn't see the Mercedes, but he tells Paula to climb on top of the food truck and scan the parking lot. She gives him the thumbs-up. Joe finds a pickup with the logo of a local construction company and attaches the GPS device just under the rear bumper.

He pulls out of the parking lot and onto Farmstand Avenue, a four-lane road heading south. Paula shifts into the passing lane to parallel the truck. She shifts into neutral, revs the engine, then falls back to ride six inches off his bumper.

Kids.

Not just any kid. A kid who had to kill her grandpa. A kid bad guys were looking for. A mixed-race kid.

That sort of thing doesn't matter now, and he didn't mean to make a big deal of it. But sometimes he can't help wondering how things have changed. Joe's dad would have keeled over if a mixed-race couple ever walked into Pendergast Cut-Rate. God forbid they'd be holding hands. The store followed the custom of the 1960s—*custom* being another word for being racist assholes. You waited on whites first, blacks second. The black kids never touched the penny candy bin. If their parents picked up an apple or a potato from the barrel, his dad considered it bought. When you gave change to a black person, your fingers did not touch theirs. You dropped the coins from a safe distance. But you still told them to have a nice day.

And Dad never knew about Cheyenne. She was a dark-skinned girl who always stopped by just before dinnertime, when Joe worked the counter. He was probably thirteen or fourteen, and she might have been a year or two older. She always asked for two pretzel rods from the canister and a Royal Crown Cola. Sometimes she bought boiled ham and cheese and acted like someone without a care in the world.

"How come you always work this time of day?" she asked him once.

"Because school's let out. Dad started here at sunrise and now he's three beers in, and Momma is cooking dinner," he said. "This is my time to work. I fill the gaps."

He jammed the change into her palm, and she let their fingers touch. Her dancing smile was a terrible, wonderful, forbidden thing that Joe couldn't shake.

Paula isn't Cheyenne, but Joe sees commonalities. They're both easy to talk to. They're both comfortable in their own skin. And they're both never far from trouble. Cheyenne marched in a few protests in her day, and he could see Paula doing the same thing. Joe enjoys analyzing people like this. Working at a bar for so long qualifies anyone for honorary degrees in psychology, sociology, public relations, hostage negotiating, forgery inspection, and a few other things for which they don't give degrees. Cheyenne ended up as a social worker somewhere in California. They lost touch long ago.

When Joe pulls into his driveway, Paula parks behind the food truck. She gets out, slams the door, and points to a spot in the front yard. "You were standing right there when I stepped from the boat the other night," she says. "You were looking out into space."

"Let's talk out back. I don't want you in the house just yet."

Joe means it as a joke, referencing her recent break-in, but Paula looks at the ground and walks to the backyard. With that mohawk of hers and the way she carries herself, maybe she gets insulted all the time. He doesn't want to insult her. He wants to help her in some way. Her grandpa was mixed up with those people from the Pickett Grill, which means he wasn't worth much. Joe regrets not breaking that guy's thumb and letting him scream for all it was worth. Wendell, was it? Yeah, Wendell would have been a screamer.

CHAPTER

29

THEY SETTLE INTO camp chairs on his little deck, their shadows short and squat in the early afternoon sun. Paula glances at Donna's house next door. "That's the person with the video?"

"Correct. Now get to what happened that night in my boat."

Her eyes roam around the yard. "I wish I had a little place like this. You sit outside and grill burgers and drink a beer and watch the sun go down. Maybe talk to your neighbors over the fence, find out what they do, what books they read."

"And talk about how your grandfather ended up a floater. Let's go over that before we get all misty-eyed for days of yore. You have the floor."

"You don't want to know how I did it," she says. "You want to know why."

"That's a fair point. Start with the why."

"The George Pickett Grill is involved in labor trafficking. They bring in young girls from Latin America and work them to exhaustion. I discovered this—where are we now, March?—I discovered this last summer. I lived above my grandfather's garage and saw him herding young girls into a van at four in the morning."

"Where'd they come from? I get the Latin America part, but where did they stay?"

"In his house. They were sleeping overnight. I was never allowed to go upstairs in his house. He barely let me in the front door. But after that, I got curious."

"Now you're Nancy Drew."

Her eyes turn hard. "I also visited my grandfather at the Pickett to have a friendly lunch and nose around. On my way to the ladies room, I diverted to the kitchen and saw those same girls. They were dead on their feet. Dark circles under their eyes. Feet shuffling from one spot to the other. They were in trouble. So yeah, that's me. Nancy Fucking Drew."

"I didn't mean to joke," Joe says. "Let's get on with it. You saw girls come out of your grandpa's house and saw them again in the kitchen. Then you searched the house."

"He has two spare bedrooms on the second floor. They had cots. As the weeks went on, some girls left and others took their place. I don't know where the first group went. Maybe they went into the ground. If that's the case, I wish my grandfather's death had been longer than it was. I wished he swallowed some brackish water and upchucked all over your shitty boat."

Paula clenches her fists. Joe studies her whitened fingers and understands her a bit more. Losing her mom so early, she depended on this jackass grandfather to raise her. More than likely she raised herself, got a fast car, and tried to become her mother. That look on her face when she got behind the wheel in the parking lot was something else. But some problems you can't fix with a screwdriver.

"I needed someone to help me understand what was happening," she says. "When I was a kid, we had migrant farm workers come up through Berkeley County, but migrant restaurant workers? No way was this legit. I found Mia Newsome from news stories. She runs a homeless shelter for women here in Hampton and knows about trafficking. She told me to chat up the girls. When they took smoke breaks outside the restaurant in back, I'd pretend to walk by like I worked somewhere else in the shopping center."

"They knew English?"

"A couple did. I convinced one to come to Mia's shelter. Her name is Rosa. The men who ran the grill suspected something. They'd seen me talking to the girls, and then one went missing, so they're like, 'Who is this strange woman who keeps coming by?' I guess my grandfather saw me too." She breathes in, exhales through her nose. "On Wednesday night, he found some human trafficking brochures on my front seat. We went for a ride. Him in the passenger seat. We came to your road by chance. He was looking for water and saw your boat." She stares past Joe at something else. "He wanted to kill me."

"The boat was a mess the next morning," Joe says. "You must've had quite a time. Did he hurt you?"

"He didn't have a chance."

Silence stretches the space between them. A squirrel hops onto the deck and eyes the grill. Its nose quivers. Then it scurries to the garbage can and climbs onto the plastic lid. It starts working at a small hole in the top.

"That squirrel's been busy," Paula says

"Yep."

"Are you going to call the cops on me?"

"Already had the chance, like I said. The police came asking about the boat. The lifejacket your grandpa wore had a name tag. It wasn't mine. The neighbor who gave me the boat had moved away. It listed his address across the street. That brought the police here, and they took the boat. They know this location is important, but they don't suspect me. I don't know if they're looking for you."

Paula swallows hard.

"That little garage apartment you lived in," Joe says. "It's all cleaned out?"

"Totally. And my address of record is still Berkeley County. Same with the car registration."

"Let the police think you still live there. Now what's this about an Aloysius O'Brien fellow?"

Paula brightens. "Ledyard Aloysius O'Brien. He's how you get back at Maxie Smith."

"That's a totally different problem," Joe says. "Maxie is after me about other things, and I need to take care of business. That's why I'm not turning you in. I'd be the pot calling the kettle black. You had reasons for doing what you did. I'm just an old man who's been left by the wayside and wants to go out with guns blazing before he ends up staring into space."

Paula looks past him. For a moment, Joe thinks the men from the Pickett have followed them. Then he hears a familiar voice.

"Oh my God! Whose car is that? I haven't seen one of those in years."

Donna has come to visit. And she's brought Butterbean.

30

Butterbean scampers around the yard, and everyone pretends to be amused at his mindless circles. A foghorn sounds in the distance as a container ship heads toward the Port of Virginia. The squirrel stops munching on the garbage can and looks up as if he's thinking, "Will someone say something?" It's a fair question. If Donna overheard talk about human trafficking and old men getting dumped into the water, Joe figures he might as well rent a plane and fly a banner over the beach. Donna shares everything.

Butterbean finally works himself into exhaustion, and Donna scoops up the dog. She switches on her real estate agent smile. She studies Paula as if the girl just beamed down from Pluto. "Joe, if you don't introduce me to your friend, I'm going to burst an artery."

"My apologies. Donna, this is Paula. Paula, Donna."

"And this is Butterbean," Donna says, letting the dog down. "That's some car you've got, Paula. Back in high school, I had a boyfriend who was into classic cars. He had an Oldsmobile with a backseat that was couch-sized, if you know what I mean. You keep that vehicle in such great condition. I don't know why people think girls can't be good around cars. Did you refurbish it yourself?"

"My mom was a motor head," Paula says, seeming to weigh every word. "She taught me everything I know."

"She did a great job. It looks brand new. I like little sports cars. I've got a Mazda Miata parked out front." Donna looks at Joe, then back to Paula. That smile stays frozen on her face. She wants to ask something else and is wondering how to phrase it. Odd that she didn't pull in to her driveway, which would have revealed her presence. Instead, she parked out front and came upon them suddenly.

"Did you knock on the front door?" Joe asks. "Sorry if I didn't hear."

"I was going to, then I heard you talking. How do you two know each other? Don't tell me she's your granddaughter."

Paula casts a pleading look at Joe. She seems to have no clue how to answer.

"I've been trying to get some help for the food truck," Joe says. "Paula was a customer when I went to the Moonbeam, and she expressed an interest in part-time work. I figured having someone around will help me keep things straight in my head. Having a young mind on Team Joe can't hurt. I told her about my early-stage dementia and whatnot. Didn't faze her a bit. And she's a real whiz around the grill."

"It doesn't bother me that he's going soft in the head," Paula says. "We joke about it all the time. Also, I get free food. The mac and cheese almost gives me an orgasm."

"It's homemade," Joe says. "The mac and cheese."

Donna looks across to her own place: the crepe myrtle not yet bloomed, the neatly trimmed shrubs that border her house, the tool shed that resembles a little barn. She puts down the dog and folds her arms as if something has settled in her mind. "There are things I don't understand," she says.

Joe doesn't like her tone.

"You didn't know Paula until that night at the Moonbeam, right? Yet I saw her the night before on my home security camera." Her professional smile twists sideways. "It was you, honey. I'm sure of it." She turns to Joe. "After I showed you that footage, I downloaded it onto my hard drive and magnified it. I saw that mohawk and just assumed it was a boy." She wags her finger and her smile broadens, going from real estate saleslady to crocodile. "I'm sure it was you in the picture, honey. That mohawk gives it away. Honestly, I came back here because I saw the car. But here we are. Joe will tell you, I'm never one to keep things bottled up."

Butterbean pants with that tiny pink tongue. It is the only sound, the only movement. The squirrel freezes on the garbage can. Even the birds have stopped chirping.

"I'm guessing you didn't meet Joe for the first time at the Moonbeam," Donna says. "I'm guessing you saw him that night on the road. Her smile fades and those blue eyes bore in. She's closing the sale now, looking for money on the table. "So what's the deal, Paula—if that's your real name? Are you trying to take advantage of my neighbor? Because if you are, I have a problem with you."

31

Joe doesn't care for Donna closing in like this, but he can't blame her. She's not being an asshole about it. She saw what she saw, and it has raised questions.

"I can explain why Paula was on the road that night," Joe says. "It's not like you think."

Paula's smile is somewhere between relief and amazement. It's clear she can't wait to hear what Joe has to say. Donna nods in satisfaction, ready to celebrate how she pried loose the facts. Joe looks at the deck, as if the answers are carved into the redwood. He shuffles his feet. Butterbean settles himself against Joe's leg. It's story time.

"Joe? Are you still with us?" Donna moves closer.

"I get upset when I talk about it. Just give me a minute." He has no idea what to say.

"I can tell the story if you want," Paula says.

Joe relaxes. "That'd be fine, girl. You go right ahead."

Paula straightens up and folds her hands like a schoolgirl. "This happened about eight years ago. I lived in Berkeley County at the time. I grew up in a trailer park out in the sticks. Sometimes my dad's buddies would come over and drink beer and talk shop. They worked for a company that built houses. My dad was a carpenter, and his friends were bricklayers, painters, framers—all the trades you need to build a house. On Friday nights, they would drink late. I'd listen for a while, but I always ended up going to bed. This one guy, Chauncey, was the crew chief and a real jokester. Everyone loved him. He'd always tease me and pull my hair. I had braids back then, if you can believe it. This one night— I was fourteen years old—I woke up to find Chauncey in my room. He was on the bed and straddling me."

Donna's hand flies to her face. Her mouth makes the shape of an "O."

"My dad storms into the room and tosses Chauncey off the bed. That's when I see Chauncey's pants are down around his ankles. The covers have been thrown aside. My teddy bear is on the floor." Paula stammers. A tear falls from the corner of her eye. She sniffs and wipes her nose on her T-shirt, the same one she's been wearing for three days. "Dad beat the crap out of his boss right there in my bedroom. Eight years later and I still wake up and imagine Chauncey over me. So on the night you saw me, I was having a bad time. I drove around and ended up here on Seneca Lane. It seemed like a nice, quiet road near the water. But I was upset. I don't know why it hits me on certain nights, but it does."

"It's okay," Donna whispers. "Forget it, honey."

"I parked farther up the road and wanted to walk. I guess I walked past your house, Donna, and realized it was a dead end. Then I saw Joe in his front yard. He was staring into space. I was like, 'What the hell is this old man doing in the middle of the night?' I tried talking to him, but he wouldn't answer my questions. I saw his food truck and looked it up on Facebook. I saw he'd be at the Moonbeam and decided to check it out. We clicked and I asked if he remembered me from the night before. Then I told him the Chauncey story."

Joe clears his throat. "And that's how we met. Kind of like two trains crashing together. Her being all upset and me with a case of wander-itis."

The air rushes from Donna's sails. Her shoulders slump as she walks up to Paula and gently wipes the tear from her cheek. "I'm so sorry. I didn't mean to force that story out of you. Did anything ever come of the Chauncey thing? I mean legally."

"Dad quit his job or Chauncey fired him. I'm not sure which. I know Dad beat him up pretty good. I didn't want to talk to the police. We moved out a few months later and came down here to Hampton." Paula waves her hand and laughs. It is not a pleasant sound. "That's it. I'm done talking for today."

A pair of fighter jets streak across the sky, the Raptors from Langley Air Force Base, always flying in twos. Joe gets lost in the roar of the engines for a moment. Donna says she understands and is always willing to listen if Paula wants to talk further. She mentions a counselor she knows. Since Donna danced at clubs in her younger days, Joe wonders if men followed her home or did worse, and maybe she woke up to a Chauncey or two back in the day. She leaves with Butterbean under one arm. From the look on Paula's face, the knot inside her gut isn't finished unwinding.

"That was some tale," he says.

"It was mostly true. But it was worse than that."

"You don't have to tell me the rest."

"The assault part was true. I woke up with Chauncey straddling me. I still had the covers up to my chin, not like I told Donna. And yes, I still have nightmares about it."

"Did your daddy beat him up?"

"My daddy was long gone by the time that happened. He left my mom before I was born." She swallows hard. "It was my grandfather who opened the door. And he didn't beat up Chauncey. He just fucking stood there. Then Chauncey excused himself and went to get more beer. My dear grandfather closed the door. He never defended me, never said a thing as far as I could tell. Chauncey was his boss. Six months later, we moved down here, and grandfather got the job at the Pickett. I think Sean McTavish used to live in Berkeley County. Anyway, they knew each other."

"Your grandpa went from a house builder to a human-trafficking short-order cook? I'm not sure I believe that."

"The house builder part of the story wasn't true either. Chauncey was their crew chief, but they weren't home builders. They were a gang of thieves. They'd steal stuff from trailers at the truck stop and sell it. Sometimes they'd bribe the trucker and sometimes they'd just lift it. They'd come over to our place to drink and plan their next job. I had to put up with them looking at me. I think they thought I was exotic. You know, biracial."

"So your grandpa becoming a human trafficker . . ."

"It was an easy transition. What they call a lateral move." Paula chin-points to Donna's house. "That security footage is some shit. Enhancing it, trying to see my face. Do you think she's talked to the police?"

"That's a great question. She wasn't home when the police took my boat, but they must have knocked on her door. That Hampton police officer seemed pretty sharp. She would have done her due diligence and canvassed every home."

"Since you're the new kid on the block, maybe they came to you first," Paula says. "Plus, you have that shady backstory, being a badass bouncer and all."

Joe chuckles. "I am far from the new kid. I grew up less than two miles from here. This place was a little different in the sixties and seventies. I used to know it like the back of my hand, but a lot has changed."

"I was born in 1997, but I've read history books. Gone to museums. Seen old black-and-white footage. I bet your TV was powered by steam."

"Oh, be quiet."

32

THEY SIT ON the deck after talking themselves out. It is two o'clock on a Sunday afternoon, and Joe has already spent a full weekend. He's throttled an asshole for old time's sake, found a GPS tracker, fended off Donna's interrogation, and unearthed new details about Paula Jessup. The girl looks lost in her own thoughts, not caring that he could put her away for life.

"Did we unload the groceries?" he asks.

"We put them in the garage. I never knew anyone who kept a chest freezer and a fridge in their garage. Then again, I didn't know many people with garages. Only carports." She tilts her head, remembering something. "There's a plastic shopping bag in the freezer with what looks like a clump of dog hair."

"That's your grandpa's hair. I found it in the boat."

"You're serious?"

"Deadly."

"And you're keeping it because . . .?"

"In case they caught the killer and needed evidence. That was before I knew you were the killer."

"You going to get rid of it?"

"I suppose. I bought that chest freezer and fridge after signing the lease here. Figured I'd want to store my food closer to the truck and not lug it up and down the steps. When you get older, you think about stuff like that." Joe wants to stop talking about Paula's life. He's heard enough about old men straddling her bed and worthless, thieving grandfathers. "I don't have another gig until next Thursday at the Moonbeam. Maybe I'll make some calls and see if I can line up more events."

"Back to the hair," Paula says. "Do you plan to turn me in?"

"You had reasons for doing what you did. Now let it drop."

"But you're still keeping it in the freezer."

"I don't see why not."

Paula throws up her hands, upset by whatever point she can't seem to make. It seems clear that Joe forgot about the hair clump and should probably label it somehow. Otherwise, it might end up in a hotdog bun along with a side of mac and cheese.

"I like running this little food truck," he says. "It's more organized than a kitchen. Everything is in its place. And when you run out of food, you quit for the night. In a restaurant, that would be a disaster. But it happens in the food truck business on a fairly regular basis. You have to plan it right."

"You sound surprised that this has worked out."

"I hadn't planned on having it more than one night. When Maxie came to the Moonbeam, I intended to kill him. Then I talked to the bartender and realized my plan would screw up her life. Then I found out about your screwed-up life. I torqued Maxie's finger real good, but that just complicated matters. As I sit here, I'm not sure what he'll do next. That goes double for me."

Paula drums her fingers on the arm of the chair. "This Maxie. When I went to Captain Maxie's, he chatted me up. Said he knew me from somewhere but couldn't remember where. I wonder if he noticed me at the Moonbeam but can't quite make the connection."

"He say anything else?"

"There was an old newspaper story about his dad, Cotton 'Candy' Smith. He was a bigwig in Phoebus. I found a more recent story of his arrest and how he died in prison."

"That's a sore spot," Joe says. "Maxie looked up to his dad, then it all went downhill. His dad once had status. Now Maxie is trying to do the same thing with this casino project, acting like a big developer, hanging out with all the swells. He told me that at the Moonbeam, but I kind of knew it already."

"Just what happened between you two anyway?"

Joe tells her how things went downhill when he managed Captain Maxie's, how Maxie said he wasn't cut out for management, how Joe offered to be the greeter at the new casino and Maxie waved him off. "Then I socked him," Joe says. "He hit me back pretty hard, and I ended up in the ER. That's when they diagnosed the dementia. You should have seen this doctor, though. Pretty as a picture."

"I can't imagine anyone decking you," Paula says. "That Wendell went to his knees like nobody's business."

"Wendell is stupid. Maxie is not. Maxie taught me how to fight. We worked out at a gym when we were kids. He'd come into Pendergast Cut-Rate, smelling of cologne, all dressed up. I looked up to him like the big brother I never had. That little gym down the road was my only escape from the store. Now Maxie knows every punch I can throw." Joe swallows hard. "He got the better of me that day."

"But you had the Alzheimer's even then, which I'm sure led to your night manager problems."

"I didn't know that at the time. Maxie put me in the hospital with a concussion, and that's when they diagnosed it, like I said. Haven't been back there since. When you went there, did you see a redhead behind the bar? A woman of about forty-five or so?"

"Yeah, you know her?"

"Her name's Kathy. She was a friend."

"Just a friend, or did you two do the nasty?"

Joe waves his hand, as if chasing away a stray memory. "You said something about a Ledyard Aloysius O'Brien. I remember him now. That's the pissant old man who's holding out on Maxie. He won't sell his land for the casino project. How did you come by his name?"

"I'm a regular Nancy Drew."

"I'm serious. You'd have to do some digging to connect those dots."

"And I don't have the brain power for that, being a homeless chick with a mohawk?"

"I didn't say you were homeless, but now that you mention it, I assume you're sleeping in that car of yours."

"I can't stay at Mia's shelter—it's the Benedict House out in Fox Hill—because the Pickett Grill guys made my car, thanks to that damn GPS tracker. They showed up there last night looking for me, and Mia confronted them. I obviously can't go back to my apartment. So yeah, I've been sleeping in the Nova since crawling out of your boat."

"That's not a long-term plan for success," Joe says. "That car attracts attention even without a GPS tracker. You might as well stay here for the time being. Just park the car somewhere else."

"Come again?"

"You heard me. Get your ass in that car and drive it into downtown Phoebus. Park on a side street. Then hoof it back here. You got nowhere else to go. This house is laid out in a way where two people can live here and not bother each other. The main living space is on the second floor, but there's a bedroom and separate bathroom on the first floor."

"I'm aware of the layout. I broke in, remember? Why can't I just park in the driveway?"

"The cops took my boat. They'll visit again, no doubt about it. They see that car and they'll realize it doesn't belong to me, because what would an old geezer be doing with a hot rod like that? Then they'll run the plate and match the last name with your grandpa."

The silence stretches. Joe isn't sure about any of this, but it sounds right.

"If you're okay with me crashing here a few days, that's fine with me," Paula finally says. "I can tell you about my plan to get back at Maxie. As opposed to your plan, going down with guns blazing, which is just stupid."

"Maybe I won't go out with guns blazing," Joe says, "but I ain't going out in a rocking chair. That's for damn sure."

33

THAT NIGHT, JOE wakes up in his own bed, fully clothed, on top of the covers. His pants and shirt are unmarked, and he's still wearing shoes. He's slept away the entire afternoon, assuming this is still Sunday and the year still the same. His phone confirms the date, so he hasn't woken from a five-year coma. It's seven thirty on the dot.

At some point this afternoon, Paula left to move her car. Then Joe closed his eyes. Later, someone helped him off the deck and led him upstairs, opening the door to his bedroom. His pillow hid a snub-nosed .44 revolver, but someone snatched it away before he could grab it. Joe clenches his eyes, trying to crystallize his memory through sheer force of will, but the images remain ghostly and beyond reach. For some reason it reminds him of how Kathy clicked through channels on the TV—boom, boom, boom—Joe telling her to slow down because everything flew by so fast. That was toward the end, when everything seemed hectic and unplanned. She did his banking. Washed his clothes.

Something slams against the house.

And again.

It sounds like the sliding glass door to his office.

Joe rolls out of bed and spends a few minutes in the bathroom. He studies his face in the mirror and closely examines his clothes for signs of rips, holes, grass stains, or blood. If he had a wandering episode sometime this afternoon—screaming down Seneca Lane like a wild banshee—he managed to keep himself clean. He stomps downstairs to announce himself and finds the bathroom door closed. He taps softly and puts his ear to the crack. Incoherent mumbling comes from inside.

Help me. Help me. Please, please help me.

Joe pushes open the door and sees Paula sitting on the toilet, her jeans at mid-thigh, listening to music on tiny earphones. Her arms wave, as if conducting an orchestra. She sings along, hopelessly out of tune. Joe watches from the doorway, then peeks around the corner into the spare bedroom. Paula has stacked several boxes in the corner. He looks to his office and sees a square of cardboard duct-taped over the whole in the sliding glass door.

"What the hell. Are you perving on me? Wait, do you know where you are?"

Paula has taken out her tiny earphones and is pulling up her jeans.

"I heard you calling for help. That's why I opened the door. I didn't mean anything by it."

"It was lyrics to a song, jackass."

"You don't sing very well. It sounded like moaning cattle. Also, I heard something slamming against the wall. That's why I came downstairs in the first place. I wasn't spying. You can have this bathroom to yourself."

"I patched the hole in the glass door and wanted to see if it would hold up, so I slammed it shut a few times. That was after I came back from moving my car into Phoebus and dragged your dementia-ridden ass off the deck because you were snoring loud enough to scare the squirrels. If I hadn't done that, you would gone head over tin cups on the deck. Also, your gun is on the kitchen counter. You tried to take it from under the pillow, and I had to grab it."

"I doubt that the squirrels were scared, and thank you for making the temporary repair to the door. I'll have to see about getting a new pane of glass from the landlord. Or maybe I'll just fix it myself. Or maybe that's your job, since you're so handy with useless old men." He lets the silence settle for a bit, wondering why he had reached for the gun. "I'll be more careful about opening bathroom doors. You might want to choose songs with different lyrics that don't set off alarm bells—and work on your singing. I know the *Mad* magazine lyrics to 'Button Up Your Overcoat.' You wonder why something like that sticks with you, but it does."

"Just don't let it happen again, okay? Because if it does, dementia or not, I might just be out of here."

She washes her hands in the sink and buries her face in a towel. Something shudders through her.

She thought I was going to rape her.

"My mistake," he says. "It won't happen again if I can help it."

Her eyes close. Her voice is a whisper. "I didn't mean to say 'dementia-ridden ass.' That was stupid. And don't worry—I'll remember to lock the door when I'm in there. Did you at least look at your whiteboard before charging down here? While you were sleeping away the day, I did some homework. Everything is changed around."

CHAPTER

34

PAULA HAS ERASED the entire whiteboard. Gone is the recipe for his homemade mac and cheese and the sodas he sells. Gone are the dates listed for his Thursday and Friday gigs through December. A strange diagram has replaced this useful information. A series of rectangles runs along the top of the whiteboard, next to squiggly lines that appear to be ocean waves. The rectangles are black. A red square is in the center. A dotted line is below that. Underneath this mess of squares and squiggles is a brand-new to-do list.

> *Take the card from the customer and swipe as normal.*
> *Drop the card behind the counter.*
> *Play dumb. You're good at that.*
> *Slowly bend down, like your knees are creaky. Again,*
>   *you're a natural.*
> *Swipe the card on A SECOND READER UNDER*
>   *THE COUNTER.*
> *Return the card and tell customer to have a nice day.*

As Joe rereads the steps, Paula tromps upstairs and flops on the couch. She acts like he'll be impressed. Finally he says, "These are instructions for double-swiping a credit card. What kind of sleazy restaurant do you think I ran?"

"I don't think you ran a sleazy restaurant. I think you're going to run a sleazy food truck."

"I'm an honest businessman."

"You torque fingers like people crack eggs. You offer your spare room to the girl who killed her grandfather." She cocks her head, as if her words somehow bring the murder into focus. "Let me walk you through the diagram. Start up here with the squares I've drawn." Paula stands up and points at the whiteboard like an eighth-grade algebra teacher.

Joe throws up his hands. "What if I can't find my mac-and-cheese recipe?"

Paula pulls out her phone and shows him a photo of the old whiteboard. "Everything is there. Your precious recipe isn't going anywhere."

"That photo is too small. It's like a postage stamp."

"You can enlarge it. This is a phone. It's the twenty-first century."

"What if you erase it just to spite me?"

"Oh, for Christ's sake . . ."

"Fine. Show me this nonsense, and maybe I can make sense of your squares."

"I've been working on this all day," Paula says. "So these squares I've drawn, they represent land that Max Smith has already purchased or agreed to purchase. This is south of Virginia Beach, where he plans to build his casino-hotel complex. He's got the beachfront side secured. On the other side, he's got parcels with road frontage. This is Corsair Highway. It runs past a small airport that has vintage airplanes or something. It will be the sole highway access for the complex. The one guy who hasn't sold owns the red square."

"Ledyard Aloysius O'Brien. You told me. Why do I care about him?"

"Because you're going to outbid Maxie for that parcel. My plan will allow you to accumulate enough cash to get a loan. We just have to work fast. That's where the credit card scam comes in. If you want, I can explain it now, or we can wait. You don't have another gig until next week, so we have time. I know this is a lot for you take in."

"A lot for me to take in?"

"Given your delicate condition," she says. "So fragile."

"Good god on a Popsicle stick. My condition has nothing to do with this. I got a plan for Maxie, and it don't involve any wheeling and dealing. I'm not the credit card–scam type. I'm the break-your-eye-socket type. Ripping off other people and their credit cards is plain foolhardy."

"Can I ask you a question? Actually two questions."

"Sure. Ask the hard one first."

She juts out her hip, enjoying the attention. "Let's say you do it your way. I'm assuming you want to kill Maxie. Let's say he ends up dead and no one catches you. You have committed the perfect crime, and you return to this house and your food truck as a free man." She looks around the room. "What's next? You have nothing to live for. Someone with your problem needs to keep the mind busy."

"By playing the long con?"

"Whatever occupies your mind. We make O'Brien a legit offer. Tell him we're raising the money and we'll have it soon." She taps her finger on the whiteboard. "We know this much: For some reason, he doesn't want to sell to Maxie. My guess is, it's not about money, because Maxie would offer him more than enough. Maybe O'Brien doesn't like gambling. Maybe the land has been in his family since Pocahontas. Maybe he wants to buy a houseboat and live on the water, and until then he won't move. We need to find out what's on his mind. That said, we still need some money to show that we're serious bidders."

Joe lets this sink in. It's not bad thinking on her part. If this O'Brien wanted to sell for a high price, Maxie would have paid it. "What's your second question?"

"How would you feel about me living here while we do this? In return for me helping with the credit card project—"

"Scam."

"In return for me helping with the credit card *scam*, how would you feel about watching my back with these Pickett Grill types who won't leave me alone?"

"That's two questions, and neither one is easy."

"You handled Wendell. Sean McTavish doesn't go for violence. These men like to boss around girls, but it's different with men."

"They might have guns," Joe says.

"I don't think you're afraid of guns, and I need you to watch out for me. The way you bent back Wendell's thumb was something. I can still see it in my head. He's a scary dude, and you put him on his knees. Also, they don't know this house. I feel safe here, assuming you don't open any more bathroom doors."

He's relieved that Paula has moved past the bathroom incident. She might have other Chauncey stories to tell. He puts a hand over his heart. "On my honor, I will not bother you in the bathroom from this day forward. Maybe you can spend some of these ill-gotten gains on singing lessons because . . . damn."

"I appreciate the sentiment, but I'm locking the bathroom door from now on. And don't get up on your high horse about being my protector. It's not like you wear a cape or something."

"Since I'll be your protector, let me turn the tables here," Joe says. "What's your long-term plan? Pretend I take care of those two idiots from the Pickett, and you never have to worry about them again. Do you wanna sell spark plugs and gas caps for the rest of your life?"

The question stops her cold. She looks at the ceiling, the floor, anywhere but straight ahead. Finally, she exhales and says, "I haven't thought that far out, Joe. I just haven't."

"Bullshit. Someone who sleeps in their car has plenty of time to think. It's like being in jail. You stare at nothing and imagine the future. You're what, twenty-two years old? It's too early to start thinking about regrets. You have a long road to travel."

"Maybe I'd like to work with Mia," she says softly.

"That's something. You could mow the lawn, trim the shrubs, clean the floors, and make beds for the homeless women. Whip up some oatmeal in the morning. You'd be like a girl Friday. Except you'd need to set your sights a bit higher."

She pauses. Something passes before her eyes. "I saw those girls. I know Rosa's story. I understand how this human trafficking works. It amounts to slavery, and it's right out in the open. You pass girls on the street or in a shopping center. I can't get over that. I want to help every one of them, just put them in the car and take them somewhere."

"So you'd be like Mia's partner," Joe says.

"Maybe. Mia is a lot to handle. We get along when we talk, but I don't know about working with her every day. She's like a big sister or an aunt. It's not always good to work with your big sister. Plus, her budget is a shoestring. She couldn't pay me."

Joe has no comeback for that, and Paula seems to sense it. After a few seconds of silence, she shrugs and starts down the stairs. Joe calls after her. "Let's file this conversation away for later. Remind me to bring it up again."

"Because you'll forget?"

"Hell, yes. Forgetting is what I do best."

35

THE NEXT MORNING, Paula is awake and around before seven. Cooking his bacon and eggs as music pounds up through the floorboards, Joe hears her from upstairs. She must have abandoned the earbuds to avoid being surprised again. He expected some kind of chickenshit disco garbage sung by a woman with only one name, but this music is mournful and steady, like someone walking to their death with a bass guitar to keep them company.

Minutes later, she comes to the bottom of the stairs and calls up. "Smells like you burned the bacon. Are the burners turned off?"

"I like my bacon crisp."

She's wearing blue work pants and a cream-colored, short-sleeved shirt. Her name is written in script inside an oval underneath the logo for Brady Auto Parts. She does a little twirl. "You like my uniform? I think I look very professional."

"Especially with the mohawk."

"Mr. Brady thinks I'm going through a phase," she says. "He has me on a Sunday through Wednesday shift because we sell a lot over the weekend. I called in sick yesterday, but I can't keep doing that."

"How long is your normal shift?"

"Eight to five, with an hour for lunch. Today's Monday, so it should be slow. Maybe I could pick up some parts for your Hyundai. I'm sure we have a rubber band or two. Or maybe a hamster wheel. Also, the food truck has a rattle. Seriously, that jalopy needs a tune-up."

"The Hyundai's got a nice little motor. Just because I don't have chrome ding-dongs hanging everywhere doesn't mean my car sucks. Where'd you park your hot rod?"

"In Phoebus, like you said. Barrow Street near the library. I can walk there in ten minutes, and I just sent you a photo of your old whiteboard so you don't freak out. Recipes and reminders are all there. Also, I gave you homework. I came upstairs last night and taped a couple of printouts to your whiteboard. Old news stories about Maxie's father. He went by Cotton 'Candy' Smith."

"I know who he is. He died in jail. It was a painful subject for Maxie. I remember when the man was arrested."

"Mia says painful subjects are always weaknesses," Paula says. "You said it yourself. Maxie wants to be a legit businessman. He wants to sit on committees at the Chamber of Commerce, get invited to all the nice parties. He doesn't want controversy. I know you said that, but we should keep that in mind. That's where he's vulnerable now."

She turns on a heel and saunters out the door. The car fires up with a rumble, and she's off.

Joe has to chuckle when he reads that story about Cotton Smith from back in the day. The papers painted a picture of a small-town dandy. He was nothing but a thug, trying to make a fast buck on the backs of working men, and Maxie is his father's son. Still, Paula might be on to something when it comes to Maxie's ambitions. He likes being in the limelight now, and that wasn't always the case.

Joe sits down with his laptop and rereads the latest email from Jennifer. Why shouldn't doctors know about their little exchanges? Not that it matters. Joe doesn't plan on seeing a doctor all that much. He has three types of pills, which is three kinds more than he's ever had, and doctors can't do much more except ask him questions and nod soothingly.

Hello there, Jennifer,

I received your last email, and don't worry. I won't mention anything to the doc. It's nice that you're doing this, although I'm not sure how much you can help. Don't get me wrong—anything helps, but I got what I got.

I made a new friend. Young enough to be my granddaughter. She's helping with the food truck, keeping me straight. She's had a bit of trouble, but I think she'll be fine.

He steps outside and sees that Donna isn't home. Maybe Monday is a good day to sell houses. He takes the food truck to get gas, avoiding the commercial strip of Mercury Boulevard because the truck doesn't handle well in heavy traffic He heads to his old neighborhood of Buckroe Beach. The corner lot that was once home to Pendergast Cut-Rate is nothing but hard dirt and scattered pebbles now The heartache and tears shed after fourteen-hour days have leaked into the ground. Maybe passersby can still hear his mom crying as she climbed the stairs to their living space on the second floor. Maybe kids who play on that corner can hear Joe's footsteps as he stomped up to the attic, where he slept on the hardwood floor and dreamed of a life without stocking shelves.

Or maybe it's all gone.

Joe is looking for a gas station, but now he remembers it closed years ago. He keeps driving toward the beach, where his dad once rented a garage for storing supplies. When Joe was fourteen, Dad trusted him to drive the station wagon a few miles to the garage, usually on Saturday nights, to pick up extra dry goods, bread, and Danish for the Sunday morning shoppers. The Buckroe Amusement Park was still operating back then, and sometimes Joe would stand in the garage and listen to the roller-coaster screams. There was another park next to it, one for black people. He can't remember the name, but they had musical acts and the whole nine yards. He longed to see Cheyenne strutting around in a bathing suit, telling people about this white boy at the grocery story who jammed coins into her palm.

Today, Buckroe Beach is still a good place to sit in the sand and enjoy the water. Nice, new homes line the road that face the beach, and they have a farmer's market on Saturdays. He turns away from the water and finds his way back to Phoebus, where he gets gas at a different station. When he gets home, he sees Jennifer has replied to his email.

Joe:

I'm glad you made a friend. Tell me more about her. Maybe I can help. I'm an all-around Good Samaritan.

JOE AND PAULA

CHAPTER

36

THE DAYS PASS and Thursday arrives. Charlie, the bartender at the Moonbeam, greets Joe like an old friend. Her braids dangle like strings of a beaded curtain. She pours him a pint of pilsner and insists his money is no good. Joe leans on the bar and swirls the beer around in his mouth.

"I was thinking about what you said last week," she said, "about that theater being segregated back in the day. Black people having to sit up in the damn balcony and all that."

"It was worse in the early sixties. I think they did sit-ins and such. Different time back then."

"And your dad being Klan."

"I'm not proud of that. He said if he didn't join, it would have meant trouble. People find all sorts of reasons to do bad things. It's easier than doing the right thing." They lock gazes, her with those dark eyes. "You're wanting to know if I joined the Klan. The answer is no."

"I wasn't wondering, but thanks for the answer." She checks out the room beyond him. "Looks like we'll have a good crowd tonight."

Joe follows her gaze. Paula is hanging around somewhere, trying not to be seen, ready to help with the grill or drinks or credit card rip-offs—whatever comes first. The place is full of office types who have time to drink beer on a Thursday. Joe checks his watch: fifteen minutes to opening. On Sunday, after Paula showed him the new whiteboard, Joe decided to do what she wanted. He ordered a second card reader shipped overnight and practiced his technique: swipe on the regular reader, drop the card, swipe on the second reader, return card. He needed liniment on his creaky knees after a couple of days, but Paula says it will be worth it. She wants to buy high-end electronics with the stolen cards and resell them. She's talking tablets, laptops, and smartphones, small pieces that will accumulate a few thousand dollars quickly.

Joe played along. But he knows they won't pile up enough money to buy out this O'Brien guy. A few thousand dollars here and there doesn't amount to much when you're talking real estate.

And it's risky—so many ways this could go off the rails.

Some nosy customer sees you double-swiping a card and calls you out. A penny-pincher questions the price of a tablet or laptop when you resell it. But Paula believes in it, and Joe wants her to believe in something beyond those two goons who want her dead. She says credit card swiping is a victimless crime. The credit cardholders (also called "victims") will call the company and have the charge removed. They won't care as long the company doesn't make them pay.

The idea of a victimless crime makes Joe nervous as hell. There is no such thing, but Paula believes that such a unicorn walks the earth.

"The pilsner is selling tonight," Charlie says. "The pilsner always does well when it's warmer." She pours herself seltzer water from the bar gun and squeezes half a lemon over it. The tendons in her forearm pop out. "With your truck, I bet different things sell better on different nights."

Joe likes how they're talking shop. "I want to diversify the menu a bit," he says. "Maybe get some crazy toppings for the dogs and sausages—cream cheese, dill relish, barbecue baked beans, that sort of thing. Then give each one a different name. See how that goes for a while."

"I like that idea," Charlie says. "You can jack up the prices too."

"I'm not trying to make money," he says. "This keeps my mind busy as I head into retirement. If I sit around all day, who knows what trouble I'll get into?"

A group of office workers with loose ties and pent-up energy sidle up to the bar. Charlie starts to excuse herself, then turns back to Joe. He's leaning forward, and they almost touch noses by accident. Her voice lowers to a whisper. "You're not nervous, right? I don't want anyone to get a bad vibe like last week."

"Not nervous, no."

"I have a sixth sense about these things, that's all. Don't hesitate to reach out. If we get a crowd tonight, you'll have your hands full."

The food truck sits in its assigned spot, the engine rumbling. The crowd seems happy, anxious to stretch their lines of credit. Two Crock-Pots are plugged in, with mac and cheese bubbling around the dewy lids. It was Paula's idea to get creative with the toppings. Put cream cheese on a dog and call it the Philly, she said. Get some spices together and make a Cajun dog. Fry up some onions and green peppers in garlic butter and charge extra as a topping for the Italian sausage.

Thanks to her job at Brady Auto Parts, the past few days have settled into a routine. She leaves house early in the morning and gets home around six. Twice this week, she brought home takeout, Chinese and Mexican. She tends to wolf down food like there is no tomorrow, and maybe there isn't. Maxie could send someone to the house any day. Sean McTavish might follow the food truck to see where Joe lives.

His phone buzzes with a text from Paula.

You ready? I'll give you the go-ahead.

Joe frowns. What does that even mean? The younger generation can't talk to people anymore. They hide behind text messages and smiley faces. He calls her number and says, "By giving me the go-ahead, what am I supposed to do?"

The wind rustles through the connection. "You don't want to pick someone who looks like they're living paycheck to paycheck. Look for kids in expensive jeans and older men with popped collars. I'm up by the theater, walking your way now. Remember, rich folks with big fat lines of credit won't notice when a couple of computer tablets show up on their statement a few weeks later."

"I see some girls with blue jeans that have big holes in the knees," Joe says. "I should avoid them. They look poor."

"Actually, they may have money. The holes are designed that way."

"What do you know? I bet you don't know anything about the theater, and there you are, standing in front of it."

"I'm standing behind it, and I know theater just fine, Joe. I've seen shows here."

"Back in my day, they separated blacks and whites. The blacks had to sit in the balcony. Sometimes I went up there because the seats were better. Also, the blacks threw popcorn on the kids below, and it was fun to watch. Since you're a tweenie or a mixie or whatever, I guess you would have hung from the rafters."

Her breath catches. "Hold on. McTavish and Wendell just walked past me on the opposite side of the street. They didn't see me, but they're probably wondering if I'm with you. Dammit."

Joe wonders if he told her about meeting Cheyenne in the empty seats, talking and sharing dreams. Or was that Charlie just a minute ago? Yes, that was Charlie. He raises the customer window to get started for the night. "Thanks for the heads-up on those two. Maybe I'll break that guy's thumb this time."

37

PAULA CUTS BEHIND the theater through a grassy area. She wants to keep away from the main drag, so she takes a parallel side street, angling between buildings until presented with a clear line of sight to Joe's Takeaway in the parking lot. Four people stand in line. Joe goes through what appear to be routine motions.

McTavish and Wendell sit at an outside table. McTavish looks at his phone, taps his foot, and points across the water to the backed-up traffic at the Hampton Roads Bridge–Tunnel. Maybe he's talking about where they found her grandfather in the brackish water. Brady's Auto Parts has a TV in the break room, and Paula has spent the past few days sneaking glances at the news. The police have ruled the death a homicide and said they are investigating several "avenues," whatever that means. Joe says they haven't asked questions about the boat, but they haven't returned it yet. Paula wonders if she left a strand of hair, some skin. Something they could test. Joe insists he cleaned it out.

McTavish goes inside the bar and comes out with two beers. Wendell pulls one glass toward him and leans over it.

Brains and brawn, those two. McTavish seems to control the trafficking flow at the Pickett. On the day Rosa escaped, she explained it as Paula sped from the parking lot.

"McTavish doesn't slap the girls, but he decides if and when they get slapped," Rosa said. "You don't talk back, and you never walk into the dining room. Sometimes the police come for lunch, and we stay in the supply room until they leave. Once I had to climb on a ladder to get supplies. It broke on the third step, and I fell backward. My ankle swelled up, and we thought it might be broken. Mr. McTavish drove me to the emergency room on one condition: that I say I was injured in a fall at home. He played the concerned neighbor. When the hospital asked for an address, I gave them your grandfather's house. I told them I was a distant relative staying there temporarily. The ankle wasn't broken, but they fitted me with a walking boot to help it heal. Mr. McTavish docked my pay for missing work, and I was out three hundred dollars. He scolded me for making eye contact with the nurse, said I was trying to 'send messages,' whatever that meant."

The Pickett sits between a manicurist and tanning salon in the shopping center. Rosa said the manicurist also rotates crews of girls, and McTavish talks with the owner sometimes. Paula will always remember the look on Rosa's face that night. She blew cigarette smoke through those dragon nostrils and kept glancing over her shoulder at the Pickett. She wasn't convinced freedom could be real.

The line has disappeared at Joe's Takeaway, although several potential customers study the menu from a distance. Paula calls him, since texts seems to piss him off. "Are you seeing McTavish and Wendell?," he asks. "They're sitting at one of the tables. And you're standing in the middle of the market."

"I don't know what that means. Have you found anyone who looks like they could use some added credit card debt?"

"This dude looking at my menu acts like he has money. He's not wearing socks in March, and that alone should qualify him for a rip-off."

38

JOE TURNS HIS focus to McTavish and Wendell until a customer catches his attention.

"A couple of dogs, yeah?" The man wears a polo shirt and white beach pants, canvas shoes, a rope belt, all of it coordinated. He slaps a credit card on the counter like it's a gold doubloon. "Some slaw too," he says.

"Sure thing. Drinks are in the cooler if you want one."

"Nah. I'm all over these beers. This truck looks familiar, but I can't place it."

"It used to belong to Captain Maxie's down in Norfolk. I worked there." Joe points to the bouncer story in its plastic cover. "Worked the door for many years, then managed the place. Maybe I checked your ID at some point. When I retired, the owner let me have this food truck, but I had to rebrand it."

"That was damn nice of him," he says.

"That's what people keep saying. Condiments are on the table."

Joe slides two hotdogs and a container of slaw toward him. He takes the man's credit card and promptly drops it. He wasn't doing the scam. He really dropped it. Shaking his head, he bends down and comes nose to nose with the swiper. It's a black rectangle no bigger than a box of .22 ammo, with a gutter for swiping. It's duct-taped to the wall, and a power cord runs to Paula's laptop, which sits on the floor to receive the data. Joe figures what the hell. This guy's a goon. He lines up the card, swipes down and the red light turns green. Joe stands up, swipes the card through the regular square on his smartphone and comes face to face with five people lined up at the window. They suspect nothing.

That was easy.

And now that he's thinking about it, Paula is right about one thing. If he kills Maxie and gets away with it, what then? The doctor said dementia affects everyone differently. Some have a long, slow slide and others get hit right away. What if he has another couple of years, or five? He buys that land from Ledyard Aloysius whatever and watches Maxie's dream crumble.

Of course the credit card scam can't accumulate enough money. What then? *Rob a bank. Knock over an armored car. Pull a jewelry heist.* Because that's probably what it would take. But he knows there's another option, if he wants to take it.

A big beefy guy leans in at the window. "Hey, buddy. Let me try one of those Italian sausages. You got any peppers and onions to put on that?"

"I don't right now, sir. But come next week, we'll have that and more," Joe says. "You think frying up those peppers and onions in garlic butter is a good idea? Because you look like an expert when it comes to sausages, if you don't mind me saying so."

The guy throws back his head and laughs. His full beer slops over the cup. "You got that right. I'm already three beers in, but I know my food."

He pays in cash. The next three customers, all men, have debit cards, and Joe double-swipes the last guy, who looks like he might be a middle manager. Business picks up and Joe settles into a rhythm. He decides to double-swipe every third customer, regardless of how they look. It provides a sense of order and keeps him sharp. He makes a point of chatting up every customer—*"those are nice earrings"; "your Flyers are looking good right now"*—that sort of thing. Paula remains AWOL. The two guys from the Pickett drink beer at their table.

One.

Two.

Double-swipe.

One.

Two.

Double-swipe.

Eight thirty comes and goes, and still no Paula. Joe calls her. He doesn't want to get into some ridiculous eighth-grade texting exchange.

"I'm fine. What's wrong?" she says. "I found the Mercedes van that McTavish and Wendell drive. It would be awesome if someone set a fire in the wheel wells and let the rubber burn. I'm just sayin'. We should send a signal if they're staking you out. Sooner or later, they'll try something."

"Don't go setting any fires."

"Don't worry. I'm armed."

"You have my gun?"

"It might be in the glove compartment of the Nova. I wanted to make sure you didn't do anything stupid."

"Get your ass back here. Then put a smile on your face and come help me out. And don't do anything with my gun, or I'll shoot you myself. You're working with me now."

"I am? Why, Mr. Pendergast, this is so sudden."

"Don't be a smart-ass. I could use some help. I've been doing this for a solid hour, and I'm restocking the grill as we speak. The coleslaw is selling like crazy, and I have no idea why. Maybe it's too warm for mac and cheese. You can work the grill, but stay in back. Keep those two morons from seeing you. I'll handle the customers. We probably have two hours left."

"How's it going with the credit cards?"

Joe rolls a handful of hotdogs onto the grill. He lowers his voice as the meat sizzles. "Got more than I can count. But I need you to tell me what happens next after all this feeds into the computer on the floor."

"You stick it on a floppy and put it in your VCR."

"That sounds outdated."

"Christ on a crutch. I'm joking. We've discussed this. You keep forgetting."

39

THE NEXT MORNING, Paula rolls out of bed early to figure out how Joe did last night. She attaches the card reader to her laptop with a USB cord and opens the file. She arranged everything so Joe only had to swipe, and now data spills onto the screen for eighteen credit cards. She sits cross-legged on the bed, her head swimming with possibilities, as Joe clomps downstairs. He stops at the landing and clears his throat.

"Are you decent in there?"

"When the door is open, you don't have to worry. When the door is closed, you worry."

"I'm going into the garage to check on supplies," he says.

"You got the lunch thing in downtown Newport News."

"Yes, it's Friday. Are you coming with me?" His voice carries a hint of hope. "Not that you have to."

"Someone's got to supervise. You went a little wild last night with these cards."

"It helps that I'm naturally awkward."

Last night, Paula calmed down after getting inside the food truck. McTavish and Wendell never seemed to notice her. Joe ran out of Italian sausage first, then brats, then hotdogs. He seemed to enjoy bantering with the customers. Maybe he was reliving his days from working the door at Captain Maxie's. The good bouncers have a way about them.

His leans into the open doorway. "So I did good last night swiping cards?"

"Looks that way. Did you get any dirty looks? Anyone ask questions?"

"When I dropped the card, most people went to the condiment table. I had all the time in the world. Especially later in the night when the beer was flowing. People wanted their food and didn't care what you do. I assume the next step is we start buying things online?"

"We can't order online," Paula says. "The credit card-holder might get an email saying their order has shipped, and then we're screwed. We need to make over-the-counter purchases with cloned cards, which is a bit of a risk, but it's doable."

"Cloned?"

"Yes. I have a couple of expired credit cards. I can overwrite the stolen information onto them. So I present a card with my name on it, but it's really someone else's information and credit limit. It's still a risk because the numbers on the physical card won't match what the cashier sees when they run it, but how often do they compare? Also, we pick busy times when everyone is in a hurry."

"Then what?"

"We buy smartphones, laptops, and tablets, and sell at a discount. We have to come up with a cover story that explains how we came by this stuff. Some people might ask. We make up flyers. We spend a day going through the parking lot of a big-box store and put pieces of paper under windshield wipers. Maybe stick some on telephone poles. We get a burner phone to use as a business number. It's not like we have five hundred items to unload. It's just a handful. People will have to come to this house unless we set up elsewhere. I haven't thought that far ahead."

Joe leaves the room, opens the door to the garage, then stops and turns. "Is this how they did it at the Pickett? Ripping off people and sticking flyers under windshields?"

"I honestly don't know. This all comes to me second-hand. Rosa saw it."

"The girl you rescued."

Paula smiles. "Yeah. The girl I rescued."

Thoughts seem to be knocking around inside Joe's head. "So we're ripping people off and whatnot, but like you say, they call the credit card company and get the charge removed. And if we wait three or four weeks, they won't be able to pin it down. They'll forget all the times they charged stuff."

"That's the theory."

Joe disappears into the garage. He still seems to have something on his mind.

A few minutes later, her phone chimes twice. It's a text from Mia.

Call me. Now please.

When Paula calls, Mia tells her, "I need to speak with you privately."

As Joe putters around the garage, Paula goes into his office, opens the sliding door, and walks into the backyard. "No one is around. Go ahead."

"I've been doing more backgrounding on Joe Pendergast. Remember that retired Norfolk detective who seemed to recognize the name? He called me back. " Papers shuffle on her end of the phone. "Joe Pendergast was questioned in an incident that involved a police officer getting shot. He said, and I quote, 'Joe Pendergast is not a man you want to fuck with.'"

"Joe is suspected of shooting a cop?"

"The incident was complicated, but he said Pendergast has a hair-trigger temper. He could work the door all night, joking with the customers, even being nice to people who get sideways with fake IDs. Then something could set him off. I've known this detective for years, Paula. He is genuinely worried that I'm in the vicinity of Joe Pendergast. Which makes me worried for you."

"I can't see him having a hair-trigger temper," Paula says.

"Exactly my point. It comes without warning. He's nice and friendly, then he turns. I know you can't go back to your old apartment, and you can't stay here. But don't hang around him. Rosa told me about this credit card swiping plan. It sounds kooky. And it won't give you enough money to buy the O'Brien land, which Rosa says is your goal."

"It's a good goal."

"It's a fine goal," Mia says. "I'm on board with blocking a scumbag from opening a casino, but you won't raise enough money, and it's risky."

"We'll see. We spent last night working at the Moonbeam Brewery. He double-swiped nearly twenty cards."

"We?"

"I'm staying with him."

A pause before Mia speaks again. "Excuse me, what?"

"Let's see. I moved in exactly a week ago. I've been going to work at Brady's and helping Joe deal with this Maxie." Paula lowers his voice. "Joe was going to kill him. You can say what you want about credit card fraud, but I'm preventing someone from getting killed and preventing Joe from rotting in jail or getting killed himself. These are my choices."

Mia sputters for a moment, the words piling up in her head. "Let's just slow down and look at the facts. You are in the same house with a very dangerous man who—oh, by the way—has early-stage dementia. Do you know one symptom of early-stage dementia? Bouts of rage. Even if you two are getting along, he could wake up one night and forget you're staying there. He walks around in the dark, sees a shadow, and shoots you dead. Get out of there today. Do you know anyone in Berkeley County? That's all woods and valleys."

"In Berkeley County I could live in a shack and work on a manifesto."

"I'm serious. Get out of there tonight."

"I want to stick with our plan."

"Which involves massive credit card fraud and an unreachable goal. Also, what happens to Ledyard Aloysius O'Brien if he sold? For an old man, with his home gone, he needs another option."

"Good point," Paula says. "I'll brainstorm."

CHAPTER

40

O N THEIR WAY to the lunch gig, Joe drives past the Newport News shipyard. Paula hunkers forward in the passenger seat and stares at the maze of buildings behind the fence and the occasional aircraft carrier rising above everything. She seems lost in thought.

Joe stops at a red light. The lunch spot is up ahead, marked off by orange cones. He wants to talk about this credit card scam, how it won't give them enough money, and to propose a plan B.

But then Paula asks: "Did you like doing bouncer stuff? You got in a lot of fights, I bet."

"Not really. In a bar fight, one of two things usually happens. The first guy makes a mistake and gets decked, and the fight is over before it starts. Or both guys end up wrestling and go to the ground, and they get tired. I'll tell you one more thing: I'd rather break up two guys than two girls. Women could always fight."

Paula seems to consider her next words very carefully, like she's got something on her mind. "What happens if the fight doesn't stop? There's always a guy who thinks his girl got slapped around or pinched in the ass, and maybe she did. Maybe he doesn't care if the bouncer comes after him. Maybe he takes a swing at you. Then what? That's probably why that magazine named you best bouncer in Hampton Roads."

The light turns green and Joe has to laugh. "That stupid magazine story will follow me to my grave, I swear. But you should read it. There is more to being a bouncer than breaking up fights. I gave people second chances if they deserved it."

"Like how?"

"If someone flashed fake ID, they either got up in my face or they started to cry. The ones who cried, I often let them walk away. Sometimes you need to do that. They'd come back to me a year or two later and thank me."

"What about cops? You ever tangle with them?"

"I always got along with the police. And they have guns. You'd have to be stupid to mess with them."

After Joe parks the truck, Paula sets up the condiment table and the cooler with sodas and water. She wipes down the laminated menu and speaks softly to him through the customer window. "You'll see I put the skimmer and laptop back in its place right below you. How many cards to you think we can do over lunch?"

"I'm thinking zero. Two things about the lunch crowd: They're sober and they're in a hurry. I can't be dropping cards all the time. Also, we need to have a conversation about your plan."

"Oh?"

"I appreciate the thinking. It's a decent way to get a few thousand dollars. But not to raise enough money to buy the O'Brien land."

"Funny that you mention it," Paula says. " I was thinking the same thing. We'll need another source of cash. You have any old baseball cards or comic books you can sell?

Old people—I mean, old people like yourself—tend to have stuff lying around that's valuable."

"What a warm heart you have. No, missy. I don't have anything like that. I do have a bank account in the low six figures. And I might decide to blow my wad on the land purchase."

Paula blinked. Did he seriously have that much cash? It took a moment for her to find the words. "But then you'll be broke," she said.

"Not if I keep doing this well with the food truck."

"That's ridiculous, Joe. You can't throw your savings away. Even I know that."

They leave it at that.

A rush of customers hits at eleven thirty. Everyone wants a hotdog. The mac and cheese makes a strong comeback. The little nip in the air probably helps. Joe couldn't double-swipe a credit card if he wanted to, and he doesn't—not really. The whole buy-and-resell thing is small potatoes, and he doesn't want to cheat his customers. The line moves too fast, and the customers are alert, waiting to rush back to their desks. Paula works the grill, and their teamwork sees them through the first hour, but Joe can tell she has something on her mind. When they have a break, she finally speaks up.

"I think being a bouncer would be a tough job," she says. "You have to make a lot of snap decisions. I could see how you might hurt someone. And I could see how you might have a run-in with the police from time to time."

"Now we're back to bouncer stories again. What is it with you? Something specific on your mind?"

"No, forget it."

"It's funny," he says, "trying to switch the subject. Last week at this time, I was stealing your backpack."

She chuckles, but Joe notices the sag in her shoulders. She's given up asking whatever it was she wanted to know.

"We should go visit Ledyard tomorrow," she says. "Keep pushing this land sale. Let's see what he wants for it. Then we can work on plan B that doesn't involve your savings account. But I've got some homework to do first."

CHAPTER

41

L EDYARD ALOYSIUS O'BRIEN lives halfway to North Carolina, in the middle of nowhere. At least that's how it appears to Paula on Google maps. She wants to drive the Nova, but Joe insists she leave it parked on a side street in Phoebus. Not only is her car recognizable to those two goons from the Pickett Grill, but she might get pulled over for being a speed demon. They'd run her license and ask Joe for ID, and pretty soon they're connecting Joe's address with a girl named Jessup, and off they go. Paula says that sounds too much like a cop show, but she lets Joe drive his little Hyundai. Mia's warning about hair-trigger temper aside, the guy drives like an old lady. They're in the slow lane of the interstate, being passed with impunity. As a minivan rolls by, Paula glares daggers at the stick figure family pasted on the back window.

"Maybe we should have taken the food truck" is all she says.

"The food truck handles like an aircraft carrier in a sea of Brunswick stew."

"The guys at the auto parts store know all the good mechanics. They'd get me a deal on shocks and struts and a front-end job."

"Could they paint some flames on the side? Jack it up in back?" The Hyundai whines in protest as Joe guns it to sixty. "Then you can work on this little gem. Get me a new lawnmower engine for under the hood."

The interstate takes them to Virginia Beach, where they head south on a two-lane road. Paula opens up her laptop and starts tapping keys. Yesterday, after returning from the Newport News lunch gig, she waited until Joe took a nap, and visited Donna next door. They talked about the O'Brien land, and Donna packed two hours' worth of real estate advice into twenty minutes. Then, with an odd gleam in her eye, she offered Paula a tour of the basement. Paula begged off and went back to Joe's. She surfed for information on Ledyard Aloysius O'Brien and came across a newspaper story from 2015 headlined "A Death at Sea: The Chris Brown Tragedy."

"I found this story," she says now. "Been meaning to tell you about it."

Joe looks at the farmer's fields, at a plane flying overhead, everywhere except the road. The Hyundai dips across the yellow line from time to time. They still have a good fifteen miles to go, and Paula wonders if they'll make it.

"I found this story that mentions O'Brien," she says again. "If you agree to keep your eyes on the road, I might read it for you. Anything to help you concentrate."

"Was he arrested?"

"Why do you always think people get into trouble? Maybe he won the lottery or competed in the Olympics back in the fifties. It turns out O'Brien was a tugboat captain working in and around Norfolk. Something like fourteen years ago, this nor'easter came up the coast, and he was dispatched to Norfolk Naval Shipyard to keep a submarine from breaking loose. A guy on his boat, Chris Brown, was lost at sea that day. This story came out ten years later. I think Chris Brown was a high school baseball star."

"I could have played sports in high school," Joe says. "Dad made me work at the store. But that's how I got to know this girl, Cheyenne. She would come in while I was working the counter and buy two pretzel sticks and a Royal Crown Cola. Sometimes I'd drop the change in her palm and she'd try to hold hands. I only think that happened once, but that memory is hard-wired."

Paula sighs. "Will you listen? So this tugboat is bumping up against the submarine, holding it in the pier or whatever, with O'Brien at the helm. Chris Brown leaves the pilot house to check on something. O'Brien sees him and they wave. When he looks back a few seconds later, Brown isn't there. Everyone assumed he went back inside. This is what O'Brien says in the story: 'We didn't even know he was missing until my first mate asked if Chris was in the pilot house. He wasn't, and it was the worst feeling I had in my life. Worse than losing three wives. His body showed up the next morning, all broken apart. I had to identify him because Chris had no parents. We scattered his ashes past the Chesapeake Bay Bridge–Tunnel so his spirit could look toward the open water. I was sixty-five years old and probably had a few working years left, but I quit the business and moved inland to my family homestead.'"

Paula fiddles with the touch pad and minimizes the screen. "Isn't that awful?"

"I'd say more interesting than awful," Joe says. "He lost three wives, but he doesn't mention kids. I wonder if this Chris Brown was the son he never had. If he was sixty-five back then, he's close to eighty years old now. He should be living in a nice retirement home. Which makes me think our plan has a problem."

"What's that?"

"How do we convince O'Brien that we won't turn around and sell to Maxie once we buy his land?"

"We put something in the deed saying we would never sell it. Make it legal. Maybe some other things, who knows?" Paula fingers a piece of notebook paper in her front pocket. Donna told her how to handle that question, but she wants to surprise Joe with some razzle-dazzle real estate knowledge.

"Then we own a piece of land in the middle of nowhere," Joe says. "We have no plan for it."

"I hoped we wouldn't discuss that right now. You might think I'm being a bit harsh."

Joe grins. "Be harsh, little lady. Somehow I'll get by."

"We buy the land, then when you pass on to your reward in heaven, you bequeath the land to me. Maybe the food truck too. I can live there. By then, Maxie will have probably kicked the bucket, and his casino project will be toast."

"I like how I get my heavenly reward while my old boss kicks the bucket," Joe says. "Are you going to build a house on this land?"

"I'll think of something."

They talk some more, figuring out their pitch. Thirty minutes later, the GPS tells them to take a dirt road that cuts through a grassy field. The Hyundai bottoms out on the uneven terrain, and Joe winces as the undercarriage scrapes against hardscrabble dirt. A scarecrow stands guard where the field crests, and Joe starts down the other side. Two structures are up ahead: a double-wide trailer with the windows busted out, and behind that, a yellow school bus sitting on blocks. The bus has a little chimney that leaks smoke. A barrel-chested man with a long gray hair and a beard stands in front of the double-wide. A yellow tabby cat sits near him. It is the biggest house cat Paula has ever seen, and Berkeley County had its share of big cats.

As the car approaches, the man breaks the breach on a double-barreled shotgun and slides in two red shells.

Then he snaps it back into place.

CHAPTER

42

JOE ISN'T THE least bit scared of the old man and his gun.
This guy isn't going to shoot anyone. He's an aging, white-
whiskered dog that needs to snarl from time to time. Old
dogs are seldom a problem. The dangerous dogs have eyes
like cold tar that hold your gaze right before they lunge. Ledyard Aloysius O'Brien hasn't lunged since the Eisenhower
administration. That cat of his might be another story.

The Hyundai slows to a crawl as Joe waits for a signal. When O'Brien shifts his feet and moves the shotgun to
crotch level, Joe opens the door.

"Don't make any sudden movements," Joe says, not
looking at Paula. "I don't think he'll shoot."

"That cat might eat us."

"Fair point."

Joe gets out of the car, palms facing outward. "If you're
Mr. O'Brien, we'd like to talk with you, sir. We mean no
trouble. A person wants to buy your land, and we'd like to
make a counteroffer." O'Brien tilts his chin toward the sky
as the tabby cat twitches its tail. Joe swallows hard and continues: "We have money to put on the table. If we could just
sit down and have a conversation, we—"

"You want to build a casino too?" The old man's raspy voice speaks of too many cigarettes, or perhaps shouting into the night at ghosts who fell overboard. "Because if you want to build a casino, I got no time for you. This land has been in my family since the Pungo Witch. She went on trial back in the dark days. I got forty acres that go into the trees behind me. It's not much, but it's something."

Paula steps forward. "We have no plans to build a casino, although we're not exactly Quakers ourselves."

O'Brien grunts a laugh. "Look at you, girl. Hair done up like an Indian."

She rubs her mohawk and looks toward the red Jeep. "It's low maintenance. What's that Jeep got under the hood?"

"An engine."

"I bet it's good for this field, but it'll rattle apart on the interstate. Not good for long drives, those Jeeps. They knock the fillings out of your teeth."

"I don't take long drives anymore. Haven't taken long drives in a while." For a moment, O'Brien almost seems ready to unpack a few things from that sentence. Then he falls silent.

"You moved back here after Chris Brown died," Paula says. "Let me guess. You couldn't be on a tugboat anymore because you'd always think of him."

Joe had been thinking about that episode in O'Brien's life since Paula read him the newspaper story. It gave him an idea. He spoke up. "But the fact is, you still think of him here in the woods. You look in the trees at night and see him waving that final time. We're old men, Mr. O'Brien. I know what it's like to look back on your life. You replay moments and wonder what might have happened if you didn't get in the car that day, or if you hadn't bumped into that long-lost friend, or if you stopped to help someone instead of passing by. For men like us, being alone isn't good. You got too many dreams to be alone with. You need to be around people and share your thoughts, even if it's small talk." He points to Paula. "I haven't known my partner here very long, but she's already been a big help, Indian haircut and all. And we sincerely want to purchase your land, but we want you to be comfortable with us."

O'Brien's face turns to stone, as if to shield himself from Joe's observations. "You read that newspaper story. Damn internet. Stuff never gets old. But they did right by Chris. He was supposed to play big-league baseball one day. The story wasn't just about how he died. It was about how he lived. A decent and hard life, although they glossed over a lot."

"Some men are worth more than one story," Joe says. "Me? I got one magazine piece to my name, and I was lucky to get that."

"He was named best bouncer in Hampton Roads one year," Paula says, jerking her thumb at Joe.

O'Brien shuffles his feet and sniffles. "You are a pair of odd ducks."

"We run the best food truck in Hampton Roads," Paula says. "Joe's Takeaway puts out simple food and we turn a good profit. Hotdogs, sausages, and homemade mac and cheese."

O'Brien holds up his hand to stop the sales pitch. "None of which explains why you want to buy my land. The other guy is offering me a mint because he's got this project."

The two of them had talked about this on the drive down, what to say if they were asked. They'd batted about some stories, but here and now, the truth seems best.

"We want to stop him," Paula says simply.

O'Brien comes right back. "Why?" he asks.

"Because I used to work at his bar," Joe says. "I was pretty good at it. Then I became the night manager. A couple of months ago, he tossed me out the door because the books weren't balancing. Turns out I got early-stage dementia—emphasis on the early part."

O'Brien gave a little grimace. "That's too bad," he says.

"You know what's too bad? I begged him to keep me on. I volunteered to be a greeter in the new casino, wear a monkey suit and shake hands with people. He turned me down and I decked him. He decked me back. It's safe to say we're no longer friends. And now I want to show I can beat him with something other than my fists. He thinks I'm a dumb lug. I worked for him forty years, and he thinks I'm a dumb lug." A sob catches his voice and he has to stop. It isn't fake. Paula looks away.

O'Brien leans the shotgun against the double-wide and hooks both thumbs in his belt. He turns back and studies the bus, the trees beyond. A sigh sputters from his lips. "I look at this land of my fathers and forefathers and wonder what they would say. They would never give it up. Hell, they settled it. The guy who's offering me all this money treats me like a customer at his casino. He wants to talk about price, like I'd die on a hill for thirty pieces of silver. But I got nowhere to go. I got maybe ten-plus years left, if I'm lucky. "

"Wish I had ten years," Joe says, not speaking to anyone in particular.

The giant tabby stretches to its full length and saunters toward them. Its amber eyes assess Joe before turning toward Paula. It walks in a figure eight between her legs and sits on her foot. Paula reaches down and scratches the top of its head. The cat pushes its head higher, urging her on.

O'Brien lowers the shotgun. "Dale Earnhardt likes one of you. That's relatively rare, and so I'm granting permission to continue your story. But you need to tell me the details before he changes his ever-loving mind and scratches your eyes out. Why is your offer better than this other guy's?"

Paula smiles like a woman about to unveil her secret weapon.

43

PAULA LIKED WHAT Joe had done, playing the age card, talking about ghosts. She was going to describe what Donna had suggested, but Joe interjects—he'd had an idea during the drive down.

"You'll never admit you need anybody," Joe says. "I know I don't. Look at where you live. You're purely self-sufficient, I'm sure, but men like us enjoy being around others of our generation so we can tell lies to each other. We're all heroes of our own stories."

The cat rubs its face against Paula's shin. She pets it and tries to hold O'Brien's gaze, but the old man is studying Joe now.

"We're offering more than just money for this land," Joe says. "Are you familiar with the Willoughby Spit area of Norfolk? Some developer took a grand old hotel there and transformed it into a retirement community. It's called Smith-George Shores. You can get up on the roof and look over at the Navy base in Norfolk, and farther down, the Port of Virginia."

"I know where you're talking," O'Brien says.

"Okay, then. You can watch ships come in and out. Aircraft carriers, those giant container ships, sometimes even a submarine. You can see barges and watch when they dredge. When the carriers come in, the sailors stand along the rail in their dress whites. When NASA sets off a rocket at Wallops Island on the Eastern Shore, you can look to the sky and see it."

"I know where you're talking," O'Brien says again. "Didn't know about the NASA part. What's the point?"

Joe squints hard, as if the details are slipping away and he needs to say them aloud. "We will pay you a fair price for this land and for your first year's lease at Smith-George. I live near there, so you know where to find me if it doesn't work out. You can walk around to your heart's content, and I'm sure they can accommodate Dale Earnhardt here."

"Number Three's a little picky," O'Brien says. "He eats a lot."

"Yes, that is the biggest cat I've ever seen," Joe says. "What do you say?"

"After you fund the first year, what then? I guess I'm supposed to die."

"We're giving you a head start on your golden years," Paula says, chipping in, realizing this isn't a bad idea. And you'd have all the money from the sale. "That's more than the other guy wants to do. Did he even talk about where you might stay after selling this land?"

O'Brien rubs his gray beard. Donna had advised her to go with the flow in any sales talk. If something unplanned comes up and it sounds good, adjust your approach. The idea is to get a handshake deal as fast as you can and finalize the details later. If the client agrees to the big picture, the rest takes care of itself. Donna kept asking what Paula had in mind, but Paula had said it was all conceptual at this point.

The old man clucks his tongue and the cat scampers over to him. Paula steals a glance at Joe as if to say, *"Are you done now?"*

"I have another incentive," she says. "Virginia has an Open Space Preservation Program. We can get an easement on this land. That will be part of the sale. It can never be developed. Forever and ever. You'll have peace of mind that no one will plow it over for casinos or anything else. Your family's history is more important."

O'Brien looks beyond them to the crest in the field. He seems to see something other than open space. "I currently live in a school bus," O'Brien says. "I put a lot of work into it, and I'd like it to remain on the land. This double-wide trailer is just a decoy. The scarecrow up on the crest has a surveillance camera mounted in one of the eye sockets. The moment you turned off the highway, I saw you. But how would this open space deal work? Sounds like I'd need a lawyer."

Donna said not to balk when lawyers enter the conversation, so Paula says, "I'm sure something can be worked out. We'll keep everything you want to keep. Joe and I have a friend in real estate, and she knows this program. And if you want to hire a lawyer, that's fine by us. Does the school bus have hot water and a toilet?"

"Of course it does. I'm not a hillbilly. I got a woodstove that burns compressed pellets, granite countertops in my kitchen, and a mist-type shower that gets into the DMZ, if you know what I mean. All my wrinkled parts. It'd do fine by you, missy. That landing strip on top of your head must hold the water."

Silence follows. Paula imagines that both men are dealing with their own images. Finally, she claps her hands. "I think we're making progress. Is it fair to say you'll hold off selling to Max Smith until we can talk further?"

Joe sets his feet as if he's ready to throw a punch. "We'll pay you one hundred thousand dollars, plus ten thousand more for dealing with Maxie, plus whatever it costs at

Smith-George for one year. That's the offer. Also, you will have rights and privileges to live on this land if you don't like the retirement home atmosphere. Or you can visit here."

"Maybe I can be a co-owner," O'Brien says.

Joe nods. "We can work with that," he says.

O'Brien motions behind him. "One hundred thousand sounds interesting. How about I give you a tour of the school bus? This ain't a done deal. I want both your full names so I can do some research on who the hell you are. Number Three likes you, and that's the best thing you got going right now. He couldn't stand the woman who came here representing that Max Smith."

"Woman?" Joe stiffens as if shocked. His hands turn to clenched fists. "He sent a woman here?"

"A redhead," O'Brien says. "She came here and tried a come-on, but I don't think her heart was in it."

44

So Maxie sent Kathy to talk to the old man, Joe thinks. That made sense. Kathy does more than run the night kitchen for Maxie these days. She always had one eye on those poker games and all that money. Thanks to Kathy, Maxie owns an apartment complex in Virginia Beach, where he launders poker cash. He rents several units to employees at triple the usual rate. The employees don't live there, and the "rent" pours in from the poker tournaments. He created a shell company to fund capital improvements at the apartments—again, a place to stash poker money. It looks like a legitimate pile of cash set aside for new roofs, gutters, and landscaping, and it was all Kathy's idea.

Paula jabs him in the arm. "Let's go see the bus, partner. Don't go zoning out on me."

O'Brien is already halfway there, his cat leading the way. Joe starts walking that way, keeping his voice low and tight. "You didn't tell me about any open preservation law. And you talked to Donna behind my back? I guess that's where you disappeared to yesterday. Thanks for keeping me in the loop, *partner*. If we're going to do this thing, we need to be open with each other."

Paula lowers her voice to match his. "What about the nursing home? You didn't share that. Besides, Donna doesn't know the details of this. I gave her a generic example of how someone might block a development." She nudges him in the shoulder. "I'm not pissed. That idea about the nursing home was perfect."

"It came to me in the car on the way down, but we were talking about the pitch at the time. I get good ideas sometimes."

"So who's this redhead? I saw your reaction."

"I think I know."

They follow their host to the bus and board it, like a couple of third-graders, and come face to face with the woodstove as they step inside. A couch and end table take up the middle of the bus. Next up is the galley, with a two-burner propane stove, overhead microwave, and sink. O'Brien wasn't kidding about the granite countertops. The counter extends to form a two-seat breakfast bar with stools. Beyond that, a sectioned-off area looks to be either a bathroom or bedroom. It leaves space for a narrow hallway that extends to the rear. O'Brien pulls out a stool from the breakfast bar and invites them to sit. Joe imagines Kathy stretched out on the couch, one leg hooked over the back, asking O'Brien if he wants a poke in the hay.

"So this redhead," Joe says, unable to contain himself, "what was her name?"

"She didn't give a name," O'Brien says. "She sat where you are now and said she was representing Max Smith and wanted to make me an offer. She said everything was on the table, and by everything she meant just that." He smiles sadly. "You could tell she had rehearsed her lines. I know a come-on when I see it. Back in the day, I danced to Bill Haley and the Comets and sweated through my shirts. I've also outlived three wives and don't fancy a turn on the couch like I used to. She didn't stay much more than twenty minutes. Had a cup of coffee and left."

"This sofa is covered in cat hair." Paula rubs her hand on the cushion. "Not meant for lovemaking."

"I enjoy a good book and sippin' whiskey," O'Brien says, ignoring her. "An old movie now and then. Tell me your names so I can look you up on the computer."

"Joe Pendergast," he says.

"Paula Robinson."

O'Brien frowns. "I'll find a lot of Paula Robinsons. You got anything else to tell me?"

"My middle name is Michelle."

"Where did you graduate high school?"

"I dropped out, but I got a GED."

"You got a job somewhere?"

Joe holds up his hand. "Let me stop you right there. I'm the one steering this transaction. Paula here likes to talk, but I've got the skin in the game. I worked for Max Smith, and you can find the magazine story they wrote about me. There's even a picture of me standing behind the bar. Max Smith is quoted in there."

A laptop sits on the kitchen counter. O'Brien jabs at it with two fingers, and it takes a good five minutes for him to find the story that named Joe as Best Bouncer in Hampton Roads. O'Brien whisper-reads, then continues to search.

"This might go faster if the cat walked across the keyboard," Paula whispers.

Finally, O'Brien settles himself and says, "You look like the real deal. I can see the redhead in the background of this picture."

"Yeah," Joe says. "She was around back then. Her name is Kathy."

O'Brien shrugs. "Like I said, her name is neither here nor there."

Joe doesn't hesitate. "I feel the same way," he says.

CHAPTER

45

PAULA WANTS TO talk numbers and establish a time line for closing the deal. She still doesn't want Joe to clean out his savings account, but there is no time to worry about that. Donna's advice was clear: *"Keep pressing and get a deadline, even if it changes later."* Joe hunkers forward on the couch and stares at the floor. He must be imagining Kathy flaunting her boobs, letting old Ledyard see the goods. Joe made a show of blowing her off just now. Translation: she still means something to him.

Paula realizes she knows nothing of women in Joe's life. He hasn't hung framed pictures of his mom, former wives or girlfriends, or long-lost daughters. You learn a lot by what people hang on their walls or what they don't. Years ago, after Paula's mom died in that car wreck, a newspaper reporter knocked on the door of the trailer. He wanted to do a "color piece" on Michelle Jessup because she seemed to be well liked, which was news to Paula. Her grandfather wasn't around, and the reporter started firing questions. Was it hard for her being a single mother? Did she have a drinking problem? Did she always like fast cars? When Paula asked why he chose those questions, he pointed to photos on the wall that showed Paula with her mom but no other kids, and another of Mom mixing margaritas with a weed wacker, and a third looking out from under the hood of her Nova with a grease-smudged face. Paula smiled and kicked him in the shins. He had limped back to a ridiculously small Ford.

Joe's lack of energy puts a damper on the conversation, but O'Brien holds up his end and even smiles a couple of times. "I get the concept of open space preservation," he says to her. "That's fine. But I don't want it overgrown with weeds either. That wouldn't be a fitting memory. I want it kept up. Maybe put something on it that makes sense."

"An open space easement is just one option," Paula says, trying to channel Donna. "I'm currently between apartments and would love to settle down here."

"Settle down?" O'Brien grunts a laugh. "You're like sixteen."

"I'm twenty-two and have been around the block a few times, thank you very much. And I'd be happy to work with you when it comes to future uses." Paula looks right and left. "I like this school bus. It's not much to look at from the outside, but I can see living here."

O'Brien turns away from the laptop and looks out the window. "Chris would have liked it. His happiest days were in high school. He was cock of the walk—captain of the baseball team, a girlfriend who was a cheerleader—the whole nine yards. I renovated it in honor of him. He always took the bus to school, even though he had money to buy a car. If it were up to me, I'd put up a statue of him."

Paula doesn't want to press, not with O'Brien going down in memory lane. She's curious about what happened to his three wives, but that will push him farther away from sales talk. She asks about the woodstove, where he dug the well and if there is a secondary source of heat, which turns out to be solar panels on the roof. She gets him talking about the Pungo Witch, a story that goes back to the 1700s. Just as she's ready to talk money, O'Brien closes the lid to his laptop.

"I'm done talking now, missy. I probably talked more in the last half hour than I have in six months."

"Then let's shake hands and say we have a deal in principle," Paula says. "We can always tweak the numbers."

"How about we just shake hands and agree to talk again?" O'Brien smiles again. He seems to like her, but this was a lot for the old man to take in at one sitting.

On the drive home, Joe steers with two fingers and whistles a series of random notes. "That boy falling off the boat was a real tragedy," he says, "but it must be nice to have a close bond with someone, even for a short time. A true friend never betrays you."

"Speaking of which, this Kathy was your squeeze," Paula says. " Did she get upset when you had the big blowup with Maxie and left?"

He seems to consider the answer very carefully before speaking. "Maxie wanted to toss me out on my ear. Kathy had the idea of giving me the food truck. Not that she was a saint. She'd hitched her wagon to Maxie, not some washed-up bouncer who couldn't manage a bar. So when Maxie dumped me, so did she. But was she upset? Nah. For her, it was more like a business decision. She left me the food truck because she felt bad, I guess. And she took me to the emergency room that night after Maxie and I exchanged knockout blows."

"Have you talked to her since then?"

"Not a lick. Don't care to."

"You ever been married or seriously hooked up before you met Kathy?"

"I've always lived alone." A pause. "I think I'm done talking about this now."

Paula allows the subject to settle, then says, "You named a price without even asking what he wanted. Do you have that kind of money?"

"I have a hundred twenty thousand and change in my savings. I can go to one hundred ten as a start, then do the whole thing if that will help. It don't matter. I'll be dead in a few years, and I can live on credit card scam money."

"Slow down, Joe. You want to keep some of your money. What about prescriptions? Doctor visits?"

"Doesn't matter. This is more about you than me. My time is past, missy, but yours is just starting."

Joe looks to his right. Suddenly, he turns into a grassy field marked by a pair of tire tracks that curve into the distance. Paula grabs the seat as the car bounces over a hump in the earth. "Joe, where the hell are we going?"

"I want to see where this casino will get built. Maybe Maxie put up markers or something." The Hyundai's front bumper smacks against the hard ground. "I bet Kathy will work there. She'll be a blackjack dealer and wear a short skirt. Goddamn it.

"Joe, slow down."

"I slow down enough these days." He tugs the wheel and car swerves sharply right. Long grass scratches against the doors. "Let's see what's over here. I bet he's got the entrance to the casino mapped out. That's where I would have stood to greet everyone, as if they were friends. Like I ever had friends. Like I ever had anyone who expressed anything to me besides fear or pity. What a pathetic idea I had, begging for a nothing job at a casino."

Paula braces one hand against the dashboard. She has no idea what's happening, but it's clear that Joe suddenly isn't tracking. "Take it easy. You could bust an axle in this field."

"O'Brien will pull us out. He's got that Jeep. Besides, Hyundai's got a great warranty."

Something crunches under the tires. Joe's eyes have turned hard and glassy, as if he sees only a tunnel and nothing to the right or left. The ground rises and falls. Paula can no longer see the highway. She lowers the window and smells water, trying to remember the map of Maxie's holdings, knowing that it gets swampy at some point. Joe leans over the wheel and squints into the sunlight.

"What are you thinking about, Joe? Tell me what's on your mind." She wants to calm him somehow. Bring him back to here and now.

He says nothing. The tall grass falls away and tires squish through mud. Up ahead, thin trees poke out through the muck.

"We're heading into a swamp," Paula says. "We're going to get stuck. Snap out of it."

She reaches for the wheel and tries to turn the car. A mistake. Joe snarls—that's the only word for it—and squeezes her fingers together. She pulls away in a panic, thinking of Wendell and his nearly broken thumb. The car lurches forward in fits and starts, the front wheels spinning furiously. Paula unclips her shoulder harness and lowers her window. As she tries to slither out the opening, Joe grabs her collar and pushes her back in the seat.

"Stop it." She pushes him off. "Just calm down."

The back of his hand cracks hard against her forehead. It's so fast that Paula replays it in her mind a few seconds later. *Did that just happen?* His hand flicked out with incredible speed. A knot of pain forms in her forehead and blossoms around her eyes. Tears pour down her cheeks. She looks down and sees blood on her favorite blue shirt, the one she wore to impress O'Brien, one of four shirts she owns, other than a white blouse for which she has no suitable skirt. The car lurches forward again, and her head slams against the dashboard.

"Put your damn seat belt on," Joe screams. "What's wrong with you?"

"Turn around, please," she pleads.

"I'm turning around. Put your damn seat belt on." The sight of blood seems to have jarred him back to reality. He does a double take, as if she just appeared in the passenger seat. "See what happened now? You got yourself all messed up."

"Right, Joe. My bad. We should probably get back to the house and take care of this."

"Of course we should. Crazy kid. Where's the highway? You got me all screwed up now with your yapping."

The Hyundai tacks to the left. Paula spots the ribbon of asphalt, and Joe heads for it. The Hyundai bounces onto the highway. He doesn't bother to look for other cars. Paula tilts back her head and pinches her nose. Her cheeks sting. Joe pushes the car to fifty-five and sits back. After a few minutes, he looks over at her with concern etched on his face.

"That was crazy," he says. "Are you good now?"

"Yeah, Joe. I'm good now."

"We'll get back home, fix that bloody nose," he says. "I can't tell you the number of bloody noses I've seen. But what about that cat, huh?"

CHAPTER

46

HALFWAY HOME, JOE flinches behind the wheel and sees the world as if everything is brand new. The road is clear and he's driving the speed limit. His muscles are stretched and sore, as if he just finished a workout or beat someone to a pulp. Paula has stuffed tissue paper into her bloody nostrils and sits there like a bump on a log. Fool girl, taking off her seat belt in the middle of a field and hitting the dashboard. Asking about Kathy as if it's her damn business. He wants to tell this girl how things work when you get old, how you spend time replaying the worst moments of your life. Thinking of how you might have joined the Army and hit the tail end of Vietnam, or took over Pendergast Cut-Rate and married Cheyenne and had a couple of kids.

How you might have controlled your temper for thirty goddamn minutes.

Or said no to Maxie that one time.

So many mistakes. So many paths not taken. The kid's a pain in the ass, but she bores in like a power drill. *"Ever been married or seriously hooked up?"* Listen to her talk.

It's not that Joe never had women in his life. They always hit on him at Captain Maxie's, to be on good terms with the bouncer. A few stuck with him for a week or two, but they'd always say, "This is fun right? That's all it is." Or words to that effect. None held a candle to Cheyenne. That smooth skin, those doe eyes a lighter shade of brown. Cut down too soon. Hit by a car during a protest march while was in college somewhere in California. He remembers that now. The obituary didn't come with a picture, so he has always imagined her at fourteen. Paula has no idea how it was back then. She'll probably be in jail before turning thirty. Hell, she might be in jail next week. Either that, or she'll get elected to Congress. Joe laughs out loud, surprising himself.

"Something funny?" Paula's voice is thick and nasal with all that wadded tissue.

"I was picturing you being a politician and shooting your mouth off. It's funny. I don't know why I think of these things."

She leans against the passenger door and stares out the window.

Moody kid, not that it's her fault. Her momma dies young and daddy is already gone. Then crazy grandpa takes charge of her life. Plus, that pervert who came into her bedroom. That can mess someone up for a long time.

"You never talk about your daddy," he says.

She studies the road.

"If you can ask me about Kathy, I can ask about your daddy," Joe says. "What's fair is fair."

"You'll get no answers because I never knew him."

"You said he lit out. What happened?"

"Said he couldn't be a father. At least that's what Mom said."

"Was he the black one or the white one?"

"He was black. Mom was white."

"Did that prejudice you against black people up in Berkeley County?"

"The black people I knew in Berkeley County are some of the nicest people I ever met. The family who lived near us had a little truck farm. They hired local pickers along with some migrants that broke off from the wave that came from Florida. Most migrants went up the Eastern Shore, but a few come our way. They picked tomatoes when they were green and hard as baseballs. Dropped them in a basket. I picked with them sometimes, but I was a lot slower. The family's name was Childress. They'd leave me and my grandfather all kinds of produce at our trailer. Whatever was in season."

"But your daddy left, and people tend to talk," Joe says. "They'll say a black man can't take responsibility, wants a new woman, that kind of thing."

"Oh no, Daddy wasn't fooling around on my mom. He was sick."

"Sick like perverted?"

She snorted. "All you think about is sex. No, sick like cancer or something. I think he went off to die so Mom wouldn't have two people to take care of. I was about to be born when he left. He figured it was easier that way because he wouldn't have to love me. Mom said he could put up a wall around himself and not let anyone in. He hated showing weakness." Paula glances Joe's way. "Some men are blockheaded like that. They think they have to show strength, and then they do something stupid."

"Can't argue the point," Joe says.

"I had one picture of my dad, and his eyes seemed to be yellow."

"Jaundice," Joe says. "Liver disease. That could kill a man slowly. He would know the clock is ticking."

She unpacks the bloody tissue from her nose. "Your clock is ticking. When you found out about the dementia, did you ever think of driving off into the sunset and dying?"

"There ain't no sunset, girl. You drive off into the sunset and find a new set of problems. Another town that's screwed up, another group of people just like the one you left. There is no beautiful backdrop that allows you to relax. You got to deal with your shit, which I've mostly done and still got to do." He pauses, thinking. "I give you credit for one thing, though."

"I can't wait for this answer."

"That gun I keep under my pillow. I bought it for Maxie, but I also figured to check out when the time came. If I woke up not knowing where I was, or if I needed to get myself committed or some shit, I'd walk upstairs and end it. But I think you're like medicine to me."

Paula chokes back a breath and holds it. Joe wonders if that bloody nose bothers her.

"You got me fighting back in a different way," he says. "Buying a man's land, showing Maxie he shouldn't have crossed me. It makes me feel good to think about it. He'll realize I was more than a pair of fists. And when we stop him, I'll enjoy seeing how he'll try to build another house of cards. It's harder to ruin a man than to kill him, but it's worth it. Maxie is older than me. Clock's ticking on him too. Thanks to you, I'll beat him using my brain. That'll stick in his craw to his dying day."

"I wish I could go back in time and tell my dad he could have stayed. Be a different person, a stranger. Someone who stops him on the street and says he has a daughter in his future, so he should stick around."

"If you had stopped me on the street years ago, you'd be scared," Joe says. "Not like now."

She wipes her cheeks. "Yeah, I'd be scared of you. Big-time bouncer and all. You're not worried I'm going to ghost you?"

"What's that mean, to 'ghost me'?"

"Just up and leave without saying goodbye."

"I hope you don't do that," Joe says. "I really do."

THAT NIGHT, THEY sit on opposite ends of the couch and order takeout pizza. Joe offers to pay and asks if she wants garlic knots or cannoli. She presses her nose and wonders if she'll end up with raccoon eyes from his hard slap.

"It doesn't matter," she says. "Just pizza will be fine."

"I'll get garlic knots just in case," he says.

Maybe this afternoon was a perfect storm. Pushing him on Kathy, on women in general, and driving near the casino site at the same time, imagining Kathy as a blackjack dealer in a short skirt, kicking himself for groveling at Maxie's feet. It all hit him at once. *Like I ever had friends. Like I ever had anyone who expressed anything to me besides fear or pity. What a pathetic idea I had, begging for a nothing job.* A minute later, he's asking about her father and seems genuinely concerned she might up and leave.

But what if something else sets him off tomorrow? That fucking slap. His hand had lashed out with a mind of its own, as if she tripped a sensor that Joe couldn't control. And afterward he had no idea he'd hit her.

"You want to watch some true crime?" He flips through channels, concentrating on the TV.

"It doesn't matter. I have a question."

"I'm flipping channels. Hold your britches." He goes past the channel and throws up his hands in disgust. It takes every bit of self-control for Paula not to cover her face. "Go ahead," he finally says. "Ask your question."

"You would never hurt me on purpose, right?"

"That's a hell of a question. Of course I wouldn't hurt you. I'm just upset with the TV here. You know me and technology never got along. I can't even do computer banking, especially after doing a shift at Captain Maxie's. I'm all tuckered out."

Are you talking to me or Kathy?

"Joe, did you ever hurt other people?"

He finds the channel and settles back in the couch. "Sure. All the time."

The answer is so casual that she wonders if he misunderstood the question. But that's not a question you should ask twice. The true crime show is about a series of murders on the Colonial Parkway near Williamsburg, which happened ages ago. Paula pretends to pay attention and surfs her phone for tips on dealing with people who have dementia. A quick read reveals no easy answers.

Dementia hits fast or slow.

Someone with early-stage dementia can hold down a job, go on vacations, and function normally for long periods of time.

People with dementia sometimes lose their filter and say whatever is on their mind.

They can get antsy around sundown.

Medication can slow the decline, but not stop it.

The only constant is a death sentence.

Watching the show eats up sixty minutes. The pizza comes, and Paula steers the conversation toward the food truck, asking Joe if he might offer pizza one day. Joe says it's a possibility, but pizza might not go over well in downtown Newport News. Those city workers want something for lunch that isn't messy, that they can eat with one hand.

Good, she thinks to herself. *He's back in the present.*

"I guess I'm gonna hit the hay," Joe says after the show ends. "It's ten o'clock. I got to clean this house tomorrow. This white carpet is going to drive me crazy. Hey, I made a joke. Crazy, get it? And you have to work. Someone needs to pay the bills around here."

"That brings up a point. Do you want me to kick in for rent and utilities?"

"I'm joking, girlie. Keep whatever pennies they pay you. You're earning your keep by leading this scheme. When it comes to cloning credit cards, learning about land easements, how to keep developers at bay and such, I can't do that. I'm just an old bar bouncer."

"Best bouncer in Hampton Roads," Paula reminds him.

He dismisses her with a wave of his hand. "After I close my bedroom door, drag this couch across the room and jam it up against the doorknob. I'll put a chair on my side. This wandering business has me worried. I don't want to find myself on the street tonight."

"How about I stack a couple of chairs from your dinette in front of the door?"

"Right. Better idea."

He takes his pills, then goes into the bedroom and clicks the door shut behind him. She grabs a chair and jams it against the knob, rattling the door in its frame.

"Did you put a chair on your side too?" Paula asks.

"I did."

"Good night, then. Don't dream about pulling chairs away, because then you probably are." As she starts to walk away, Joe clears his throat. He starts to say something, then catches himself. Then he says it anyway, and his voice is small. "I think I might have hit you today," he says.

Paula doesn't hesitate. "No way. I'd have kicked your wrinkled ass. Like you said: my head smashed against the dashboard while you were driving in the field."

"I don't know why I drove into that field."

"You wanted to see where Maxie's casino was going. Sometimes they put up wooden stakes so you can tell. Except we didn't see any stakes. Just swamp water. But it was worth scouting out."

"Before you go to sleep, lock your door."

She scampers downstairs, uses the bathroom, and goes to her room. After the door snicks shut and locks, she calls Mia, who apparently never sleeps. The woman picks up on the first ring.

"I was wondering about you," Mia says. "Please tell me you've moved out of the house with the crazy bouncer. That nice boss from Brady Auto Parts can find you an apartment in Norfolk. Or crawl into one of the concrete bunkers at Fort Monroe. Something. Anything."

"Opinion noted," Paula says.

"Sorry. It's been a night. One challenge of running a homeless shelter for women is that homeless women come with kids. I've been playing child psychologist all night, and now I know why I never wanted a family. What's up?"

"I'd like to know more about Joe's police record. We had a minor incident today."

"Define *incident*."

"We were driving and Joe had a foggy spell. He drove into a field. When I got upset, he smacked me in the face. I'm fine. It's just a bloody nose, and I think he realized it later. He's been as nice as pie all night."

"Jesus fucking Christ. He hit you?"

"Just a bloody nose."

"Paula, he doesn't get *foggy spells*. He has dementia. You are in the same house with a dangerous man who could go off the rails in the blink of an eye."

"I'm good for him. I'm preventing him from killing Maxie." She can hear Mia trying to calm herself, taking deep breaths. "Rosa spilled the credit card scheme to you, which I don't appreciate, but it seemed to be an easy way to accumulate money and keep people from getting hurt. This O'Brien fellow, we'll do right by him. Joe wants to blow his savings on the land deal, which I don't like, but we'll work through it. And Joe likes the idea of scheming. It gives him something to live for. In the meantime, I'm protected from the terror twins at the George Pickett Grill. But tell me about his record. It might help me talk to him."

Mia steps away from the phone. Paula hears papers rustling. Mia comes back on the line and says, "This concerns a guy named Virgil. Where is Joe now?"

"In his bedroom. I put a chair in front of the door in case he starts wandering."

"Oh, that's great. What a foolproof solution."

"Don't be an ass. It was his idea."

48

Virgil Post went by Verge. He had been in his mid-thirties, an accountant for a small defense contractor, married with three kids. Verge liked to gamble and was a regular player in the illegal backroom poker tournaments held at Captain Maxie's in the early 1990s. Mia texts a photo of a pasty-faced white guy with weak eyes and a receding hairline.

"Verge looks like a real winner," Paula says, trying to sound tough, figuring this story will end with poor Verge dead in a ditch.

"He was a decent poker player," Mia says. "Won more than he lost. But he was a poor loser. After a bad night, he would sometimes insinuate that the games were rigged to keep him from winning more. He'd leave the room and go into the bar and start talking about rigged poker games. Many people attested to these drunken ramblings, but no one blew the whistle on the games. They were illegal, of course, but no one cared. It's men playing cards. No one's forcing them. It's a victimless crime."

"I've heard that one before. Go on."

"One night in the spring of 1990, police find Verge's BMW parked off the road south of Virginia Beach not far from the North Carolina line. It's fully engulfed in flames. Verge's body is in the trunk, shot twice in the head. His hands are tied behind him. He was last seen being escorted from Captain Maxie's by Joe Pendergast, who was in his heyday as a bouncer back then. Joe was escorting him very aggressively, witnesses said. Police examined Verge's body and discovered he was missing his tongue. The next day, they get an anonymous tip to check out a double-wide in trailer park near where the car was found. That double-wide's owner was one Donald Gold, a drug addict and a poor poker player who owed money to Max Smith. He also had a violent streak and tended to answer the door with a gun. Even the great Joe Pendergast has had trouble collecting gambling debts from Mr. Gold. The anonymous tipster said the police would find Verge's tongue in a Mason jar under the front steps of Gold's trailer. When police went to the trailer—"

"Gold answers the door with a gun," Paula says. "He gets killed and the story ends."

"You're half right. Donald Gold answers the door with a gun and fires one shot. The police take him into custody without killing him, but a cop is shot. He ends up paralyzed from the waist down. Donald Gold gets convicted for the shooting, of course, and they also get him for killing Verge, because the tongue in the Mason jar is right where the tipster said it would be, along with a washcloth covered in Verge's blood. It's all neatly wrapped up."

Paula takes a breath, holds it. She doesn't care about Verge or Donald Gold, and that scares her. She doesn't care about carving up her grandpa. Isn't something supposed to happen by now? Some kind of reckoning where you break down in tears and vow to be a better person? Or feel bad about what you did, even if you were defending yourself?

"Do the police think Joe put this Verge in the trunk of his own car, drove to the vicinity of Gold's trailer, shot Verge and cut out his tongue, set the car on fire and planted the tongue on Gold's property?" Paula is trying to see Joe doing all these things.

"There were witnesses at Captain Maxie's," Mia says. "This detective remembers it very clearly and took good notes. Verge walking around the bar, trashing the so-called 'rigged' poker games in a loud voice, and Joe watched him like a hawk. Max Smith came out and was seen talking to Joe. Their conversation was very animated. Joe kept nodding, as if Maxie was giving him detailed instructions. Then Joe comes to Verge and is heard saying, 'Let's go for a ride.' He grabs Verge by the arm and they walk out together. Joe admits escorting Verge from the bar that night but denies ever saying, 'Let's go for a ride.' Witnesses later changed their minds and said they didn't hear Joe say anything."

Silence.

"Paula, are you there?"

"I'm here. I'm thinking."

She's thinking of that unearthly snarl that rose from the depth of Joe's throat just before he hit her, and the way his hand cut through the air. She imagined him working around Verge's mouth with a paring knife, pulling out a slippery piece of tongue, then sneaking up to the trailer and planting the evidence. But the story had holes: If Joe drove the Verge's car to the middle of nowhere and set it on fire, how did he get back to Norfolk? Maybe Maxie arranged a second car.

"This doesn't bother me," Paula says. "I'm feeling nothing. I did the same thing."

"You defended yourself against a man who wanted to kill you. Speaking of which, why don't you go to the police? I was thinking about this last night. Say you were scared at first, but tell them all about the George Pickett Grill, your grandfather's involvement there, rescuing Rosa. I'll back you."

"I don't think the police can protect me. And they certainly won't protect Joe. He'll get dragged into it because of the boat. The Pickett twins will find out where he lives, and they'll come after him. This isn't over."

"You did what you had to do in that boat. What Joe did was different."

"If I had to do over again, I would have cut out my grandfather's tongue."

"Jesus, Paula."

"Yeah, I don't know why I said that."

But I would have. I hated him, she thinks.

CHAPTER

49

JOE REALIZES HE hit her. He remembers it, his hand lashing out, making contact.

He stares into the darkness of his bedroom and is certain of it. But good Christ, she wouldn't stop talking. He wanted to calm down, like she was telling him to, but things take more time now. Thoughts don't always translate into immediate action. Everything gets backed up and nothing comes out of his mouth. It's brain sludge. Portions of his brain are being turned into mush, and it clogs the pipes from time to time. You can go days or weeks without a clog, then suddenly your thoughts are stuck. Sooner or later, you get a hard clog and don't think about anything.

But now the pipes are clear, and it all comes rushing back. He jabbed her with the two knuckles of his right hand—pointer finger and middle finger—and hit the bridge of her nose. It was a hard shot, delivered to get attention, to show the seriousness of the situation, to move things along.

But why was I driving in that field to begin with?

Joe starts to cry.

Silent tears of frustration and pain.

"You can't see this through," he whispers into the dark. 'You're out of time. Just go kill him and be done with it."

When the pipes get clogged up again, he might decide that a jab isn't good enough and crush Paula's voice box. He needs to have a sit-down conversation with this girl and confront some hard truths. Let her use his savings account, plus those stolen credit card numbers, and just go on her own. He grabs his phone off the nightstand and googles *how to say goodbye*.

Jennifer has sent him an email. It came two hours ago.

Gosh, Joe. We haven't talked in nearly a week. How is your new partner working out? I feel protective of you. I don't want anyone to take advantage of you. I hope and pray you're staying upbeat and dealing with life in a positive way. I checked the Facebook page for Joe's Takeaway and it seems you're staying busy.

Just one piece of advice: Don't overextend yourself. It looks like you've got two gigs a week, and that seems like the right pace.

Jennifer

He checks emails and sees that they last exchanged messages on Sunday. Today is Saturday. How did six days go by? Driving through fields and hitting up an old man to buy his land and smacking a young woman who wants to help, that's where it went. Meanwhile, this Jennifer comes out of left field. She's supposed to help him handle the dementia, yet she wants to know about Paula. He hits "Reply" and starts thumbing the screen.

Jennifer,

Thanks for your note and sorry I haven't written sooner. Things get so busy. My "partner" is a great help. She has a lot of energy. Her background is a bit downtrodden. Not to say she's poor, but she's some bad breaks. I have no worries about her.

Joe

Jennifer's reply comes back less than a minute later.

I understand completely. What's her name?

Joe almost thumbs a reply telling Jennifer to mind her own fucking business. Then he takes a deep breath and stops. Just pretend he didn't see this. If she asks later, he'll say he fell asleep before replying. In the meantime, let her hang. *Ghost her.* That's what the kids say.

50

Paula gets up early the next morning. After a quick shower, she towel dries her hair and throws on khaki pants and a navy-blue polo shirt with the Brady's Auto Parts logo. The store gets busy on Sunday, and she wants to get there early. Or maybe she just wants to avoid Joe. She sneaks upstairs and removes the chair from his bedroom door, thinking about Verge's tongue in a Mason jar. A cop paralyzed for life. Some dumb schmuck framed for murder. A long workday will give her space, allow time to sort her thoughts.

But shortly after she comes downstairs, Joe is already out of bed and making noises. As she comes to the front door, he stands at the top of the stairs.

"I was waiting to be let out," he says. "Almost climbed out the window. I was hoping we could have a conversation before you leave. This is about our business arrangement. I'm having second thoughts about the feasibility of the whole thing."

Paula keeps one hand on the doorknob. "A little hesitation is understandable. Just take it easy today. I'll get takeout from that Mexican place on the way home, and we can talk over dinner. Text me what you want. This is a marathon, Joe, not a sprint."

She opens the door and a fist slams into the side of her head.

Wendell.

He steps inside and Sean McTavish edges in behind him. Bright spots pop through her vision, and pain comes in waves. The room spins and now she's on her knees. No, she's flat on her back. McTavish pulls out a gun. He grabs her strip of hair and twists.

"We missed you at the Moonbeam on Wednesday, but then someone posted a selfie on Facebook and tagged Joe's Takeaway. In the background was our Paula, working the grill like nobody's business. You were hiding back there." McTavish laughs and pulls at her hair.

Paula winces in pain and waits for the room to stop spinning. This was inevitable, she tells herself. These two goons would eventually find Joe's house or follow her here. McTavish holds the gun loosely by his side and is about to say something else when footsteps clomp down the stairs.

"You don't bring a gun into my house," Joe says.

The same quick hand that smacked Paula in the face reaches for the gun and twists it away. Moving fast, mechanically, Joe tosses it aside, sets his feet, and delivers a punch to McTavish's midsection. McTavish doubles over and vomits a brown batter onto the tiled floor. Wendell takes a kick in the nuts and drops like a stone. Paula's vision starts to clear.

"Easy, Joe," Paula says.

Joe picks up Wendell by the collar and slams him against the door. He lands on top of his boss, and they are nothing but a pile of arms and legs.

"Do you want to keep the gun?" Joe asks her.

"Huh? Excuse me?"

"The gun. I can throw it away, or you can keep it. Some people are gun types and some aren't." He bends down and rests a calloused hand against her cheek. "Looks like he rung your bell. Now we both got scrambled brains."

McTavish breathes in a wheezing singsong that sounds painful. He pushes Wendell aside and tries to sit up. Joe slaps his face and asks how these two found the house. McTavish waves his hand as if the answer is simple.

"The police asked us if Tony Jessup owned a boat. They impounded it, said it was on Seneca Lane. And your food truck is in the damn driveway." He squints at Joe in disbelief. "Did you kill Tony Jessup, old man? Because we can't figure you out. You got no dog in this hunt. Do you know George?"

"George is just a name to me."

"George runs the manicure place next to the Pickett," Paula says. "Another human trafficker scum."

"I could use a manicure after this," Joe says. "But no. I don't know George. Now both of you listen up real good. Maybe you come back here at a different time with bigger guns and you'll do better. But know this: I got nothing to lose. I'll make it hell for you to come at me, and you'll have to decide if it's worth it."

"But before that, look this way," Paula says.

The two idiots turn their heads on cue. Paula takes a photo with her phone. "This image will be stored in any number of mobile devices, tablets, laptops, and the cloud. If something happens to us, the police will gain access to everything. They'll find your image. It will have the date. It will have a revealing caption. And it will show that you were in this house. Then they might take a look at your business operation."

They watch them go, Wendell cradling his arm in an unnatural position. Paula tries to get up, and a wave of nausea washes over her. She sits down hard. Joe rests a hand on her shoulder. Silence passes.

"I got to get to work," she finally says.

"Let me drive you. You look dizzy."

"I'm good, except he pulled out some of my hair."

"You don't have much to begin with," Joe says.

Paula opens the door. The front yard is clear, and no strange cars are parked along the road. "You wanted to talk about our business arrangement," Paula says. "We might as well get that out of the way since I'm late anyway. Is this about emptying your savings account?"

"Our business arrangement can stand. I thought I was uncomfortable with it, but now I feel better." Joe pats the top of her head. "I get you took their pictures. But what's the cloud?"

"Don't worry about it," she says. "I handle the tech stuff, remember?"

51

I T TAKES HALF the morning to clean up the foyer, but Joe works with renewed energy. He hadn't torqued a gun out of someone's hand in a long time, and it felt like riding a bike. It felt good. He texts Paula and asks her to get a burrito at the Mexican place on her way home.

After eating two hotdogs for lunch, he goes back to the foyer and sees spattered blood on that damn white carpet. He's scrubbing on his hands and knees when the doorbell rings. Pushing up with a groan, he looks through the peephole and gets a fish-eye view of Donna in a flouncy sundress. She holds a plate covered in tinfoil and smiles when Joe opens the door.

"Hey, neighbor, I guess you had some excitement this morning." She peers at the sudsy pink spot on the carpet. "Cleaning up blood, I see."

"Whatever makes you think that?"

She cocks her hip. "I danced for a few years, Joe. I've seen the aftermath of bar fights, including when they were fighting over me, not that such a thing happens anymore." She shifts to the other hip, as if rehearsing a move. "What's going on with you? Paula came over the other day to talk about land sales. Open space preservation. She mentioned a name, and it's interesting, Joe. It's extremely interesting. I wondered if you two are collaborating on a business deal, even though you don't know her that well."

She studies the tinfoil-covered plate as if it contains hidden answers. "She's an interesting girl. The other day in the backyard, she described that man coming into her room years ago. It had the air of authenticity, but some people are good liars. When she visited, I went through her purse when she went to pee. Do you know her last name? Because it's extremely interesting."

"You've established that she's interesting. Get to the point, Donna."

"Her last name is Jessup. The same as the dead man found floating near the HRBT. I saw the police take your boat away. The dead man was in a boat before he was found in the water. And that girl was walking along this road before the body was found, looking very agitated. Now she's curious about open space preservation and drops a name. Ledyard Aloysius O'Brien. That's a unique name. It wasn't hard to find the land he owns, and it was even easier to find who owns all the land around him."

"Max Smith, my former boss, is buying up land around the O'Brien place, if that's what you're asking. I already know."

"Incorrect." She pulls out a sheaf of papers that look like copies of a website. "I'm in real estate, and I know how to look up this stuff. It isn't Max Smith. The land is being bought by a holding company called Paradise Unlimited LLC. All sales have taken place in the last few months. O'Brien is effectively surrounded, which makes it interesting that he wants to preserve open space—at least according to Miss Jessup. The registered agent for the LLC is Kathy Culhane. I googled her. She works for Max Smith at Captain Maxie's.

You also worked for Max Smith at Captain Maxie's, as you just said. Now Max Smith is pushing a big project, and this Ledyard fellow is a piece of the puzzle, and you're mixed up with him somehow."

"Kathy Culhane," Joe whispers. "That makes sense."

"Why is that?"

"It just does, Donna. Don't let it concern you."

"It doesn't mean Kathy Culhane is controlling the project. LLCs are limited liability companies. They can be used to shield names of people who are actually in charge. It's very possible that Max Smith wants this Kathy to be the person of record on this thing. That way, if something goes haywire, Kathy's name is all over the paperwork."

"I didn't realize that," Joe says.

"But how is Max Smith connected to this dead body they found out by the HRBT? That's what I can't figure."

"They're not connected," Joe says. "Those are two separate things. Two runaway trains in my life going in different directions. And I don't know where it's all going."

"Except you've got blood to clean up," Donna says. "And two men came away from your door earlier this morning looking all beat up. I love to connect dots, Joe, and I'm worried about you. We've known each other a few short weeks, but you're my neighbor and that counts for something. We've got a boat involved in a murder, a young woman gallivanting around with the same last name as the victim, the same young woman interested in preserving road frontage to block a proposed casino, not to mention strange things written on an easel in your living room. I can't keep this straight, and I'm not the one with dementia."

"I sympathize. What's under the foil, Miss Detective? A bomb?"

"I figured you needed to chill out, so I made you some funny brownies."

"Define *funny*."

"I have a rather extensive pot farm in my basement. Paula could have seen it if she wanted to, but she wouldn't bite. She might have thought I wanted to get her in the sack, but that was not the case. I don't swing that way."

"A pot farm. You. The seller of real estate."

"Pot will be legal in a few years in Virginia, mark my words. And I want to hit the ground running. For now, it's a good reason to avoid the police. They didn't see my security footage of Paula on the road that night. I told them my camera was out of commission."

"I see."

"Another thing, not to change subjects. I've been reading up on the connection between marijuana and dementia. The research hasn't come to any conclusions, but some say its calming effect could help dementia patients, especially when it comes to anxiety and bouts of rage."

"I have rage? Me?"

"I saw those guys leave this morning. One looked like his wrist was broken, and it almost made me upchuck."

"That's not rage, Donna. That's practice. But you might as well come in."

Joe has never tried pot. He was never keen on alcohol. His parents didn't keep booze in the house as a general rule. Mom hid a bottle of blackberry brandy under the cellar steps for when Dad yelled at her, so Joe always associated alcohol with crying jags. Working the door at Captain Maxie's, he saw more than his share of ugly drunks. But after eating two and a half of Donna's brownies, a soft cloud settles over him. He switches to listening mode. Donna is talking about the so-called gentleman's clubs outside military bases and how the work made her patriotic, and then she got a job selling RVs to fat old men in flannel shirts before getting her real estate license, and then became involved with her married boss for six months, then forged her own path, because being a people pleaser only brings stress and she's done with that.

When she comes up for air, Joe says, "You got the jabbers. Maybe you ate a few brownies before knocking on my door."

"I made a double batch," she says, cheeks bulging. "The first has White Russian, but this is Lavender Haze. It's supposed to make you feel focused and aware. The THC content is around twenty percent, I think. Very balanced."

They're sitting on the couch an arm's length away. Joe sinks into the cushions, but he's not tired. He asks what else she grows.

"I didn't grow this stuff. I bought it. Same with the White Russian, which you should try. I mean, you just should. Twenty-five percent THC, and it gives you a mental boost. Are you feeling it yet, Joe?"

"Hard to say. I need to finish cleaning up that carpet."

"I'll do it for you. I like to work through my buzz."

Donna skips down the steps, humming a nameless tune. The sound of a brush scraping against carpet is the next thing he hears. Joe finds it soothing, and the pieces of his life seem to fall into place. Maybe these brownies will prevent him from smacking Paula again, although he can't go around like this all day. After a while, Donna comes up the steps, clapping her hands in satisfaction. "All done," she says. "That white carpet must be annoying, though. Every stain will show up big time."

"I'll try to keep the blood to a minimum."

She flops back on the couch. "After Paula left the other day, I did some research on Ledyard Aloysius O'Brien. He was a tugboat captain of note. I came across this story about a young man who fell overboard during a storm."

"Chris Brown. That story is everywhere."

"I cried when I read it. Mr. O'Brien sounded heartsick over it. Being a tugboat captain was his passion, and so was that boy. O'Brien said he never had kids, and I bet Chris Brown was like his son."

Joe hadn't read that far down in the newspaper story, and now the conversation at the school bus replays in his head with renewed clarity. O'Brien renovated that bus in honor of that boy, and maybe that's the key. A one-year lease at a nice nursing home got O'Brien's attention, but that won't close the deal. Chris Brown will. Joe concentrates and sees himself back in that bus, O'Brien talking about the boy. His brain makes a connection.

"Well, shit," he says. "It's simple."

"How's that?"

"With O'Brien. It's simple. But I have to think about Paula too. She wants to live in that school bus, but she doesn't have a plan for herself. She deserves a future too. She should follow her passion."

"Not sure where you're going with this, Joe."

"It's simple."

"You just said that."

"It is, Donna. Paula never had a sister, but there's a woman acts like her big sister. Mia Newsome. Runs a homeless shelter. Paula looks up to her. And Paula could do what I'm thinking about. She'd need some help, but she could do it. I haven't gone around the bend yet, by God."

"You mentioned a school bus. I'm confused."

"Try to keep up, Donna. This man, O'Brien, lives in a renovated school bus. It has a woodstove and everything. He told us—let me think—he told us he'd put up a statue of Chris Brown if it were up to him. That's it, Donna. That's how we close the land sale to O'Brien. And I know why Paula should live there. That's the more complicated part. I got to call people first."

"Before doing closing land sales, you should run it by me," Donna says. "I'm a professional."

"Damn right you are. This is good pot."

Donna hoots in laughter as Joe gets on the phone.

52

Paula gets back to Seneca Lane around six with dinner from the Mexican place. She finds Joe sprawled on the couch with a note taped to his shirt like some homeless dude who showed up at the ER.

Paula:

I gave Joe some pot brownies and he zonked out. No worries. I think it helps his condition. Anyhoo, you should tour my basement operation. When Joe wakes up, you need to ask about the O'Brien thing. He had some inspiration and spent time on the phone.

Your friend, the nosy neighbor lady

The brownie pan on the counter is two-thirds empty. Paula finishes what's left and starts feeling relaxed a few minutes later. She goes downstairs for a nap, making sure to lock her door. When she wakes up, Joe is yelling as if the house is on fire. She opens the door to find him standing there, fist raised.

"Whew. I didn't know if you were okay in there." The note is still pinned to his shirt. He seems not to notice it, but calms down after a few deep breaths.

"The things you miss when you have a day job," Paula says. "So Donna grows pot in her basement and brought you brownies? And you had inspiration and got on the phone. That could be good or bad."

"I called O'Brien and sealed the sale. We're not only buying his land, but we're also building a statue of Chris Brown."

"We? A statue?"

"He said he'd erect a statue of that kid, remember? Also, you will live on that property, but that's not all. You're going to open a shelter for homeless women. You can call it whatever you want. Benedict House South maybe. But it will be more than a shelter. You'll run a clearing house for these girls that get tossed around to different places with no choice about where to go."

"Tossed around. As in trafficked."

"Whatever. Form a nonprofit. Go speak to people. You got a big mouth and you like to perform. The thugs from the Pickett Grill would think twice about approaching you because you'll have a high profile. You might even crack their operation." He pulls scraps of paper from his pocket. "It's all here. I took notes."

Paula places both hands on her head to stop the room from spinning, either from the brownies or Joe—she isn't sure. "O'Brien approves of all this?"

"I was high as a kite when we talked, but I think so. We buy the land, pay a one-year lease at the nursing home, build the Chris Brown statue, and open the nonprofit for these destitute young people. O'Brien feels that's a good use for the land. He's outlived three wives and never had kids, so it's his way of taking care of other kids. Not kids, really. Young people. You get the picture."

"Back to this statue."

"I might have said a plaque. Affixed to the building. O'Brien's name should be somewhere too. I figure you keep the school bus, get rid of the double-wide and built the anti-trafficking center in that spot. It can start out small, but Mia can help you."

"She might not want to."

"I spoke to her. Looked her up on the computer."

Paula tries to imagine that conversation. "Who else did you speak to?"

"Statue people. Plaque people. People who do fancy gravestones. Donna was here the entire time. By the way, Donna knows your last name because she went through your purse when you had to pee."

"Goddamn it."

"She noticed the Jessup name and suspects you did something bad. I didn't volunteer information, but it doesn't matter. The pot farm prevents her from going to the police. She gave me these printouts about pot and dementia. Apparently, smoking pot can help with the symptoms. Donna wanted to show you her basement greenhouse, but you thought she was lesbo."

"Have you eaten dinner?"

"Already had my burrito, but yours is in the fridge. It's going on nine o'clock. I thought you'd sleep the night away."

Things settle down after that. They go upstairs to watch a true crime show, and Joe gets a call. He gets up from the couch and walks into the kitchen with the phone clamped to his ear, using his business voice. "Yes, this is Joe's Takeaway. Yes, we have available days on the calendar. Yes, we can work curbside. Sure, Tuesday would be perfect.

Can you email me the setup details? Thanks so much. We appreciate the business."

He returns to the living room rubbing his hands in satisfaction. "We have another gig, this one in Norfolk. It's at the Wolf's Head Brewery. A small place, as I recall. There's a crematorium across the street and a place that sells leather goods next door. We'll be there Tuesday night. Their regular food trucks can't make it, and they saw our Facebook page."

"You sound very professional on the phone," Paula says. "That must be the voice you use when talking to plaque people or statue people, or managing a bar. As opposed to your bouncer voice, which I'm sure is deep and threatening."

"I didn't have a bouncer voice. I had bouncer fists."

Joe scribbles a reminder on his whiteboard for Tuesday at seven PM. He suggests Paula bring a change of clothes to work that day and come directly to Wolf's Head from the auto parts store. She says that's a great idea, not wanting to rain on his parade. But she's trying to wrap her head around everything she's heard. Run a clearing house for information on human trafficking? And he's talked to Mia? Later that night, Paula calls Mia to get the other version of that conversation.

"He's worried about you because of the George Pickett Grill guys," Mia says. "He wants you to be in a safe place, and he wants you to do something with your life. A suspected murderer with rage issues has adopted you. Congratulations."

"He's dying."

"Dementia will do that to you."

"It's not funny, Mia."

"I'm not making a joke. My dad died of Parkinson's. He was losing his memory, then one day he fell down the steps. The hospital gave him painkillers, and he never regained his faculties. He never got to reflect on his life. Joe has that chance. He wants to be remembered for something other than collecting bad debts and knocking heads. Managing that bar was his dream, and that was taken away from him. You're all he's got."

"How long did you two talk?"

"Forty-five minutes. He did almost all of the talking. He sounded a little wired."

"He had a few pot brownies. Maybe more than a few."

"He doesn't seem the type."

"The neighbor lady grows pot in her basement. This is some street, let me tell you. But this Benedict House South thing, me running a shelter and an anti-trafficking center? I can't believe he came up with all of that."

Mia hesitates.

"I'm sensing you need to finish my thought," Paula says.

"Joe said you needed a purpose in life. He suggested you run a homeless shelter for women because you look up to me. That was sweet. I took it a step further and suggested the anti-trafficking center. It would function as an information resource, offer seminars, submit white papers to conferences. I want to do more of that, but I don't have the facilities here."

"So you'd like to run it."

"It would be your baby. You'd be a better public speaker than me. I tend to be brusque. You'd turn on the charm. You have street knowledge of the criminal enterprise. You might even entice Rosa to work for you. Put the homeless shelter somewhere else on this O'Brien land, separate from the conference center."

"Jesus, now I'm running a conference center."

"You'd need all kinds of approvals. The anti-trafficking center would require a board of directors, someone to manage operations, someone to deal with the media, and you'd need to get your name out there. The death of your grand-father is problematic. But yeah, it could happen. One thing? Forget about calling it Benedict House South. Find your own name. Saint Benedict is the patron saint of the home-less, and I'm keeping him."

"I don't think I can—"

"Shut up with that language. I've seen the way Rosa looks up to you. You've got drive. Joe says you had O'Brien eating out of your hand. Selling auto parts is no way to spend the rest of your life. Joe said he planned to buy the O'Brien land with money in his savings account. You should let him do that. If the dementia worsens, he'll end up in a nursing home, and that will suck out his nest egg anyway."

"You really have no filter."

"Let him buy the fucking land. Who cares if it blocks a casino? You've got your own plans. Keep Joe Pendergast by your side as long as he's able to be there. The guy never wanted kids. He had an unhappy childhood, and working the door at the bar exposed him to plenty of stupid adoles-cent behavior. Now he regrets not having kids. You're what he has now. You need to come through for him—and for me. I'm tired of yelling at you to do better."

"No pressure then."

"Also, don't get arrested for stealing credit cards. Just stop that nonsense. That'll fuck up everything."

CHAPTER

53

WOLF'S HEAD BREWS in Norfolk isn't much to look at. The glass-front features large metal tanks that obscure most of the interior, which seems like a good idea. The two guys who run the place have lumberjack beards that young men favor these days. They thank Joe for showing up on short notice and play up Tuesday trivia, which attracts a few regulars. Joe smiles and takes it all in. People who can afford to drink on a Tuesday shouldn't blink at false credit card charges a few weeks from now. The lumberjack men, Dan and Bill, say they'll be working all night. If Joe needs anything, he should just say the word.

Joe raises the customer window at five o'clock with a steaming grill and a bubbling Crock-Pot. A line forms. Paula gets off at five, but she works in Ocean View, and it will take her at least twenty minutes to get to this end of Norfolk. Joe decides not to try any funny stuff with credit cards while he's alone. It feels odd, this new location, and he wants Paula looking over his shoulder.

Maybe she can work the window. She can probably swipe cards lickety-split.

Then again, she won't be around forever. She'll get that
land and become famous. No time for helping out old Joe
and his food truck. But that's okay, he tells himself. He
can watch her grow into a new life as his peters out. Who
wouldn't want something like that?

As he opens for business, Joe concentrates on keeping
everything straight. One order at a time, he tells himself.
Then move on to the next one. Thirty minutes pass and
Paula doesn't show. He replenishes the grill at a quarter to
six. A run on Coke products leaves the ice chest half empty,
and he rips open another twelve-pack, screwing each can
into crushed ice. A break between rounds of trivia prompts
another food run. It lasts twice as long as the initial rush,
and Joe has to restock the grill while waiting on customers.

What he wouldn't give for one of Donna's funny brownies right about now.

At six thirty, he wonders if Paula got stuck in traffic or
had to stay late at work. He texts her.

> You should have walked out the door 90 min. ago.
> You showing up tonight? It's busy.

Business doesn't let up. He learns from customers that
the microphones went dead on the trivia game, and everyone
is standing around with nothing to do. So they all decide
to eat. Joe has to keep things straight in his head and stay
calm. When the rush subsides, it's seven thirty. Paula got
off work two and a half hours ago, and now he's sure something happened. Maybe she's had second thoughts about
this deal. He might have scared her, beating up McTavish
and Wendell and talking to Mia about the future. Come to
think of it, maybe Paula and Mia have talked behind his
back. *"Yeah, that crazy old guy called me out of the blue about
this land deal. You should get out of there, Paula."* She could
be halfway to Florida, speeding off in that Nova.

At eight o'clock, he sends another text.

Where are you?

Four people stand at the window. He takes care of them and checks his phone. There is no answer. Panic rises like a slow, unstoppable tide. He needs to get out of here and do something. He lowers the customer window and goes inside. The microphones are working again, and trivia night is in full swing. Joe snags one of the lumberjack men. Dan or Bill, it doesn't matter.

"Have you seen a young woman in here, mixed race, wearing her hair in a mohawk?" Joe realizes how stupid this sounds as soon as he says it. She wouldn't come into the bar on her own.

Dan or Bill says he hasn't seen anyone like that and asks if everything is okay.

"Not really," Joe says. "I'm having trouble with my propane feed. The grill is acting up, and I may have to close early."

"Not a problem," Dan or Bill says. "Trivia is about ready to wind up. We had technical problems, but this is always an early crowd. If you need to bug out, I understand."

"I just wish my partner would have shown up," Joe says. "I'm a little worried."

"I'm sure everything will be fine. Here, take one of our cards. Your food seemed to go over well, and we might want to book you on a regular basis. Simple stuff, right? Our weekend food trucks are locked in for a few months, but we could use reliable vendors during the week."

"Thanks," Joe says, putting the card in his pocket.

He returns to the truck and closes the window. He takes the ice chest inside, folds up the condiment table, and puts it away. He scrapes down the grill and puts the cooked meat in plastic containers. He closes the Crock-Pot and sticks it in the fridge. Satisfied that he's cleaned up, he heads for the driver's seat, when a knock comes at the window. It's the other lumberjack, Dan or Bill.

"Did you see her in there?" Joe asks. "My partner never showed up."

"Uh, no, I haven't seen her. I wanted to make sure you got a business card. It's got our personal contact information. Cell phone is on the back." He slides it across the little windowsill.

According to the card, lumberjack men are Dan Floorman and Bill Bose. The owner is listed separately. As Joe reads it, he gets an odd sense of déjà vu. Then his tired brain makes the connection, and his blood runs cold.

No, no, no, no.

Wolf's Head Brews is owned by Paradise Unlimited LLC, the same paper organization under Kathy Culhane's name that's buying all the land around the O'Brien property.

Maxie has his hooks into this place.

He could have arranged this gig.

And Paula never made it.

A T Brady's Auto Parts, Paula swaps clothes in the ladies' room when the clock hits five. She exchanges her polo shirt for a black pullover. Studying herself in the mirror, she decides Joe's Takeaway needs a logo so they can sell swag. Maybe a hotdog man with boxing gloves would do the trick, building off Joe's reputation as a bouncer. Something in teal and black with a touch of red, small enough to fit on a ball cap, big enough to splash on a banner.

She reaches Wolf's Head Brews twenty minutes later and parks a block away. The food truck is out front, but Joe hasn't opened yet. The ice chest and condiment table are still inside the truck. He must be talking to the owners, playing salesman. This would be a good night to swipe a few credit cards, despite Mia's warning. This place is a one-off, and they'll never see these customers again. Let two weeks pass before making purchases with cloned cards. Concentrate on high-end electronics and rotate the locations. Assume you'll be on security cameras and wear a ball cap pulled down low. Don't go hog wild on any particular card. If someone sees a hundred dollars on their card that doesn't belong there, they won't ask for an investigation. They'll be happy if the card company just makes it go away.

And then go legit: Paula Jessup, anti-trafficking activist, head of her own nonprofit located in the middle of nowhere. Just look for the school bus with the woodstove and the scarecrow with the surveillance camera.

She kills the engine and rests her head on the steering wheel. Could this really happen? And is she wrecking her own dream by committing credit card fraud? But she can't live on that land until O'Brien and his cat move away. And she can't put her hands on much money without pulling a few victimless crimes.

"So just do it," Paula whispers into the steering wheel.

She checks her phone to make sure Joe hasn't texted her. It's only twenty minutes after five, and she's not due for another ten minutes. He hasn't sent any messages, but she checks her email just in case, because Joe is more an email guy than a text guy. Actually, he's more of a number-two-pencil-and-paper guy.

A man crosses the street toward the Nova. He stands at the driver's side door, with arms crossed. He's squat and broad shouldered, with big forearms and thick legs. Paula doesn't recognize him from the George Pickett Grill, but that doesn't mean much. She's still thinking about Jennifer the counselor. Jennifer the email lady.

"Excuse me, I need to get out," she calls through the closed window, cursing the tremor in her voice.

The man raises his hands in mock surrender and points to a late-model Escalade SUV across the street. "Max Smith would like a word."

"I have to work."

He points to the food truck. "You see the man with cargo pants leaning on the car next to the food truck? He's with us. If you don't come with me, Joe Pendergast will not be long for this world. This doesn't have to be ugly."

Screaming won't do any good. The guy is just standing there. Maybe the police would make them move along, but they'd be back. She gets out of the Nova, locks the door, and walks across the street. The interior of the Escalade SUV smells of tobacco and bourbon. Max Smith sits in the back seat. With his good hand, he pats the empty spot next to him. His glittering blue eyes are nestled in folds of skin. The broad-shouldered man gets behind the wheel.

"Let's go for a drive, Jimmy. I want to talk to the girl here." Max Smith's voice is rich and buttery. He holds up his bad hand, the little finger swathed in gauze. "I'm going to need physical therapy. Can you believe that? For a torn ligament on a little finger, Health insurance in this country, that's the real scam." The SUV pulls smoothly away from the curb. Paula wonders what it's got under the hood.

"Do I call you Mr. Smith or Maxie?" she asks. "Or maybe Max. Or just old fart."

The old man raises his good hand and Paula braces for a punch. Instead, he runs a finger along the top of her mohawk, and she tries not to shudder at his touch. "That was very disrespectful," he says. "I detest people who act smarter than they are or who talk a good game. That's why Joe and I got along for so many years. He was humble. He didn't forget who plucked him out of that neighborhood." He chuckles. "Now he forgets everything."

"He really doesn't," Paula says. "It's in the early stages."

"He managed my place for two years and performed decently. Not great, but decent. He was good with the customers. Being a bouncer for so long helped. He could make anyone feel comfortable and defuse a lot of bad situations. The back part of the operation—ordering supplies, scheduling help—he was never good at that, dementia or not." He studies her face. "You're like him. You can talk to people."

"How would you know?"

"Because Ledyard Aloysius O'Brien is very impressed with you. He says, 'That girl got more than a mohawk on her shoulders. She got sparks.'" Maxie chuckles. "When old men are childless, they think they missed something in life. Suddenly they like kids when they're eighty years old."

The SUV pulls onto I-64 toward Virginia Beach. Paula can feel its power, passing cars and barely making a noise.

"Ledyard O'Brien is not only impressed with you," Maxie says, "but he wants me to stop making offers for this land because he's selling to this mohawk girl and an old guy. You and your one-year lease at a nursing home, whatever other fucking shit tale you spun."

"It's not a tale. It's good business."

A vein throbs in his head. "Ledyard O'Brien said his two buyers ran a food truck called Joe's Takeaway. We figured if we showed up where the food truck did business, we'd run into you. And look what happens: You park practically across the street."

"Lucky me. How did you know about this gig? We didn't have time to post it on Joe's Facebook page."

Maxie ignores the question. "We figured one of you would need a break at some point during the night. Either Joe goes to the bathroom or you do. Then we take you and have a conversation. I can't talk to Joe anymore. You? I'm thinking we can work something out."

"Tell me what will happens next tonight," she says.

Maxie sighs. "We talk. Then you've got your work cut out for you."

55

J OE WANTS TO brace those two guys with the beards. Their regular Tuesday food vendor happened to call in sick, and they stumbled on Joe's Fadeaway on Facebook? He pounds his fist on the steering wheel while driving away. Knocking heads won't do any good because this is a different sort of fight, and he needs to think it through. The two lumberjack boys might be clueless. Maxie could have called the food truck guy directly and told him not to report. It doesn't seem like a rabbit hole worth exploring. At a traffic light, a car blares its horn, and Joe sees that the light has turned green. His vision goes a little sideways, as if everything is on a distant stage and he's seeing the road from the cheap seats.

Go home, he tells himself. *When you get pissed, you get confused.*

He pulls into his driveway around nine thirty and sees Donna standing in her front window. He breathes a sigh of relief that his nosy neighbor is patrolling the ramparts. She runs out to meet him. "Christ, I was worried about you," she says. "I've been getting these texts."

Joe hasn't checked his phone in some time. Digging around in his pocket, he says, "Please tell me you've heard from Paula."

"Paula? No. I'm getting texts from someone named Jennifer. She says she's a friend of yours and is worried about you."

"Jennifer my counselor? That makes no sense. She wouldn't have your number, and she doesn't know what's going on. She volunteers for some Alzheimer's support group, and we trade messages from time to time. It's just an email thing." Joe checks his phone and sees three missed texts, all from Jennifer.

Hi Joe: Just checking to see if everything is OK.

Joe, me again. Looping back to make sure you got my previous message. Maybe we should talk on the phone.

PLEASE call me.

He stares at his phone until Donna gently pries it from his hand. "Your messages came in the last thirty minutes. Mine came ten minutes ago. She says she's been counseling you on the dementia diagnosis and wants to make sure everything is fine, and could I please check on you. I saw the house was dark and your food truck was gone, so I didn't do anything. Tuesday isn't a normal work night for you."

"I had a one-time gig at Wolf's Head Brews in Norfolk."

"A hole-in-the-wall place. It's been around for a few years."

"It's owned by Maxie. Sort of." Joe explains the LLC connection, how Wolf's Head conveniently lost their usual Tuesday food truck and how Paula never made it to the gig. "She's missing," Joe says. "I can't find her."

"Have you checked hospitals?"

"I guess that's a good idea."

"Does Max Smith know you're pursuing the O'Brien property?"

"Not from us. Maybe this is about me torquing his finger. He doesn't like me 'out in the wild' because I know every bad thing he's ever done. Maybe he's taken Paula, and this is supposed to send a message that I should keep my mouth shut. He's taken people before, people who owed him money, people I couldn't collect from."

Donna shakes her head. "I'm not following."

Joe takes a breath. "Look, Donna. I busted heads for Maxie going on forty years. He runs illegal poker games in the back room of Captain Maxie's and sometimes makes high-interest loans to losers who want to keep playing. They didn't always pay him back, so I had to knock on their door or knock on their heads. Sometimes they hid from me. In those cases, the late payer would get pictures in the mail: their wives at work or kids at school. That wasn't my thing, terrorizing people. I either hit them or I didn't."

Donna retreats a step, as if Joe might grab her. "I thought I was a badass for having a pot farm."

"I need to call Jennifer and figure out why she texted you. Don't go anywhere. I want you to hear this." Joe punches in the number and puts it on speaker. A woman answers in a soft voice.

"Jennifer? This is Joe. You were texting me. You wanted me to call. I feel a bit odd. This is the first time I've heard your voice. What's on your mind? The texts seemed kind of urgent."

Silence.

"Jennifer? Can you hear me?"

"Hey, Joe. It's Kathy."

"What? Kathy, shit, I didn't mean to call you."

"I'm Jennifer," Kathy says.

"Say again?"

"You need to process this, Joe. Maxie asked me to keep tabs on you. I posed as a volunteer counselor so I could check in from time to time. That's why I didn't want you to tell the doctor. I'm Jennifer. I've been emailing you."

Joe swears under his breath, thinking how she handled his banking toward the end of their time together. She had all his passwords. "You could get into my email," he mumbles to himself. "You could see what I was doing."

"I also installed an app on your phone that allows me access your texts," she says. "You can yell at me later, but right now, you need to focus. This has gotten out of hand."

Donna's hand goes to her mouth. She mouths, "Are you fucking kidding me?"

Joe searches for what to say next and comes up with one word: "Paula."

"Maxie has her. He's driving around with Jimmy. You know what happens when he drives around with Jimmy. You have to back off on this O'Brien property. O'Brien called Maxie a lousy businessman and sang the praises of you and Paula. Maxie flew into a rage. He said he should have seen it coming."

"How could he have known what we were planning?"

"Paula came to Captain Maxie's one night. I was working the bar and didn't know her from Eve. Maxie recognized her from somewhere and asked me to keep an eye on her. I overheard her talking on the phone. She mentioned the name of Ledyard Aloysius O'Brien, and I strongly suggested that she leave. But then I told Maxie that this girl mentioned Ledge's name over the phone. He went ballistic and found the girl's car on parking lot security footage. A friend in the police department ran the license plate, and he got her full name."

"So he got her name, so what? That wouldn't connect her to me."

"But the two of you visited Ledge," Kathy said. "You impressed him. Ledge told Maxie about your visit. A Joe and Paula who ran a food truck, he said. Then Maxie flew into a rage and arranged for you to do Wolf's Head tonight."

Joe allows himself a smile. "And you were watching all this time, *Jennifer*. Sending me an easel to write down notes. Telling me to label my toothpaste so I wouldn't shave with it. Just a nice person who wanted to help someone." He fights to remain calm, rattling off this list, the things she has done.

"I was ordered to do it, Joe. And part of me wanted to do it. I could make sure you were doing okay with the dementia and the food truck and everything else. I would have pushed back had I known it would turn out like this."

"We all live with our choices," Joe says, deadpan. "How can I find Paula?"

"He's taken her to his apartment complex in Virginia Beach. You should go there and tell him the O'Brien deal is off. Make the call to O'Brien while Maxie is standing there. Back off on the purchase. That will calm him down for now. You can't outscheme Max Smith."

"Because I'm stupid?"

"I didn't say that."

"Because you're too busy buying up land around O'Brien's place and owning the Wolf's Head to boot?"

"Huh? I have no idea what you're talking about."

Donna punches him in the arm. "Paradise Unlimited LLC," she whispers.

"Paradise-something-something LLC," Joe says. "Your name is on that organization."

There is dead silence, followed by the clicking of a keyboard on Kathy's end of the phone. A few seconds later, her

gasp sounds real. "He got me to sign a few papers for the bar
a while back and I . . . damn it, I'm the registered agent for
the Paradise? Joe, I'm seeing this for the first time. Now if
this all goes sideways, my name is out there."

"We all have our problems," Joe says. "I gotta go." He
thumbs off the phone.

CHAPTER

56

THE SUV STARTS to shimmy at eighty miles per hour. They're on I-264 heading east toward Naval Air Station Oceana, the master jet base for the East Coast. When Paula was a senior in high school, her grandfather urged her to join the Navy so she could fly jets. He promised to wave from the house if she flew over Hampton. It made no sense at the time, but now she wonders if he wanted her out of the way while he herded exhausted girls in and out of his house. They might have grown closer had they lived at more of a distance, their relationship based on convenient perceptions instead of hard and ugly truths.

The SUV takes the exit ramp like a squirrel skipping along a limb and lurches to a stop. Max points to the right, and Jimmy nods as if he suddenly remembers where to go.

Something pings under the Escalade as it accelerates. Jimmy leaves off the gas as the transmission prepares to shift and the engine whines in protest. Then he stomps on it. Paula's momma would be cuffing his ear, telling him to grow a set and drive like a man. When Paula was seven or eight, Momma took her on Sunday drives through the back roads of Berkeley County. She'd point to the former youth center where she'd met Daddy, a building since converted into a warehouse. When Paula asked why the county didn't have a youth center anymore, Momma would shrug and mumble something about drugs.

Sometimes she'd take Paula into the hills to spot deer in the twilight. A bottle of applejack always sat between the seats, and Paula might take a sip or two. Momma took bigger swigs and swallowed with fluttered eyelids and breathless, toothy smiles. After they saw a few deer, their eyes shining green in the dark, she'd speed back to the trailer park, shifting heel to toe through hairpin turns, promising to teach Paula about driving when her time came. In between their trips, the car always seemed to be perched on red jacks, Momma squatting underneath, her steel toes sticking out, swearing at a shock or a strut, barking her knuckles, asking Paula for WD-40 or a socket. Paula was always afraid the car would slip off the jack and crush Momma against the concrete slab. She would imagine that pretty brown hair all mushed up with blood.

When Momma died two years later, they held an open casket viewing and it looked like someone put a statue in there. Momma wore her navy-blue Sunday dress with a frilly collar, her hands folded just so. Ten-year-old Paula figured the funeral director burned the real body from the car crash and substituted a dummy.

Maxie directs the Escalade onto a side road that leads to an industrial park. The hulking shadows jolt Paula back to present, away from Momma and her tools and flashes of her old life. She waits for them to stop and the door to open. She will run until her lungs burst. She will find the dark and hide in the shadows. She'll make Jimmy work for it. But the industrial park is nothing but a shortcut. They emerge onto a four-lane highway, turn left, then take an immediate right into an apartment complex. The buildings are ash gray with black shutters. Each one is three stories tall, with an open stairway running up the middle. It looks like every apartment complex you'd ever see, but it is brightly lit. She can't hide here.

The Escalade stops at the leasing office, a smaller building painted in the same gray and black scheme. Jimmy cuts the engine, gets out, and opens Paula's door. He sets his feet, prepared for her to run. Max turns and chuckles. "She doesn't get out here. We take her to apartment 102. That's vacant, right?" Turning to Paula, he says, "you'll hang out in one of my units. It's not bad. We'll have a good time."

"How long does the good time last?"

"Until you tell Mr. O'Brien this land grab is over. Then you can leave, no hard feelings. Knowing Joe, I figure you're the brains of the outfit. If you go thumbs-down on the sale, Joe can't bring it home on his own."

Paula gives up her wallet, and Max goes inside the leasing office. Paula turns to Jimmy. "I need my car. It's parked on the street up in Norfolk and might get towed if I leave it there."

"You and that car of yours," Jimmy says. "A parking ticket is the least of your worries." He shuts the door, gets behind the wheel, and drives further into the complex, watching her in the rearview mirror.

CHAPTER

57

DONNA INSISTS ON driving, and Joe doesn't put up a fuss. He's a bit spooked after the trip back from the Wolf's Head, where everything seemed distant, as if on a stage. When does a moment become an episode? When does an episode never end? The snub-nosed .44 rests in his lap as Donna slams through the gears of her sports car. The barrel is pointed toward the door, just in case. He holds his phone in his other hand. Kathy promised to text him with updates, but Joe already knows how this will end. He feels for the plastic bag inside his jacket. It is cold to the touch. He pulled it from the freezer as Donna ran to get her car.

"Kathy might be an unwitting dupe," Donna says. "Maxie could have forged her signature on papers or got her to sign something when she was busy. She sounded genuinely surprised that her name was on that LLC."

"It would be just like Maxie to hide behind a shell company." Joe says. "And Kathy wasn't vindictive when we broke up. She was just sad. Yeah, she spied on me. Maybe she thought I'd run the food truck into the ground or lose all my money. Maybe she wanted to watch over me, like she said. I guess she knew everything I was doing on my phone." Joe gropes for more words. "Maybe she still cared."

"There's an app," Donna says. "Parents who want to watch their kids' phone activity can download it. Same goes if your spouse is suspected of cheating. If she handled your banking when you lived together, she already had passwords. Did she withdraw any money after you broke up?"

"I don't think so. My savings account has been fairly static since the big blowup."

On a late Tuesday night, the Hampton Roads Bridge–Tunnel is nearly empty. Donna comes roaring out the other side, doing seventy-five. She glances in the rearview mirror and starts to say something. She catches herself, then goes ahead anyway. "How did it end between the two of you, Joe? We talked about O'Brien and the LLC, but not about what happened between you and Kathy, or you and Maxie for that matter."

"I was managing Captain Maxie's and the books weren't balancing. Supplies were running short and work schedules got messed up. Maxie confronted me about it. Going soft in the head, he said. Then I groveled, pleading for a job at his new casino as a greeter, playing off my bouncer reputation. He turned me down."

"Joe Louis worked as a casino greeter in Vegas after he retired," Donna says. "He wore a cowboy hat, the whole shebang. He posed with people and put a fist on their chin and signed autographs. He supposedly enjoyed it, but they paid him well, gave him housing, not a bad deal."

"I regret making the offer, but at that moment I would have done anything to stay. When he insisted on firing me, I snapped. Hit him with a right cross. He hit me back and I ended up in the ER. That's where they diagnosed the dementia. Kathy visited me in the hospital and said we couldn't stay together, that Maxie wouldn't stand for it."

"Were you two in love?"

Joe realizes this is the question she wanted to ask all along. "At first, we had fun at work. Then a water heater burst in her apartment and she moved in with me. It was meant to be temporary, but we started fooling around. This may surprise you, but I was always pretty good in bed. I had plenty of women hit on me when I worked the door. I got better as I got older too."

"Because you were safe," Donna says.

"People have seldom described me as safe."

"From a relationship standpoint. A younger woman sleeps with an older guy who has been around the block, and the older guy considers himself lucky. Also, working the door at a bar allows you to see a lot of women. You don't go pie-eyed at every young hottie. You play the game and decide which one to take home. I can see how you'd be good in bed. You get exposed to different techniques."

"You don't have much of a filter, do you?"

Donna grins. "You thought that was a dementia problem, blurting out embarrassing things in public? Hell, Joe. You're early stage. People with dementia can hold down jobs and do other things. Plus, you've got my pot farm going for you."

The little car speeds along I-64. Traffic is light. "We're talking like this to avoid what's ahead of us," he says. "Like soldiers who make small talk before a battle."

Joe wants to say how much he appreciates Donna trying to pump up his confidence. She might think they can rescue Paula and return home as if nothing happened. She'll tend her pot farm while Joe and Paula double-swipe credit cards and make life easier for a lonely old man in a school bus. Joe has to smile because sometimes that's all you can do. His past might be foggy, but his future is crystal clear. He has one more door to knock on.

"You may not believe this," Donna says, "but sales training prepares you for moments like this."

"That so?"

"Everyone has a vulnerable spot. Something always makes them sit up and take notice. I once sold a house to a couple because it had a woodstove in the garage. Who cares if there's a woodstove in the garage? But the wife worked on pottery. She had this dream of going out to the workshop in cold weather and firing up a woodstove. That sealed the deal."

"I don't think Maxie cares about woodstoves."

"My point is, everyone cares about something."

"Like I care about Paula," Joe whispers.

Donna isn't listening. "Think, Joe. Where is Maxie vulnerable?"

Joe indulges her, and in that one moment something connects. He thinks about his whiteboard and the two old news stories Paula had taped to the bottom of the easel, about Cotton "Candy" Smith.

"I see you have an idea," Donna says.

"I do. Maxie has gone legit. He's coming out of the shadows. He has to appear in public before planning commissions and zoning boards. When you work with someone for a long time, you don't notice the transition, but it's very real. Now bear with me. Maxie's dad was a big kahuna in Phoebus back in the day, a godfather to all. Then he went to jail. Maxie wants to be like his dad minus the jail time. He wants to be accepted like a big shot. The last thing he wants is bad publicity. He told me this at the Moonbeam that night. I forgot."

Donna taps the steering wheel. "This is good. If the police were called to a disturbance at his apartment complex, Maxie would cooperate," she says. "He wouldn't want to be perceived as uncooperative."

"What kind of disturbance did you have in mind?"

"A bomb threat. A fire. Something that makes people run into the parking lot. If Paula is there, she'd have to come out." Donna downshifts into third while approaching a truck, then slams it back into fourth in the passing lane. "This is the fun part. Let's make something up."

58

APARTMENT 102-F IS the most remote building in the complex. Jimmy rests his hand on Paula's shoulder and steers her into the main room. It has a couch and two end tables. A flat-screen TV with a game system and two controllers sits against the opposite wall. A dinette is to the left, a hallway to the right. The carpet and walls are eggshell white. There are no photos, posters, or anything to suggest humans live here. It could be a terrorist's apartment. After a moment, Maxie walks in behind them and closes the door.

"You'll be here for the night," he says. "Then we get an early start tomorrow."

"An early start doing what?"

Jimmy disappears down the hallway. Maxie stands in the center of the room and smiles in a half-cocked way. "Maybe I didn't make myself clear. You need to make a call. Tell that old man you have no plans to buy his property." He holds up one finger. "And further, tell him what a nice guy Mr. Max Smith is, how he has best interests at heart for Ledyard Aloysius whatever."

"I'll say Mr. Smith will pay for a five-year lease at the Smith-George Shores so O'Brien can retire in comfort. With his cat."

"I'm not paying for any fucking lease at wrinkle city. I want that guy to be gone, him and his half-ass school bus. He'll eventually die, but I don't want to wait. I've offered him three times what the property is worth. We sent Kathy over there, and he acted like he wasn't interested. Maybe I need to hire the Chippendales." Maxie looks around the room. "God, this is a dump."

"It was Joe who sealed the deal, not me."

"I don't really care. You need to pull the plug. I'm a civilized man, but I don't want to wait on this prick. He doesn't have family or friends. We can't see him leaving the land to someone else. He doesn't have a will. Kathy did manage to finagle that piece of information."

"You're a civilized man," Paula says. "Yet here we are."

He smiles with those crocodile teeth. "Settle down on the couch and go to sleep. You'll wake up tomorrow with a clear head, make a phone call, and put this unpleasantness behind us."

"And then you'll let me go?"

"Answer me a question first."

"Sure."

"I took your ID back there. Your last name is Jessup. But I already knew that. Back when you visited the bar, I had a guy run your license plate. I wanted to make sure you didn't have five different driver's licenses, like a pro. But you're not a pro. You're just some kid on the run."

"Why would I be on the run?"

"Your last name is the same as that old guy they fished out of the water by the HRBT. My guy who does research took two minutes to figure out that guy is your grandfather. The cops say he was murdered. Well, they say it's suspicious, which means he was murdered. Your grandfather's boss at this greasy spoon was crying for the TV cameras. How come you're not on the news, mourning for old grandpa?"

"I don't like publicity."

"The George Pickett Grill has always been a seedy joint, and you need the money to buy O'Brien's land. Also, I doubt you live in Berkeley County like your license says. So you're working some angle. I'm wondering if you killed your grandfather and stole his money to buy O'Brien's land."

"Nice try, but a clean miss."

"But it's something," Maxie says. "You are not mourning him. I can see it in your eyes. Some angle is involved, and you're lying low."

Paula considers how much to tell him. "The George Pickett Grill is engaged in labor trafficking. They bring in girls from Latin America and elsewhere, work them like slaves in the kitchen, then ship them off to God knows where. My grandfather was part of it, having graduated from being a small-time thief in Berkeley County. I suspect his death is related to the trafficking, and if that's the case, he deserved to die."

"I take it you two weren't close."

"Sometimes these girls stayed in Grandpa's house. I had an apartment above his garage and saw them get herded into a van. I kept seeing their faces in my sleep."

"That's dirty business. Was he fucking these girls?"

"I don't think so, but thanks for the image."

"I'm just saying, you call it labor trafficking. Maybe it was more than that. I assume this is still going on, even with your grandfather out of the way."

"I would assume. The Pickett is a seedy joint, to use your phrase. That guy who's been crying in front of the TV cameras, he controls where the girls go. They suspect I know something because I lived next to my grandfather. They tracked me to Joe's house and tried to muscle me, but Joe didn't stand for it. Joe kicked their asses."

Maxie chuckles. "I bet he did. Why don't you blow the whistle on that place?"

"If the police raid the Pickett, the men plead ignorance. They'll say the girls showed them fake papers. Only the girls get in trouble. The police would need to commit resources to a place like that, play the long game, figure out who does what."

Maxie goes to the window. Paula allows herself to think he might do something about the Pickett. He might draw the line at human trafficking and try to play the hero. She can almost see the wheels turning inside his head. Then he turns away from the window and claps his hands as if a great solution has presented itself.

"That's too bad for you. Make that call tomorrow, and you can leave here. You got a nice car that hopefully hasn't been towed. I would suggest driving away in it. Go on the run. There's no future sticking with Joe Pendergast." Maxie calls for Jimmy, who trots in from the hallway. "Give her the pills so she goes to sleep. I have to leave."

Paula sits on the couch and hugs her knees. "What pills?"

"They'll keep you from doing something stupid, like trying to break out," Maxie says. "Knocking on the walls won't help because all adjacent units are empty. But just to be safe, I don't want you hurting yourself."

Jimmy goes to the kitchen and comes out with a glass of water. "Don't make me work for this," he says. "Just swallow them."

"You're going to kill me," Paula says. "You won't let me drive off into the sunset. Even if you do, that's a myth. You don't find a sunset. You find another town with the same problems with people just as bad."

Jimmy stands before her, hand outstretched. "Just take the pills."

59

DONNA STOPS AT a convenience store and buys two burner phones. She drives to within five miles of the apartment complex and pulls onto a side street. A text from Kathy says Paula will likely be in Building F.

That's because Building F units are vacant. Leased to employees at Captain Maxie's, but no one lives there. Poker game proceeds pay the rent. Money laundered that way. *Sorry I can't help more. Didn't want for this to happen.*

Donna settles her shoulders and slaps the steering wheel. "That's it. We camp out at Building F, and everyone will evacuate because of a bomb scare We look for Paula. After firefighters and police get on the scene, we can walk up to her. Easy peasy. Max Smith won't put up a fuss in front of everyone."

The air is close in Donna's little sports car. Joe checks the load on his revolver. He should have worn a heavier jacket. Virginia stays cold in early April, and he's starting to shiver. "Maxie won't be alone," he says. "He surrounds himself with young wannabe toughs, guys with gym muscles who aren't used to getting hit. But they'll be trouble. They follow him like puppy dogs, driving the car, opening doors.

This could be many things, Donna, but easy peasy is not one of them." He puts the gun in his pocket and hugs himself against the chill going through his bones.

Donna calls 911 on the burner phone and puts a hand over her mouth. She speaks in a raspy voice that sounds like she's been possessed by a demon. "Someone has planted several bombs in the Garden Fair Apartments Virginia Beach. They were upset at rigged poker games held at Captain Maxie's, the bar in Norfolk. The same person owns both places and this person is pissed. He's former military and got his hands on C-4 or some shit. The bombs will go off in half an hour. Get everyone out of the apartments. Someone will get killed over those damn poker games, you wait and see."

She cuts the connection and breaks the phone in half. Tuesday was garbage collection day in this neighborhood, and she drops the pieces of the phone in an empty can that lingers at the curb. Joe checks his pockets to make sure he still has the gun and the package from the freezer.

"C-4? That was a little over the top," Joe says.

"Let's just go."

They pull into the apartment complex. Donna drives to the far corner and finds Building F. She pulls into a parking spot to wait. A minute later, two police cruisers arrive with lights flashing, but no sirens. A third follows. An officer gets on a loudspeaker, and the cruisers turn on spotlights. Windows light up, doors open, and people spill into the parking lot. A man with a shaved head opens the door to a ground-floor apartment. He holds Paula by the upper arm. He walks in long, regular strides away from the growing crowd, and Paula struggles to keep up. She's wearing her hoodie, walking like she did that night on Seneca Lane when she appeared in Donna's security video as a mystery woman.

"I think that's the only coat she owns," Joe says. "I should get her another one."

"Why doesn't she scream for help?" Donna asks.

"She doesn't want attention from police. Trust me."

"Because of having the same last name as Anthony Jessup, that dead guy in the water? What happened there, Joe? I haven't asked, but since going through Paula's purse that night. I've been trying out different theories in my head."

"Paula's not a bad kid, but she got herself in some trouble, that's for sure," Joe says. "I'll tell you after this is all over. Let's follow them and see where they're going. The guy's she with is called Jimmy. He's not to be trifled with."

They climb out of the sports car and move through the crowd. Paula and Jimmy walk toward the leasing office. Maxie does business from there, and he might be inside. He'll probably come out in a minute or two, backslapping the police for their quick response. It will be interesting to see if Donna's call about the bomb threat being connected to illegal poker games causes any trouble in the long run. But Joe isn't worried about that now.

As they approach the leasing office, Joe trots ahead. He pulls out the .44 snub nose and sticks it in Jimmy's back. "You know what this is. Release the girl and let's walk to the office."

"Joe Pendergast. I hear you're sick."

"I got no quarrel with you, Jimmy, but we can't stand here and talk." Turning to Paula, he asks, "You okay?"

She stares at the ground, shaking her head. Her voice is barely a whisper. "They were going to give me pills, but I spit them up. Now they're pissed at me. But then—Christ on a stick, Joe. I can't believe you found me."

"Walk away. Donna's behind me."

Jimmy chuckles. "You're making a big mistake."

Paula runs to Donna. Joe steers Jimmy away from the front door. "Is Maxie inside?"

"I don't owe you any answers, and you won't shoot me."

"I'll take that as a yes. Walk ahead of me."

"Where to, old man?"

A dumpster sits behind the leasing office. It is shielded on three sides by a brown security fence. Jimmy walks toward it, then plants his feet. "Wait, you want me to climb in there?"

"I'm sure Maxie's garbage is very sweet smelling. Keep walking." Joe figures a dumpster is a suitable place to stash this guy; he can wedge the lid locked long enough to keep Jimmy out of the way.

Jimmy mutters an impressive string of curses as he starts through the container's side door. At the last second, he turns and throws an elbow at Joe's jaw. It misses by an inch and Joe instinctively clocks him with the butt end of the gun. Jimmy grunts but doesn't go down, and lunges at Joe. Joe catches the younger man's forearm and shoves it against the sharp edge of the side door. Jimmy gasps in pain, a satisfying sound. Joe clocks him one more time and throws him into the garbage. Jimmy lies still, whimpering, it sounds like. Joe closes the side door and latches it.

Joe breaks off a couple of thumb-sized branches from a nearby shrub. He wedges the branches into the holes where a padlock would go and does the same for the top lid. It won't hold forever, but he doesn't need forever. Anyway, he doesn't have forever.

He walks to the front door and steps inside the darkened office. Shapes harden in the gloom as his eyes adjust. Two chairs face the front desk, and a sofa is pushed up against the left wall. Joe realizes he's never been in this room. A hallway leads to the back of the building. It ends in a closed door labeled "Private." Maxie's voice comes from behind this door. It sounds like the police are on the phone. Maxie tells them to search wherever they want because he has nothing to hide. He acts like he's somewhere off-site, telling the police, "I'll make it when I can." Hearing that lying voice makes it real for Joe. The short walk down this hall could be the last steps he ever takes.

He waits for the conversation to end and opens the door. Maxie says nothing. Both hands are flat on his desk. Joe closes the door behind him, and the two men lock stares. Joe levels the gun at Maxie's head.

"This was you?" Maxie asks. "A bomb threat?"

"You don't have Paula. Jimmy is out of commission for the time being. It's just us."

Maxie wears heavy, black glasses that went out of style in 1965. Joe always joked that the old man needed bullet-proof glasses to go with his hard head. Now Maxie removes his glasses and places them gently on the desk. This is him saying the jokes are over. No more kidding around like a couple of brothers. He takes off his blazer and hangs it on the back of the chair. He comes around the desk and stands with his feet apart, weight distributed. When they were young, Maxie taught Joe how a boxer should stand. That's how Maxie stands now.

"This was a dumb move, Joseph."

"I've made dumber. Like begging you for a job when you wanted to dump me."

Maxie waves dismissively. "You wanted to kill me back at the Moonbeam Brewery. I saw it in your eyes. The girl interrupted it then. Was she part of it?"

"She was just a girl then."

"Now she's more than that," Maxie says.

Joe shrugs. "She believes in holding onto life. Maybe because she's young and at a crossroads. Kids like that either flame out or grow up. I intend to help her grow up. We need that O'Brien land. It's not just a way to block you, although it is that. We need it for other things."

"We?"

"It's her future. Did you plan to kill her tonight?"

"Of course not. I want her to call O'Brien and pull her offer. Then she can walk free. She can help you with that shitty food truck until you don't know which end is up. You're a fucking crazy thug, you know that? What did you do with Jimmy?"

"Locked in a dumpster out back."

"Jesus. With police all over my property and him probably making a racket."

"Yeah, I've become a royal pain in the ass. You're saying Paula could have walked away if she called off the land deal?"

"Of course." Maxie looks to the corner of the room. He can't hold Joe's gaze.

"Bullshit. You were going to kill her."

"Why would I kill a girl I don't even know?" Maxie says. It's not a real question. Joe knows Maxie, knows how he thinks, knows how he operates. But Joe answers anyway.

"Because she knows me. You'll assume she's talked to me, that she knows about your poker games. You'll assume she knows about Verge, about that cop who is paralyzed. It's one thing for me to run my mouth. I'm a disgruntled ex-employee with a dementia diagnosis. But she might be more creative. She could post something online. Get it out in the open. You can't have her walking about."

Maxie spreads his hands. "So nothing has changed. You still want to kill me."

"A lot's changed. Before, I wanted to kill you and let the chips fall. Not so much now."

Maxie sighs. His shoulders deflate, and he doesn't want to talk anymore. Joe lowers the gun an inch or two. He knows it's a mistake even as it happens, because for a man like Maxie, an inch or even less is enough.

60

MAXIE SLAPS AT the gun and it clatters across the floor. Joe didn't want it anyway. The police might be milling around and would hear a gunshot. And maybe a bullet was too quiet an ending, too impersonal, too cold. Maybe they needed to fight it out, fight out all the shared history between them.

Now in the stilled moments before the first punches are thrown, Joe knows he wants to win. It's not enough to go out with guns blazing. He wants to see what happens with Paula, with Donna and that damn dog with the silly name. *And don't think for a moment it will be easy,* he tells himself. Maxie's injured finger will make him even more dangerous. Years ago when they were kids, Maxie cracked his wrist while they were sparring in the gym. His eyes had turned white with rage, and he beat Joe into submission with his left hand.

"There's no bell to stop us," Joe says. "You really want to do this?"

Maxie answers by throwing an elbow that whistles past Joe's jaw. Joe steps back, balances himself and throws a roundhouse right. His fist bounces off Maxie's granite forehead. The guy can still take a punch, but he's standing straight now, and Joe follows up with a left uppercut into that hard belly. Maxie shakes his head like a Rottweiler and charges. When they were young, Joe was a beanpole of a kid, and Maxie always muscled him into turnbuckle. Joe would duck under the bigger man's punches and get to the center of the ring, where he could stick and move. But those days are gone. They are two men in the final throes of life, joints cracking like hard candy, circling in a drunken dance.

Joe takes a kick to the groin and drops to one knee. Sausage fingers dig into his eyes.

"I'll blind you," Maxie whispers. "An old dog that has to be put down. That'll be you."

Joe imagines Paula living in that school bus. He sees her talking to politicians, leaning into a bristle of microphones at a press conference. She could do it. She's at a crossroads now, but she could do it—she *will* do it. Joe believes in her. Down on one knee, he shoots upright and rams the heel of his hand against Maxie's jaw. Maxie falls back against his desk, leaving himself exposed. Joe puts everything into a chopping punch to the liver and watches his old boss flop across the desk. A lamp topples to the floor, throwing a crazy light across the room.

"You done, boss?"

"Fuck you."

Maxie pushes himself up. Joe sets his feet and delivers a short right to the jaw, then two more punches to the stomach. Maxie falls again, and this time the air whooshes from his lungs. He rolls around like a flounder out of water. Joe hits him twice more in the tender skin just below the eyes. With his knee, he pins Maxie's good arm against the floor. Joe reaches for the throat and finds the Adam's apple. Maxie knows it's over now. He's whacking Joe with his bad hand, kicking for all he is worth. Joe knows he has to end it, but he wishes he didn't. Maxie will always be his older brother. If it were just two old men and their dying dreams, they could both walk out of here. But Maxie won't let Paula live, and she deserves a chance to make her dreams come true.

"This is how I did Verge," Joe whispers through gritted teeth. "The gunshots were just for show."

Maxie gags. The office door flies open and bangs against the wall. He expects the police to rush in, and that would be acceptable. But it's Paula and Donna in the doorway, coming to see if he needs help. He didn't want them here, didn't want them to see any of this.

He turns back in time to see Maxie grabbing a heavy bookend. It smashes against Joe's head, and pain flashes like tiny firecrackers, but he still has Maxie by the throat. He squeezes. A gurgling sound escapes Maxie's throat. That bookend hits Joe again and again, but he holds onto that throat like a pit bull.

Maxie whacks him one more time and goes limp. Blood drips into Joe's eyes, and small hands pull him away. Paula's hands. He's come to recognize them. Joe reaches into his pocket and tosses out the package from the freezer. She'll know what to do.

"Stay with me, Joe. Answer me one question."

So many questions. He'll pay a year's rent on the beach house and give Paula the food truck. She won't have to double-swipe those credit cards. Donna will find a way to help. And Kathy will do the right thing. She still cares. He needs to keep his head above water and not fade away.

"You got to lay low," Joe says, finishing his silent thought. "You can't get caught."

"Joe, what you talking about?"

"Your future. All the questions."

Donna stands behind them. She's found the snub-nosed .44. Paula takes it and grabs Joe by the collar. "I'm not talking about the future, you old man. We need to find Jimmy. He could ruin everything. I'll—I'll take care of him for you. If I have to, I will."

"He's gone," Joe mumbles. "In the garbage." Now he remembers Jimmy's cut wrist, the trickling blood, how still he'd been after Joe tossed him in, after that last knock on the head. He'd thought Jimmy was whimpering, but maybe he'd imagined that.

"I'll go look to make sure," Paula says.

"You'll do nothing of the kind." *You're too good for that,* he thinks. *That's not your life. You don't need to see a guy in a dumpster who died there, even by accident.*

JOE AND THE GIRLS

Seven Months Later

THE DECEMBER WIND drives a dusting of snow across the stubbled field. Red and green lights hang from the scarecrow's skeletal frame set against a Santa hat and a garland necklace The lens of a new surveillance camera protrudes from its mouth like a black tongue. As Paula attaches the last string of lights, Donna pats the scarecrow on the cheek. "There is something about twinkling lights intertwined with a creepy doll that brings home the true meaning of Christmas."

Paula plucks two hemp gummies from Donna's coat pocket but doesn't take her eyes off the highway. "I still dream about a Mercedes van coming along this road. In the dream, I watch as they approach. It's like I'm helpless. I wonder if they'll try one day."

"You are many things, Paula Jessup, but you are not helpless." Donna looks toward the school bus. There is movement in the windows. Let's go eat breakfast. I think he's making pancakes."

Wooden stakes marked with orange tape lead the way. Paula can't see the big picture from the ground, but Donna assures her it represents the boundaries of the proposed Pendergast Anti-Trafficking Legal Center. The local planning commission has blessed the drawings, and a zoning variance turned out to be, in Donna's words, easy peasy. Up at the Benedict House, Mia is screening applicants to serve as volunteer subject matter experts. They will answer to Paula, who will serve as executive director. Donna will handle day-to-day duties as operations manager and deal with the media. Rosa will parlay her inside knowledge gained from suffering at the George Pickett Grill to become a field investigator. In January, she will begin pursuing a criminal justice degree at Old Dominion University.

"Do you think we can really do this?" Paula asks.

"We're still a year away," Donna says. "We're amateurs, but we'll learn. We can lean on Mia, and I'll feel better once we have a board of directors. And we need to work on the name. The Pendergast Anti-Trafficking Center is a mouthful, and he hates it."

Stepping inside, Paula finds Joe furiously scribbling at his whiteboard. Wisps of smoke rise from an empty frying pan on the front burner. He has divided the whiteboard into grids that match days of the week. Under each day is a list, but Paula can't make out the words.

"Morning ladies," he says.

"Joe, you've got a hot pan on the stove with nothing in it," Paula says. "Is everything okay?"

"You ever make pancakes back in Berkeley County?"

"Uh, no. Can't say that I did."

"Well if you did, you would know the surface has to be hot before you pour the batter. Otherwise, we'll be sitting here until the rapture. Why don't you two food critics grab a plate and take a seat at the counter? I got whipped butter and two kinds of syrup."

"For the record," Donna says, "I was not criticizing your kitchen skills. What's on the board?"

"A menu plan for the not-to-be called Joe Pendergast Anti-Trafficking Center. These girls will need to eat, and if I know Paula here, they'll be slurping ramen noodles from sunup to sundown, along with some high-sugar soda, and wondering why they feel wrung out half the time."

Joe arches his back to loosen the stiffness that has plagued him since the fight with Maxie back in April, followed by several months of sleeping on the third floor of the Benedict House. Joe wasn't tied to Maxie's death, but their highly visible breakup earlier in the year might have made him a suspect. So he laid low and emptied his savings account in installments, giving Donna the money to purchase O'Brien's land. O'Brien and Dale Earnhardt the cat are currently enjoying their new retirement community, but he's promised to come back to review the project.

The project.

At first, Joe wondered where he might fit in such a place. Homeless young women, trafficked and exploited, and him a single white male who'd never had kids. But then he thought about it some more. In a way, he'd been preparing for this job all his life. Working the door at a bar for several decades, he'd run across all types of kids. He knew which ones deserved second chances and which ones needed a kick in the ass.

"And I can cook for them," he whispers.

Paula cocks her head.

"Never mind," Joe says. "I'm just talking to myself. Hey, someone's coming."

A small corner of the flat screen TV shows the surveillance camera, where a lone figure walks toward the crest, wearing a heavy coat and a ball cap pulled low. Paula goes to the door, with Donna behind her. The figure reaches the crest, passes the scarecrow, and starts down the other side. Once within earshot, Paula flips open the door and yells, "Take off your hat and identify yourself. This is private property."

Kathy Culhane removes her ball cap and wipes sweat from her brow. Her hands are hooked into the straps of a backpack. "I brought the last of it," she calls out. "No one followed me. I'm sure of it."

She comes inside, places the pack on the floor and unzips the top. Folded stacks of cash spill onto the floor. Maxie had laundered poker money through the Garden Fair Apartments in Virginia Beach, but he could only clean so much at one time. He kept the bulk of his winnings in a chest freezer in the restaurant kitchen, one with a false bottom, an old lesson he'd learned from his father.

Kathy walks into the kitchen and gives Joe a peck on the cheek. "You making pancakes, hon? I think that frying pan is hot enough."

"Thank you," Joe says. "At least someone around here gives me credit for knowing what I'm doing."

The pile of money sits on the couch. Kathy waits for Paula and Donna to sort it, but the two women just stand there with crooked smiles. It's the fourth time Kathy has brought a stash of Maxie's money from the bar to the trailer, and each time she's donned a ball cap to hide her face, to make sure no one followed her.

"You're not going to count it this time?" Kathy asked.

Donna waves her hand at the money. "We don't have to. I can see we have enough to make it work—at least the first phase. Thank you, Kathy. You're a lifesaver. I wish you could be involved in what we're doing."

"Better that I stay away," she says. "The police seem to have finished picking over Maxie's stuff, but the investigation is still open. Maxie's and Jimmy's murders will become cold cases, if we're lucky. Being a cooperative witness has its advantages."

"Especially when it comes to steering a homicide investigation in the right direction," Paula says. "As in, away from us."

"Miss Donna and I will take some credit for that too," Joe says, pouring batter into the frying pan.

Paula had to agree. Joe had done more than rescue her that night. He'd brought along the clump of her grandfather's hair, which they planted in a drawer. And Donna's 911 call that referenced illegal poker games at Captain Maxie's had not gone unnoticed. When police came to search the bar, Kathy supplied a flash drive that contained a roster of the poker players. She added Sean McTavish at the last minute.

And that launched a brand-new investigation into the George Pickett Grill.

"McTavish is trying to work a deal," Kathy says. "The police can't charge him with killing Maxie or Jimmy, but they're quite interested in the number of young women who circulate through the George Picket Grill and the manicure place next door. Federal authorities have been brought in. They want to expose a major human trafficking pipeline in Hampton Roads."

"That's excellent," Donna says. "Better yet, they've stopped looking at Paula, our soon-to-be executive director."

McTavish had tried to blame Paula for her grandfather's death, but Mia's intervention proved to be key. She insisted Paula had been staying at the Benedict House that entire week—before and after Anthony Jessup's body was discovered—and Mia's word carries weight with the police.

Joe turns to the women. He cradles Butterbean in his arms. "We have to take care of this dog. I don't want him left by the side of the road, running after a car. That's a shame when people do that with dogs."

"That will never happen," Paula says. "We're keeping Butterbean."

Joe turns back to the stove and starts flipping pancakes. Paula and Donna begin counting money. Kathy looks out the window and, for a moment, thinks she sees someone in the field walking toward them.

But it's only the scarecrow, fluttering in the wind.

ACKNOWLEDGMENTS

B RINGING A FIRST novel to life is a heavy lift, and thanks go to the team at Crooked Lane Books and editor Sara J. Henry, who put their shoulders to the wheel. Even so, nothing would have happened without the patience and support of my love and best friend, Shana. Author Rob Hart took a break from his work to edit this manuscript into shape. My Luddite self owes a debt to the great Andi Petrini for managing social media, as well as website developer EJ Toudt and photographer Heather Hughes Ostermaier. I will be forever grateful to the editors who took a chance on my earlier work and encouraged me to continue writing. Those include Michael Bracken, Todd Robinson, Steve Weddle, Anthony Neil Smith, and Kevin Burton Smith. Finally, while this is a work of fiction, the neighborhood of Phoebus is a vibrant and real place in the city of Hampton. The street names have been changed, and there isn't a bar called the Moonbeam—at least not yet—but it would fit nicely.